To Gerry
a good friend
& fellow golfer
Bill Harris

# Seeking Utopia

## *Making Life Better*

**William G. Harris**

This is a work of fiction. All of the characters, names, incidents, organizations, and dialogue in this novel are either the products of the author's imagination or are used fictitiously.

ISBN: 978-1-4834-8073-2 (sc)
ISBN: 978-1-4834-8072-5 (hc)
ISBN: 978-1-4834-8071-8 (e)

Library of Congress Control Number: 2018901592



Lulu Publishing Services rev. date: 03/26/2018

Thanks to my loving wife Nancy, whose patience, motivation, and assistance were instrumental in the writing of this novel.

# *BEGINNINGS*

*A journey of a thousand miles*
*- starts with the first step.*

# 1

Mae was a tall, skinny, shy, thirteen-year-old girl. She lived on a large farm in Eastern Canada with her mother, father, and brother Daniel.

Mae was born on the farm. She lived nowhere else and knew nothing about the world beyond the gate at the end of the road.

When she was five years old, Father assigned her simple chores like gathering eggs and feeding chickens. Father added more tasks at age ten. At age thirteen she took on more responsibility. Father told her to help her mother with the housework and cultivate the family vegetable garden. Mae had no choice but to accept these new jobs. Father's word was always final.

Mae's hair was light brown and cropped short. It made her look like a boy, which she knew Father always wished she was anyway. Father did not want her wasting time combing her hair and making herself look pretty. There were more important things to look after.

The farm was large and spread over five hundred acres of rolling hills. Mae never saw the whole farm. Father, and Mae's older brother, Daniel, were the only family members who worked the farm. A mammoth task, especially at harvest time. Father hired migrant workers to help gather in the crops.

Mae never attended school and could not read or write. She knew nothing about what was going on in the rest of the world. She gathered news from listening to the radio, but at her youthful age, she could not understand what was going on. Other family members could not help because they were illiterate also. Nobody knew, or cared, what happened beyond the farm.

Mae knew there was a war going on, and that Mr. Hitler was a cruel man. Father did not like her squandering time listening to the radio. She only listened to the radio when she was alone. Mae wondered what life would be like if she did not live on the farm and instead lived another type of life, in a big city.

Mae doubted she would ever leave the farm unless she married someone who would whisk her away to a better life, but that would not happen soon. She wanted to go now.

Father knew nothing except being a farmer. His father before him ran the farm, and everyone knew Daniel would take over when Father could no longer manage it.

Despite her yearning to explore the other world beyond the fence, she knew she had no choice but to accept what farm life handed her. Mae worked hard every day, doing her regular chores and taking up the challenges of new ones.

Mae lived a simple life in the red-bricked, farmhouse, with a white wrap-around veranda embracing two rocking chairs, various-sized tables, chairs, and planted pots—home to many colorful flowers and perennials. Ornate-patterned gingerbread trim decorated the gabled eaves and dormers.

The long, two rutted dirt road leading to the house had grass growing in the middle, and cornfields on each side. The house looked forlorn sitting by itself surrounded by farmland.

The farm produced cash crops of corn, onions, carrots, and peas. It also had a small apple orchard in the back quarter. It was in a rich fertile area of Eastern Ontario.

Mae was frail at birth, but farm life enabled her to develop into an active, healthy girl. She was slender and tall for her age.

I'm a teenager, she said to herself. I must get on with my life. I don't want to spend the rest of my life living on the farm, but how can I do that when I know nothing except farm life? I wish I could learn more.

Mae hated to look at herself in the mirror. She looked poor. There was a war going on, and money was scarce. Farmers especially were having difficulty making ends meet. There was never any money to buy fancy clothes or make-up, though she wished there was.

Father insisted that Mae keep her hair short. He told Mother to cut it every month. Father wished she were a boy, even though her body was developing, and she looked like a girl.

Mae owned two dresses — a red one, which she called her Orphan Annie dress, and a white one, which she only wore on Sundays. Father told her two dresses were plenty. He instructed her to wear the red one from Tuesday to Saturday, and the white one on Sundays.

Monday was wash day. Mae did the laundry for everybody. She slipped into an old housecoat to wash her only two dresses together. She cleaned the housecoat separately.

The weekday dress used to be bright red; now it was more orange than red. Mae's white dress had also faded, looking more yellow than white. The faded dresses did not look nice anymore. Mae thought they would look better if she could wash them in a milder soap, instead of the harsh, homemade lye soap that Father insisted she uses. The overpowering soap took most of the color out of the clothes and aggravated her hands until they became raw and painful. It was pointless to ask Father's permission to use a milder type of soap.

Mae did the laundry in the kitchen because that was where the wood-burning stove was situated, and where she heated the water.

There was no running water in the house. Mae fetched water from the well behind the house. On wash days, it took a long time to heat-up the icy water — even longer in the wintertime. When steam rose from the big pot, that was her signal the water was hot enough to use. It took all her strength to lift the massive container off the stove. When it rained on Monday, then Tuesday became wash day.

Winters in Canada were long and bitterly cold. There was snow on the ground from November until March. It was not uncommon during a blistering snowstorm for the family to be housebound for several days. When it stopped snowing, Father hitched a team of horses to a plow and cleared the quarter-mile path to the main road.

Mother was not in good health and could not work long hours. At those times, Mae did Mother's work and her own and made sure Mother was comfortable and took her medicine every day.

When indoors, Mother seldom took off her old housecoat. Her feet were often cold. She wore Father's discarded work socks and slippers, to keep them warm.

When Mae worked outdoors, she wore a denim work dress and heavy work boots. Her hands, knees, and elbows were heavily callused, and her fingernails badly chipped from digging in the garden.

Mother could not stand up straight. She appeared always to be looking up at people when they spoke to her.

Notwithstanding Mother's health problems, she stayed in good spirits and accepted her role as it was. She never complained. Mae liked working with her around the house, and Mother appreciated having Mae nearby.

Mother and Mae canned vegetables after harvesting them from the garden. Mother washed and then cooked the vegetables in a large pot on top of the stove. When ready, Mother spooned the vegetables into sterilized tins. Mae's job was to seal lids on the tins and name the contents on the side of each tin. A manual canning machine with a long-handled crank sealed the tops onto the tins.

Mother instructed Mae to put colored marks on the tins to show what each tin held. Red for carrots, green for peas, yellow for corn, and white for onions. That was too boring for Mae. Instead, she drew colorful pictures of the contents on the outside of each tin. It allowed her to display her artistic talent. She painstakingly painted faces on each drawing and dressed up the vegetables in people clothes. Mother would lose patience and scold her for wasting time.

"Mae, we'll be here until next spring if you don't move faster. Stop taking so much time painting those silly pictures on each can. You only need to put a colored mark on each tin."

Mae told Mother she liked drawing the pictures. She said that it inspired people to want to open the can and enjoy the contents.

Mother reminded her, "Father will not care about the fancy pictures on the outside of the tin. Besides, it does not make the food taste any better because you put a fancy picture on the tin," Mother quipped.

Mother and Mae laughed and giggled throughout the process. They had fun together.

Neither Mother nor Mae had any formal education. Each could read a little, but not well. What little they could do, they learned from each other.

Mother's health worsened. Sometimes she could not get out of bed and stayed there for several days.

Every six months, an Eaton's catalog arrived in the mailbox at the end of the driveway. Mae liked when it came. She gloated over the beautiful clothes, adored the gorgeous models, marveled at their sleek hairdos, admired their high heels, and idolized their beautiful fashions. Mae wished she could design clothes like that, instead of painting vegetables to look like people on the sides of tin cans. Mae realized that the chance of ever ascending to the level of an Eaton model was remote, however.

How could a simple farm girl like me ever design clothes for fancy models in the Eaton's catalog? I wish I had an answer. If I stay on the farm, I'll know no other life except farm life, she told herself.

Mother cut Mae's hair when she did her own. Mae never liked the results. The way Mother hacked at her hair, Mae knew that it would never look like the ladies in the catalog, any more than her old faded clothes could compare to the beautiful garments the Eaton models wore.

When Mother was well enough, Mae offered to take her into town to get their hair done at the beauty salon. It was only a fifteen-minute walk away.

"Those things cost money," Mother reminded her. "Something that's always in short supply. Anyway, Father would never approve of such foolishness."

Their concentration centered on preparing meals, making beds, washing dishes, and tending to the many chores to keep the large house, and farm, clean and functional. There was no time to do much else.

When time allowed, Mother and Mae darned threadbare clothes to extend their life a little longer, before they got cut-up into dusters and washcloths.

When the weather was good, Daniel and Father worked in the fields every day, except Sunday. The farm produced cash crops of corn, oats, barley, potatoes, strawberries, and apples.

Mother baked apple pies from apples Mae picked in the orchard. She kept some aside to make into applesauce for canning.

Mae's outdoor chores included feeding chickens, slopping hogs, cleaning the hen house and collecting eggs. Mae gave each chicken a name. She did not like it when one of them ended up as Sunday dinner. She soon got over it, however. There were too many other things that needed her attention. She had no time to mourn over departed chickens.

The hardest job was keeping the large farmhouse clean. Father was a tyrant about cleanliness. He inspected the house like a Sergeant Major checking the barracks. When the house was not to his liking he would bellow at Mae, "This house looks like a pig sty. Clean it up."

Mae feared Father. He was the head of the house, and he made sure everyone knew it. He was a domineering, big, burly, man with a thick black beard. His hands, arms, and face, were a deep reddish color from working outdoors. Suntan lines formed where his clothes ended. The back of his neck, hands, arms, and part of his face, were well weathered.

When working in the fields, Father always wore the same old tattered, sun-bleached, straw hat. Mae never saw him wear any other headwear. The one-piece, full-bodied overalls, and a long-sleeved multi-colored plaid shirt rolled up above his elbows completed his work uniform. The straw hat prevented the sun from reaching his forehead. His forehead was lily-white, and it continued upward into a receding hairline. He had more hair on his face than he did on his head. It amused Mae when he came in at night, and she saw how strange he looked. Mae had to be careful, however. She did not want to let Father catch her laughing at him. Father got mean when he was angry, and would not hesitate to verbally chastise her, and assign extra work for her to do as punishment for mocking him.

He was a man of few words. When he spoke, he spoke in a gruff voice and short sentences. Father inherited the farm from his father. Everyone knew that someday Daniel would take it over.

Like clockwork, Father and Daniel returned at four-thirty every afternoon. They expected to eat supper at five o'clock. It was Mother and Mae's responsibility to make that happen. Father was not happy if supper was late.

Supper always consisted of meat, baked or mashed potatoes, and a canned vegetable. Desert was a homemade pie or cake. Father liked to spread mounds of butter on his potatoes and vegetables. He ate his meal using a fork, knife, and spoon. Father held the fork in his fist like a spear and cut behind it with his knife. He pushed the vegetables onto his spoon with his thumb. Father liked his dinner swimming in a pool of thick brown gravy which he soaked up with a slab of doughy homemade bread.

Mother and Mae only ate after Father and Daniel finished their meal. As the men of the house, they ranked higher and therefore felt it was their right to eat first. After everyone had eaten, and dishes washed, it was lights-out and off to bed for everybody shortly afterward.

Father and Daniel started work early each morning. They left when the sun came up over the barn, but not before devouring a big breakfast made up of three or four eggs, a tower of pancakes, lots of maple syrup, and mounds of fried potatoes. Mother arrived in the kitchen first to start breakfast. She got up at four o'clock. Father and Daniel got up an hour later.

While Father and Daniel were eating breakfast, Mother prepared their lunch. A regular meal included a sandwich, or two hard boiled eggs, a slice of pie, and a thermos of tea. Mother placed two lunch buckets at the door for them to pick-up when they left.

Like supper time, Mae and Mother sat down and ate their breakfast after Father and Daniel left each morning. Mae spent more time with Mother than she did Father. Father preferred Daniel over Mae, and he made no secret about it.

Mae felt there was little passion between Mother and Father. She never saw them hug or kiss. They lived, and worked, in their separate worlds. It seemed to Mae that the only thing they shared was the roof over their heads. They slept together in the same bed, but Mae figured that was all they did in bed together.

Mae had no formal education. There were chores to do and no time for book learning, even though she wished she could attend school. Once, when she thought Father was in a good mood, she asked his permission to let her go to school. "Father, I'm getting older now. Can I go to school? I hear the man on the radio tell me how important it is to get some book learning."

Father's voice intimidated Mae. He demanded, "Who will look after things around here if you're away all day at school?"

Mae suggested she could do her chores after school and on Saturday and Sunday.

The answer came back, "No, and don't ask me again. There is plenty of stuff around here to learn. You don't need books to teach you. Your mother can teach you everything you need to know. It is more important that you learn how to cook and sew. Knowing how to keep house will get you a good husband. More than what book-learning will. Men want wives who can cook and look after them."

Frustrated, Mae asked. "How will I find a husband if I never leave the farm?"

"If you're a good cook and know how to take care of a house, he'll find you." Mae doubted that would ever happen. When Mae approached Mother for her opinion, Mother agreed with Father, as she always did, and told Mae she did not need to learn from books. She said, "There are men out there who would be happy to have you as their wife."

Mae answered, "I do the same things day in and day out. I want to get out of this rut."

"You don't understand Mae, but someday you will," Mother said softly. "Meanwhile, get on with your chores. I need to rest."

Mother's health continued to get worse. Six months later she died. After Mother's death, Mae looked after everything in the house. It was not a comfortable life for a young girl.

# 2

Mae was fifteen years old when Mother died. The funeral took place in the big farmhouse. Father buried Mother in a remote area of the farm in a family plot. There were only a handful of mourners who stopped by to pay their respects. Mae knew nobody except Father and Daniel. They were the only family members. The other mourners were neighbors from other farms.

On the day of the funeral, Mae had no time to mourn her Mother's death. She was busy setting out food for people to eat. The night before, Mae made five platters of sandwiches, baked four pies – two apple pies, one blueberry, and one cherry. She did not get to bed until late. On the morning of the funeral, Mae awoke early and baked two dozen oatmeal cookies. At the reception after the service, she served tea and coffee. There was no time to grieve her mother's death.

The day after the funeral, life went on as usual for Father and Daniel. They awoke at their regular time, had their proper big breakfast, which Mae prepared for them, and went to work in the fields. It was as if Mother was still alive.

Life changed dramatically for Mae however. After Mother's death, Father expected Mae to take up the slack. She was all alone to tend to the many chores she used to share with Mother. She worked hard from sun-up to sun-down every day of the week.

Mae did not mind working alone during the day. Because she no longer had to tend to Mother's needs, she had more time to herself despite the extra chores. Mae took to drawing more elaborate pictures on the tins. She improved the designs from the Eaton's catalog. She sewed fancy hems and pleats into her old clothes to give them new life and style.

Mae enjoyed browsing through the Eaton's catalog. Her limited reading skills confined her to admiring the gorgeous models, wearing beautiful clothes, hoping someday she could afford them. Mae suspected that her chances of ever getting an education or looking like the catalog ladies were unlikely.

Father and Brother continued to treat Mae like a servant, rather than a daughter or sister. Mae could not understand why. She tried hard to please them but to no avail. Nothing she did for them ever seemed reasonable enough.

Unexpectedly, Father told Mae he was going away for a few days and that Daniel would oversee everything in his absence. He gave no reason for leaving, or when he would return. Mae knew better than to ask. If Father wanted me to know he would tell me, Mae supposed.

After Father left, Mae asked Daniel, "Where did Father go and when will he be back?" Abruptly, Daniel answered, "It is none of your business. Get on with your chores. Father will tell you when he's ready. He told me not to say anything to you."

Mae could not understand why Father was so secretive. It was clear that Father liked and trusted, Daniel over her. She wished she knew how to please Father, so he would love her as much as he did Daniel.

Three days afterward, Mae got up at four o'clock like she did every morning to prepare breakfast. Father had still not returned home. Something was different on this morning, however. Daniel did not come downstairs at five o'clock as he usually did every morning. Mae had prepared his breakfast, but he was not there to eat it.

Daniel eventually came downstairs at eight o'clock. He looked different. He had on a white shirt and tie, flashy black pants, black socks, shiny shoes, and combed hair. Mae had never seen him dressed like that before. She wondered where he got those fancy clothes, and why is he wearing them this morning. "Why are you dressed like that Daniel? Where are you going today?"

Daniel responded, "Mind your own business and get my breakfast."

Mae asked no more questions, although she was quite intrigued and knew that something unusual was going on. Father and Daniel obviously had plans which did not include her. Eventually, she figured she would discover what is going on.

Daniel left the house at ten o'clock. Through the parlor window, Mae watched him walk down the dirt road, and turn towards town - about a fifteen-minute walk.

Later that afternoon, Father and Daniel arrived home accompanied by a short, fat, lady.

Father said, "Mae, this is your new mother, Isabel. We were married at the Presbyterian Church in town this morning."

"Why did you not want me at the wedding Father?"

"Because you had no nice clothes to wear."

"You bought new clothes for Daniel," Mae responded.

"That's because he is the oldest boy and entitled to be at the wedding. You only need to concern yourself with chores."

Mae could not understand Father's reasoning. It confirmed what she always thought, Father was ashamed of her. Because she had no clothes was only an excuse to keep her away from the ceremony.

Right from the start, Isabel and Mae disliked each other. Isabel looked upon Mae, not as the daughter of the man she just married, but the person who prepared meals, and tended to household chores. Isabel was unsympathetic to Mae's personal needs, wants, and desires.

At least Father is away all day, and I only face his cruelty in the mornings, and at night, Mae thought. Isabel is around all day long, however.

Mae was a teenager coming into her own. She displayed a rebellious attitude towards Isabel. "I'm not a little girl anymore," she would shout at her. "You have no right to talk to me the way you do."

Isabel reminded Mae she had every right to speak to her the way she did. They battled with each other every day.

Isabel was grossly overweight. She had oversized arms and a big bosom. Isabel was often out of breath. When she walked, everything on her body went into motion. Her feet never left the floor. She had rotten teeth and bad breath. Mae did not understand what attracted Father to marry her.

Mae thought Father thinks Isabel looks beautiful. I see how he looks at her. I wish he had looked at Mother like that when she was alive.

Mae tried to tell Father how mean Isabel was to her. Father always answered the same way, “You listen, and do, whatever Isabel tells you to do. She’s your mother now. She knows what’s best for you.”

Disappointed at Father’s unsympathetic response, and in despair, Mae resumed her role as a servant girl rather than a daughter.

Isabel made sure Mae knew, unlike Mae’s mother, that she had no intention to do housework. Mae continued doing Mother’s chores and her own and was under Isabel’s rule around the clock. She had no time for herself.

Mae was troubled when Isabel ate with Father and Daniel at meal times. Mae ate alone after the other three family members finished. As the head of the family, Mae could not understand why Father did not exercise his authority and allow her to eat with the other family members. It soon became clear that Father was relinquishing his status to Isabel. She was becoming the head of the house.

Lonely and depressed, Mae often cried herself to sleep at night while Father, Isabel, and Daniel, gathered around the radio and laughed at the antics of the Amos and Andy show. Mae was not a happy young girl.

I wish I knew how to get away from this miserable life, she asked herself.

Unbeknownst to Mae, her answer came in a manner she least expected. Isabel eventually became disillusioned with farm life, and Canada in general. She persuaded Father to turn the farm over to Daniel and move to England with her. “I should never have let you entice me to move to this backward, God-forsaken, country,” she told Father. “I can no longer live here. The winters are too cold and too long. I want to go back home where I belong.”

Father asked, “What about Mae? She’s too young to live on her own.”

“I don’t care what happens to her. Arrange for her to live somewhere else,” Isabel barked at Father. “And make it fast. I don’t want her hanging around here any longer than is necessary. Her presence will keep me from leaving sooner."

Soon after Isabel's ultimatum, Father gestured to Mae and told her to sit down because he had something important to say to her. Most times Father ignored Mae. Mae wondered, why does he want to speak to me? It can be nothing good. Father never has anything good to say to me.

Father told Mae, he and Isabel were moving to England in a month.

Mae asked, "Will I be moving to England with you?"

"No. You'll not fit in. I've arranged for you to live with your Aunt Wilma."

"Who is Aunt Wilma? I've never heard you speak of her before."

"Wilma is my sister. She lives on the outskirts of a small village in Ontario, called Avonmore. I've asked her to look after you until I can find a more permanent place to put you."

Father kept talking while Mae listened intently, "You always wanted to learn from books. Aunt Wilma used to teach school until she retired last year. I asked her to give you some book learning like you always wanted. In return, you'll do chores for Aunt Wilma as you do for Isabel and me."

A week later, Mae was alone on the train destined for the tiny village of Avonmore, to meet Aunt Wilma. Mae did not know what to expect when she arrived at the station in Avonmore. It was an all-day journey on the slow-moving train that stopped at every station dropping passengers off and boarding new ones. It was the first time Mae had ever traveled on a train.

While she did not know what her future held, she was not sad to leave the farm. It was never the same after Mother died. I hope Aunt Wilma is not like Isabel. I'll work hard to make her happy, Mae said to herself.

Mae was happy that Aunt Wilma agreed to help her do schoolwork. I hope Aunt Wilma likes me. If she doesn't, she'll not want to teach me, Mae feared

Mae left the farm with everything she owned, stuffed into an old duffle bag that belonged to Father. She traveled in her pale red Orphan Annie dress. Father shoved her Sunday white dress into the duffle bag, which rode beside her on the train. The name tag still had Father's name on it.

Mae felt she would never see her father, or Isabel again. She was okay with that thought. I'm starting a new life, she happily thought to herself.

Mae looked at Father's duffle bag on the seat beside her as the train rumbled along the rails. The tattered suitcase and its near worthless contents were all that Father left her. She felt that the value of Father's bag, and its meager contents, reflected the low esteem he had for her. Life had not been pleasant for her after Mother died. It deteriorated even further when Isabel arrived to rule over her. Mae did not understand what the future held for her. Whatever it was, she hoped it was better than the life she was leaving behind. She desperately wanted a better life for herself.

Wilma was the only person on the platform when Mae stepped off the train.

"You must be Aunt Wilma," Mae said to the tall, slim lady standing in front of her.

"I am," she said. "Are you Mae?"

"That's right Aunt Wilma."

Aunt Wilma looked older than Mae expected. She wore a long grey dress, down to her ankles. The long sleeves went to her wrists. It matched the color of her hair which she tied up into a neat bun at the back of her head.

On her head, she wore a stylish brimmed hat that matched her long dress. A large hatpin through her hair-bun held her hat at a jaunty angle.

On her nose hung a pair of rimless eyeglasses. She wore no make-up. The toes of her black, low heeled shoes, peaked out from under her long skirt. A narrow black belt showed-off her tiny waist. She carried a black leather purse, elegantly looped over her left arm.

She looks nice, Mae thought. What must she think of me in my Orphan Annie dress, ruffled boy haircut, long brown stockings, and worn-out shoes?

Wilma said, "Your father asked me to watch over you for a while. I only found out yesterday, from a letter I received, that he moved to England with his new wife. He did not know what to do with you and asked me to watch over you. I don't think your

Father intends to return to Canada. He asked me to give you some education. Are you ready to learn Mae?"

Mae answered with an enthusiastic, "Yes Aunt Wilma. I want to read and write as you do."

"Very well then. I'll try to teach you a thing or two," Wilma stated. "The first thing to do is get you some decent clothes. You must feel good about yourself. It makes it easier to learn. We'll look in the Eaton's catalog when we get home."

Wilma remarked in a reluctant voice, "I did not need this disruption at this point in my life. Damn your father anyway. He has been like that all his life - accepting no responsibility for anything." Looking at Mae, Wilma mumbled, "You obviously were a problem for him. I had not heard from him for years then unexpectedly he writes, asking me to look after you so that he can flit-off to England with his new bride."

Mae, sensing Wilma's resentment, said, "I'm sorry Aunt Wilma. I'll try not to be a burden to you."

"It's not your fault Mae. It's your Father's attitude that upsets me. You and I have no problems. We don't even know each other. Pick up that old bag and follow me to the bus stop. It leaves in ten minutes. It's our only transportation home, and we don't want to miss it. It will not get back to this stop for another hour."

Aunt Wilma sounded angry that Father, without any warning, asked her to look after Mae. Mae didn't know what she could do about it, other than try her best to please Wilma.

Mae told Wilma, "Thank you for giving me a place to stay Aunt Wilma, and for offering to help me learn to read and write."

Wilma threw her head in the air, looked down her nose, and between two tight lips curtly said, "That's okay, Mae. You seem like a nice girl. We will get to know each other better as time goes on."

A week later new clothes arrived in the mailbox for Mae. It was the first time in her life Mae owned store-bought garments. Mae was liking the way her life was changing after moving in with Wilma. The relationship between her and Wilma deepened. Mae was happy to help with the cooking and housework. They traveled every second day into the village of Avonmore on a rickety old converted school bus. There was nowhere else to shop except in Avonmore. They developed a habit of stopping for ice cream before boarding the bus to return home. Once home, Wilma rested, while Mae prepared supper. Mae led a routine daily life.

True to her word, Wilma spent time every evening after supper teaching Mae how to read and write. She gave her homework to do and treated her like one of her former pupils. Mae learned quickly from the one-on-one instruction. Wilma liked being a teacher again. Mae made steady progress, and Wilma complimented her on how well she was progressing. Mae was equally happy with her accomplishments.

Before retiring, Wilma taught school in Avonmore. It was a one-room schoolhouse, with a pot-bellied stove in the center. There were regularly twenty students in the school ranging from grade one to grade ten. Wilma loved teaching and was sorry when she had to retire. Teaching Mae gave her pleasure and a feeling of accomplishment. She threw herself into the role of teacher again and loved it. Mae learned well. Wilma marveled at how quick she absorbed and sustained knowledge.

Mae awoke early every morning, before Wilma, to do the homework that Wilma assigned the night before. Wilma reviewed her homework in the afternoons when Mae was doing chores. Mae enjoyed learning from Wilma, as much as Wilma enjoyed teaching her. It was not long before she could read textbook passages, and write short stories, under Wilma's tutelage.

Wilma was more like a mother to Mae than an aunt. Similarly, Wilma came around and regarded Mae more as a daughter, than a niece. They got along well together. There was no further word from Father about Mae's living arrangements. Mae and Wilma figured that he had abandoned Mae into Wilma's care. Neither expected to hear from him again. Mae was not upset living with Wilma. She thought Aunt Wilma was okay with the arrangements also.

Wilma was not getting any younger, and while she enjoyed tutoring Mae, the age difference between them occasionally caused friction between them.

Thanks to Wilma's expert teaching skills, and Mae's determination to learn, Mae eventually reached a grade ten level education. Due to the one-on-one pupil/teacher ratio, she did it in record time. At every opportunity, Mae read newspapers and magazines that Wilma had around the house. She enjoyed reading the words describing the beautiful clothes in the Eaton's catalog, even though she still could not afford them. Aunt Wilma was kind to her. She bought new clothes for Mae every Christmas. Mae could not thank her enough for everything she was doing for her.

When she needed help in subject matters like geography, history, and mathematics, Wilma unselfishly provided Mae with all the support she needed. "You're a good student," Wilma complimented her.

# 3

Wilma never stopped being a teacher. Mae was grateful for her dedication to her profession. She gave Mae an education which she would not otherwise have received had she still been on the farm.

As a thank-you for the hours of teaching Mae wanted to surprise Wilma with a new housecoat. She asked Wilma if she could buy a bolt of material the next time they went into Avonmore. Aunt Wilma questioned why Mae wanted the fabric. Mae answered, "It is a surprise, Aunt Wilma."

"Very well Mae. I don't know what you're up to, but I like surprises. We'll buy fabric the next time we go into town."

"Thank-you Aunt Wilma."

Mae planned on making Wilma a new housecoat to replace the well-worn one she always wore. Christmas time was nearing, and she wanted to give it to Wilma as a present. The next time they went into town, Mae left Wilma in the butcher shop while she zipped across the road to the fabric shop. The shop lady knew Mae and Wilma. Mae explained that she wanted to make a housecoat for Wilma. The shop lady helped Mae pick out a pattern and some conservatively colored fabric.

Wilma didn't know Mae's intentions for the fabric. Mae wanted the new housecoat to be a surprise Christmas present, but knew it would be difficult keeping it secret. The first challenge was obtaining Wilma's height and arm length. Wilma was a very private person and did not readily relinquish personal information. Unbeknownst to Wilma, to get the desired measurements Mae deviously stood beside Wilma and compared her height and arm length to Wilma's. The results were amazingly exact.

Mae sewed the housecoat in the privacy of her room. Wilma wasn't sure what Mae was doing in seclusion every night. Mae fooled her into thinking she was doing homework.

Mae did not want to make a mistake on her first garment attempt. She studied the pattern attentively before cutting into the cloth. She had no problems completing her project.

On Christmas morning, Mae presented Wilma with a beautiful, full length, well designed and expertly stitched and hemmed, warm housecoat. Wilma was grateful to Mae for making such a beautiful garment.

"I can't believe the talents you possess Mae. You're a talented young lady. You'll go far in this world. This housecoat is nicer and made better than any housecoat I could buy from the catalog. Thank you, Mae, for your thoughtfulness."

Wilma told Mae she had an uncle who lived in Lewisville, a day's journey by train from Avonmore. His name is Charlie. Wilma wrote to Charlie, and told him about Mae's father moving to England, and that Mae was now living with her.

Charlie and his wife Mary wanted to visit Wilma and meet Mae, a niece they never knew they had.

According to Wilma, Mae's father and Charlie, even though they were brothers, rarely spoke to each other. When Mae questioned Wilma, she was not sure why. Something to do with money, Wilma said. "Charlie lent your father money some time ago, but your father never repaid it. Your father had no money. He thought that Charlie should forgive the loan. Charlie did not agree. Your father was a farmer, and that's all he ever wanted to be. He wanted nothing to do with Charlie who was a successful businessman in Lewisville. Over the years they grew further apart. I doubt if they spoke two words to each other after the outstanding loan episode."

Wilma invited Mary and Charlie to visit them in Avonmore to meet Mae. They accepted.

Mae and Wilma went to the train station to meet Mary and Charlie. Wilma introduced Mae, and everybody traveled back to Avonmore on the old Avonmore bus.

Charlie liked Mae. Mae was interested in hearing from Charlie about life in the big city of Lewisville. Mae learned that Charlie was a long-time resident, and businessman, in Lewisville. He owned a bookstore on Pitt Street, the main street in Lewisville. Mae thought she would like to live in Lewisville, instead of outside the little village of Avonmore.

When their visit ended, Wilma and Mae rode with them on the bus to the train station. Mae was sorry to see Charlie and Mary leave. Learning from Uncle Charlie about life in a big city gave Mae a thirst to seek a different lifestyle than the one she was living in Avonmore. Her ability to read and write, thanks to Wilma, enticed her to spread her wings, in new directions. She enjoyed talking with Charlie. He opened her eyes to another world. A world to this point she only read and dreamed about, but never experienced.

After a time, Mae and Wilma were not as compatible as they once were. Aunt Wilma did things her way. They were not always the ways of a young lady in her early twenties. On occasions, tensions rose between them. The arrangement was no longer ideal. Mae recalled how generous Aunt Wilma was with her time. She remembered the many hours Wilma spent teaching her how to read and write. Now she wanted to use what she learned. There were no opportunities in Avonmore. She stood a much better chance in Lewisville to start a new life for herself.

Wilma never married. She delighted in telling Mae how terrible men were. “Avoid having anything to do with men,” she warned Mae. “Men are only interested in one thing - sex.”

Mae figured that Aunt Wilma felt the world would be a better place if there were no men in it. Mae was getting feelings. She imagined it might be nice to have a man in her life. That’s not going to happen if I continue to live with Aunt Wilma, Mae deducted. Mae had been residing with Wilma for a long time. Mae reckoned it was time she set out on her own. When the time was right, Mae would tell Wilma that she wanted to move away from Avonmore. She hoped Wilma would not feel offended at her announcement.

A few days later Mae confronted Wilma. “Aunt Wilma I love you, but I’m becoming restless. I want to move to the city and look for a job.”

Mae's announcement surprised Wilma at first. She knew this day would come. However, she just was not expecting it now. Mae noted the sad expression that came across her face. The room went silent for a moment. Neither Wilma nor Mae spoke for a long time.

Mae noticed a softening look come over Wilma's face. To Mae's delight, Wilma smiled and said, "I understand Mae. There is not much around here for a young woman of your age to do. Move on with your life. You're ready to do so. Have you made any plans?"

"Uncle Charlie talked to me about city life in Lewisville. I'd like to move to the city and start my new life there."

"You'll need to find a job," Wilma said. "What are you going to do for money? You must have plans in place before you leave. The city can be a cruel place when you're alone, with no money, and no job."

"You're right Aunt Wilma. I did not think far enough ahead. I thought I'd just go to the city, find a place to live and get a job. I still have a lot to learn."

"You just learned something Mae. Knowing how to read and write, which you mastered beautifully, is only one part of your learning process. Education is on-going. Observing others, asking questions, understanding what makes other people successful and unsuccessful, and gaining knowledge from your own mistakes and shortcomings, is a life-long learning process."

"You're so wise Aunt Wilma. I'd wager your former pupils learned a lot from you and went on to become successful."

Wilma did not comment. She just smiled and blushed at Mae's flattering remark. "I've got an idea that might help you make a decision," Wilma offered.

Mae eagerly asked, "What's that Aunt Wilma?"

"You know that Charlie owns a bookstore in Lewisville. He's always looking for help. Books hold lots of information as you know. Working in Charlie's bookstore could prove beneficial to you Mae. You learn quickly and understand what you learn. Two prime ingredients for success."

Mae could feel herself welling up with excitement at Wilma's comments. She was happy that Aunt Wilma understood.

"Thank you, Aunt Wilma, for that wonderful suggestion. Through you, I've learned a lot of things. I only wish that Father was as understanding as you are. He did not want me to become too smart, and therefore I never went to school. You have changed my life Aunt Wilma, for which I will be forever grateful."

"You have done well at learning over the years that we have been together Mae. You even speak well. That will help you immensely as you go through life. I'll write to your Uncle Charlie in Lewisville. I'm certain he can find part-time work for you in the bookstore. In your spare time, you could look for a permanent job. There is a big linen mill in the city. The folks in the city commonly refer to it as, The Mill."

"Oh, that sounds good Aunt Wilma. Will you write soon please?"

"I'll write Mary and Charlie a letter tonight. We can mail it tomorrow in Avonmore. That way it will arrive in Lewisville faster than putting it into the box at the end of the path and wait for the mailman to pick it up."

Two weeks later a letter arrived in the box from Uncle Charlie. He wrote,

> *Dearest Wilma,*
>
> *It will be fine to have Mae stay here and help us in the store while she looks for permanent work. Mary and I are getting older, and we could use the help.*
>
> *She can stay in the small apartment above the store. I will give you more details when I see you.*
>
> *Love Charlie.*

# 4

Wilma and Mae rode the train to Lewisville. It made lots of stops along the way. The journey took all day. When the train pulled into the station, it was late afternoon. Uncle Charlie and Aunt Mary were waiting on the platform to greet them.

Uncle Charlie reached down and picked up Mae's old duffle bag with Father's nametag still attached. "Let me take your bag Mae and walk with me to the car. I bet you're tired after such a long trip."

"No, I'm not too tired. It is only the second time I've been on a train. I enjoyed looking out the window at all the big farms with cows and horses grazing in the fields. It reminded me of my days on the farm."

"You're about to start a new life," Charlie said. "You'll be living in the city. Life will differ from growing up on the farm or living with Wilma."

Uncle Charlie looked different than when he and Aunt Mary visited her in Avonmore. He looked shorter with a full head of wispy snow-white hair. It fluttered uncontrollably in the late afternoon breeze. He continuously snaked his fingers through it to send it back to its assigned spot on his head. It was a losing battle. He had a jovial personality and laughed at his unamusing jokes. He had a twinkle in his eyes, and his face was a roadmap of wrinkles. He had a permanent smile glued to his face.

Mae noted Charlie's shiny shoes. She had never seen such well-polished shoes. Very different from the dirty, manure stained, work boots Father used to wear. Charlie's clothes were clean, neatly pressed, and expensive.

Charlie had roving eyes. They ogled her shapely body from the tips of her feet to the top of her head. Mae felt uncomfortable with him staring at her. Mae didn't notice Charlie gawking at her like that when he came to Avonmore. Physically, Mae had developed fully, and Charlie looked at her differently than he did when she was a young lass a couple of years earlier.

Mae wished Charlie would stop looking at her the way he was this time. She dared not say anything to Charlie because he was a long-time resident of the city, and a prominent businessman, whom Mae was dependant on for a job and a place to live. Mae felt if she said anything, he might send her back on the train with Aunt Wilma the next day. As painful as it was, Mae put up with his looking at her the way he did.

Mary and Wilma followed a short distance behind Mae and Charlie. Mary carried Wilma's suitcase. They all got into a big black shiny car and drove to Mary and Charlie's place.

Mary had prepared dinner earlier. She warmed it up in the oven when they arrived.

Mary and Charlie lived in a big house filled with beautiful furniture and well-placed decorations. Mae thought it looked like something out of a fashion magazine.

"You have a beautiful home," Mae remarked.

Charlie replied, "Regard it as your home too, Mae. You'll always be welcome here."

"Thanks, Uncle Charlie. You and Aunt Mary are kind to do all this for me."

Charlie smirked, "It comes at a price for you. You must work at the bookstore and pay rent. There is a little apartment above the shop. You can stay there until you find a place of your own. We'll talk more about it tomorrow."

"Thanks, Uncle Charlie, I'm so excited I can hardly wait until tomorrow."

The next day was Sunday. Everybody dressed up in fancy clothes and drove to church.

Charlie suggested that after church, they would go to the bookstore, and he would show Mae around the shop and the upstairs apartment.

Mae thanked Uncle Charlie for taking time on a Sunday to introduce her to the bookstore and her new residence. She was looking forward to her new job on Monday, but it would help to have a sneak preview the day before.

"Thank-you Uncle Charlie. I'm looking forward to my new job. I want to thank you once more for this opportunity."

"You're welcome Mae."

Mary turned to Charlie and said, "Charlie, before you take Mae to the shop, drop me off at home after church, and I'll start preparing lunch for everybody. I don't need to be at the shop with you and Mae."

"Mary, I'll help you make lunch," Wilma offered. "It'll give us time to catch up on family news. It's been a long time since we did that. I know nothing about the book business. It'll be more enjoyable spending time with you."

"What a great idea Wilma," Mary commented.

"Okay Mae," Charlie said. "It is only you, and I left to talk business. After church, we'll drop the two ladies off at home to prepare lunch. You and I will go to the shop, and I'll show you around. We'll be hungry when we return home. Especially you Mae. You're a healthy looking young lady." Charlie glanced over his shoulder and smiled at Mae sitting in the back seat with Aunt Wilma. Mae noted that he eyeballed her as he did when she got off the train.

After church, Charlie came up behind Mae and placed his arm around her shoulders and walked her to the car. His gestures made her uncomfortable. She did not know what to say or do. Charlie said, "Mae since only you and I are going to the shop, you can sit in the front seat with me. Aunt Mary and Wilma can sit in the back seat. It will make it easier for them to get out when I drop them off. Besides which, it will be nice to have a pretty young lady ride with me in the front seat."

********************

Charlie stopped the car in front of the bookstore on Pitt Street. The entrance to the store was at street level. There was no space between where the sidewalk ended, and the entry began. Streetcar tracks meandered down the middle of the street. Because it was Sunday, no streetcars were running. The area was quiet. It looked desolate. There was nobody around except a homeless man sleeping in a doorway across the street. Uncle Charlie paid no attention to him. That surprised Mae.

"This is the bookstore where you will be working Mae."

Mae noticed that the buildings were all built close together. She told Charlie she thought the road seemed crowded on the one hand but lonely on the other. Charlie explained, "That's because it's Sunday afternoon. The street is more active during the week when the shops are open, the streetcars running, and people are shopping."

Charlie motioned to both ends of the block. "Passengers can board, and get off, the streetcars at either corner. The bookstore is an equal distance from each corner."

"That's good to know," Mae said. She glanced across the street to where the homeless man was sleeping. Pointing, she asked, "Does he have a place to live?"

"Oh, him," Charlie sneered. "He's the town drunk. He sleeps wherever he drops. You'll get used to seeing him around."

"Does he have a name?"

"Everyone calls him Stanley."

Charlie pulled out a handful of keys from his pocket. He selected a long brass key and inserted it into the keyhole of the shop door. He pushed the door open and courteously motioned Mae to enter. Charlie reached around Mae brushing against her breasts to flick on the light switch. Six light bulbs dangling at the end of three-foot electric cords came to life. Mae thought they resembled a noose.

Mae's artistic mind flew into gear the moment she stepped into the bookstore. She found the interior of the store uninviting. There were no shades over the lights that forlornly dangled from the ceiling, at the end of three-foot humble looking electric cords. Mae surmised a little paint on the walls would not hurt either.

In a happy sounding voice, Charlie proclaimed, "Welcome to Charlie's Bookstore, Mae - your new workplace. There is a small apartment upstairs where you'll live. We'll go up there in a few minutes."

"Thanks, Uncle Charlie."

"Your job will be to keep the books in order on the shelves and file them in order of subject, author's name, and title, in alphabetical order. You'll have no trouble learning the system. It is easy once you start. I'll teach you."

"That's great Uncle Charlie. I'm eager to learn. Thank you for wanting to teach me. I'll try to learn the systems as fast as possible, but please be patient with me."

"I have a lot of patience," Charlie retorted. "Now, let me show you your new upstairs apartment."

"I'm anxious to see it, Uncle Charlie. I've never lived by myself before."

Charlie and Mae left the bookshop. Mae stood on the sidewalk while Charlie locked the shop door. To the right of the bookshop entrance, was another door. Mae concluded, from the few remnants of faded paint still intact, that it used to be green. Due to lack of attention, it had become the victim of many harsh Canadian winters.

Charlie reached into his pocket and pulled out his keys again. He chose a small silver key and inserted it into the keyhole. "This is the entrance to your apartment Mae. Here is your key." Charlie snapped a silver key from the ring and gave it to her.

Mae noted that the doorway was at sidewalk level, like the bookstore door. A steep flight of well-worn wooden stairs led to the second floor.

Charlie recounted that the apartment was where he and Mary lived when they first opened the bookstore many years ago.

Mae and Charlie mounted the creaky old stairs. At the top was another door. Charlie pushed it open and stepped into the single room apartment. Mae entered through the door behind him. He closed and locked the door by sliding a deadbolt latch into place.

"Always make sure to bolt the door when you're in here. It will keep you safe." Timidly, Mae asked, "Is there a lot of crime in the area, Uncle Charlie?"

"No, but sometimes Stanley will sleep in your doorway. By keeping the downstairs door locked and this one bolted, it will prevent him from getting in. When it is cold, or rainy, he tries to get inside to stay warm and dry."

Mae was not expecting Uncle Charlie to reveal anything like that to her. She thought to herself that she did not want to live there any longer than she had to. Already she had misgivings about the area and the apartment where she would be living entirely on her own every night.

Charlie led Mae further into the apartment, "Let me show you a few things about your new home Mae. Here is the gas stove. It has four burners on top and a big oven. You can do a lot of cooking on this stove if you want to. Since you'll be living by yourself, you may not use it that much."

Charlie pushed the pilot button and lit up each burner to show Mae that all four burners worked. A blue ring of fire burst into action each time he pushed a button. "That's how you light the gas burners, Mae."

"Wow! I've seen nothing like that before. I've only cooked on a wood stove. This one is modern in comparison." Unimpressed, Charlie did not comment. He showed her how to light the oven. Two rows of blue flames sprang to life.

"That is simple," Mae said.

Charlie moved towards the top loading icebox. He told Mae that Aunt Mary would make lunch for her every day and place it in this icebox. She would arrange for the iceman to deliver ice every day and set the twenty-five-pound block of ice in the box. Charlie told Mae that Mary would empty the pan underneath the icebox every day, except on weekends. Charlie assured Mae he wanted to make things easy for her.

Charlie continued walking and talking. Gesturing towards the kitchen, Charlie pointed out the dining area. Reaching above the kitchen counter, he opened a cupboard door to reveal dishes, a few cups, and miscellaneous well-used tableware. He opened a drawer below the countertop and showed Mae the cutlery.

The kitchen consisted of a sink and single cold-water tap. Mae turned the tap handle. It made a protesting gurgling noise and spewed out rusty water. After a few minutes, it became clear. Mae figured the tap had been dormant for a long time.

A small table and two chairs competed for space in the tiny dining area. Charlie took Mae across the room to a sofa farthest from the kitchen area. He reached down and pulled up on a handle. It sprang into a double bed. "That's where Mary and I used to sleep. It is your bed now Mae." Charlie pointed to a door beside the bed. "Bed linens are in the closet."

“Over here is a small TV set. It is an early model but still works well. You can see it from either the dining room or living room.”

“How convenient,” Mae commented.

Charlie continued. Mae was becoming bored with his explanations. Mae found him boastful.

“There is a grocery store at the end of the street where you can shop for food. It is only a short distance away.”

“I’m grateful for everything you and Aunt Mary are doing for me, Uncle Charlie. I’m looking forward to starting work tomorrow.” Mae was eager to leave the dismal looking apartment.

Charlie continued talking, “I want you to be happy Mae. Someday I may ask you to do something for me.”

Mae was relieved when Charlie said, “Let’s go downstairs and drive back home where I’m sure Mary and Wilma have put together a nice lunch for us. You can stay at our house tonight. Aunt Wilma will be going back on the train tomorrow morning. You can come with me to drop her off at the station. From there we’ll drive back here to the bookstore. You can start your new job and move into your new apartment tomorrow.”

Mae responded, “That sounds great Uncle Charlie,” although she had a few misgivings.

# 5

The Lewisville train station was in the heart of the city. When they arrived on the platform, Wilma turned to her brother and said, "Thanks Charlie for giving Mae a chance to succeed. Her life did not start well. I hope you can help her turn it around. She's smart and learns fast, so please do your best to put her on the right path. I've grown fond of her, and I want her to succeed."

"I'll do what I can for her Wilma. Times are tough in Lewisville and landing a job could be difficult because she has no experience. Working at the bookstore should help, however."

"I understand. Charlie, when the time is right, please use your influence to help her get a job. Speak to some of your rich merchant friends for help. She may not have job experience, but she is well educated, I can attest to that."

"I'll help her with introductions, Wilma. She needs a general knowledge of how business works though. I'll have her start work at the bookstore today. That will be a start. So far, she has only ever worked on a farm doing menial tasks. It won't be easy for her to move from that mindset."

"Please Charlie, get her socially mobile as soon as possible. She needs all the help she can get."

"I'll watch out for her," Charlie reassured his sister.

Wilma had grown fond of Mae over the years. She hoped that she could cope with city life, but not sure whether she could or not.

Wilma's routine and lifestyle changed when Mae arrived, but as time went on it became less of an issue. They both adapted to each other over the years. Mae was a pleasant and a helpful young lady to Wilma. Wilma understood that staying in the little village of

Avonmore was less than ideal for Mae. Wilma was sad Mae wanted to move but realized if she stayed, she would end up like her — a spinster in a decaying little village.

Through tear filled eyes Mae told Wilma, "Thank you for everything you have done for me, Aunt Wilma. The years I spent with you were memorable. You changed my life and took me in when no one else would. You transformed me from a little farm girl into an educated woman. I'll be forever grateful to you Aunt Wilma."

Wilma knew what Mae was referring to. Wilma's brother and his new wife abandoned Mae and moved to England. Mae was a burden to them. As she suspected would happen, Mae never heard from Father after he moved to England with Isabel.

With tears welling up in her eyes, Wilma said, "I was happy to be there for you Mae. I have grown close to you over the years. You are about to start a new life. My best wishes for success and happiness go out to you. Be well and stay strong Mae. Uncle Charlie promised that he would help you to get off to a good start."

With more tears in her eyes, Mae sobbed, "Thank you, Aunt Wilma. I'll never forget you."

"I will never forget you either Mae. I have a beautiful housecoat to remind me of you every day. Here comes my train," Wilma blurted. "I'll get on board right away before more tears flow. Goodbye Mae. I love you."

Wilma boarded the train but did not look back at Mae or Charlie standing on the platform behind her. Mae knew that she was still crying.

She does not want me to see her cry, Mae reasoned. She's a proud woman.

The train slowly pulled out of the station. Mae got a last glimpse of Wilma through the window as it gathered speed and left the station. Wilma waved to Mae and Charlie when she saw them. She was holding a white handkerchief to her eyes.

Charlie and Mae watched the train disappear, then walked to the car, and drove to the bookstore. Mae had difficulty watching Wilma ride out of her life, but excited about a new door about to open for her.

*********************

Inside the shop, Charlie brushed against Mae and pretended to accidentally rub across her breasts as he reached around her body to flick the light switch. The dangling, low voltage, light bulbs dimly illuminated the rows of books and supplies. The shop smelled damp and musty.

"Books need replacing, shelves and books dusted, and the floor washed every day," Charlie instructed. "I will show you how our filing system works. In time, you will deal with customers, but not right now."

Charlie taught Mae how to file the books according to the title, author's name, and subject. It only took Mae a few minutes to learn the system.

"You're a quick learner Mae. Wilma told me you were. I will pay you a weekly salary. Understand this is only a temporary job until you find a permanent one. I cannot afford to hire you full time. Our busiest time of year is during the school year when children need books and school supplies. We do not do much business in the summertime. Aunt Mary does the accounting for the shop. She'll deduct the rent from your paycheck for the upstairs apartment."

"I'm grateful to you and Aunt Mary for this opportunity Uncle Charlie. Thank you again."

Mae's life rapidly changed. She worked in the shop every day, Monday to Friday, and at the end of her workday she exited from the shop, walked a few steps to the faded green door, and climbed the creaky wooden stairs to her apartment above the store. Mae reserved Saturday to do grocery shopping. She settled into a routine but was having difficulty adjusting.

Other than Aunt Mary and Uncle Charlie Mae knew nobody. She was all alone in her small apartment every evening. The weekends were the worst time when everything slowed down. The stores were all closed, and no one walked on the street. The streetcars ran on a reduced schedule on Saturdays, and never ran on Sundays. There was no one around except Stanley, who she watched lumber from one garbage can to another foraging for food or something he could sell to keep him supplied with cheap wine.

After a month on the job, Charlie asked, "How is everything going Mae? Are you getting used to city life yet?"

Mae did not want to say how lonely she was. She was new to the city, and most people who lived in Lewisville had lived there most of their lives. They all had long-time friends and neighbors with whom they associated. Mae was new to the city, and living downtown allowed her no opportunity to meet people. She felt imprisoned and alone. Mae was afraid Charlie would ship her back to Avonmore if any sign of discontent appeared. Rather than risk that, she kept her depressing loneliness a secret.

Alone each night, Mae sat in her apartment window looking out into the street, listening to the sights and sounds of the city. The smell of warm, rotting garbage, filled the air, until the garbage man arrived, with his team of horses, and open wagon, to take it away. The smell stayed around longer than the garbage.

The clip-clop rhythm of the horse's hoofs, the dumping of the cans followed by the thumping sound of them bouncing on the sidewalk, became familiar sounds every night, guaranteed to keep Mae awake.

The haunting sound of streetcars rumbling under her window each night, clanging their bell at every corner, was another annoying sleep-depriving factor.

From her window she watched Stanley every night, push a shopping cart holding all his possessions, looking for a place to spend the night.

To help pass the night, Mae talked to herself. She wished she could have somebody to talk to at night, or someplace to go. Mae lived in the heart of the business district. At night there was nothing to see and nowhere to go - not even a movie theatre where she could go to pass the time. She had no form of transportation, and the streetcars stopped running at night.

Because Lewisville was where she lived, Mae hoped that in time she would meet more people, and the loneliness she was experiencing would pass. She vowed to remain strong, and work hard, to make a better life for herself.

Charlie approached Mae one day and said, "I think now is an appropriate time to start looking for a permanent job Mae. This job at the bookstore was only temporary until you became used to city life. You have had enough time to experience city life."

If only Uncle Charlie knew the problems I have fitting into city life, Mae told herself. He has never inquired how I spend my time at night when I leave work. Mae noticed Charlie had an uncaring attitude toward others.

Charlie continued, “You’re too smart to waste your talents dusting bookshelves. I have a friend who is the Personnel Manager at The Mill. He told me they are hiring again. I suggest you go to the employment office and fill out an application.

“Before you apply for a job, you will need to have some new clothes. Mary will take you shopping this afternoon and help you pick something out. Take the afternoon off and enjoy yourself. When you get a job at The Mill, you can continue to live above the store until school starts up again, when I will need it for storage. It will save you from paying a higher rent elsewhere.”

“Thank you, Uncle Charlie. It will be fun to shop for new clothes with Aunt Mary.”

Shopping with Aunt Mary was everything Mae thought it would be. Mary had lots of money. She bought an abundance of new clothes for Mae and a few things for herself. Mae had never been shopping before where money was no object. She wondered if the day would ever come when money was not a deterrent for her either. “Thank you for buying these beautiful clothes Aunt Mary. I’m so thankful and happy.”

“You’re welcome, Mae. You have enough clothes to keep you going for a while. This outing has been delightful Mae. We’ll do it again sometime.”

“What a great idea Aunt Mary. I had fun shopping with you also.”

Upon arrival at The Mill, Mae saw the display board listing open positions. She thought she could qualify for several of the registered jobs. Mae was thankful for the time, and energy Wilma spent to educate her. Mae realized that with no schooling, there would be few jobs on the board she could qualify for, other than a position on the line sorting yarns. She was thankful to Wilma for her foresightedness to ensure that she learned well.

Mae wondered how Aunt Wilma is doing? I should write to her, she said to herself. First things first though, I must concentrate on getting a job. There are well-paying jobs listed here. I hope they are still available when an interviewer calls me.

Lewisville was a one-industry town. Most working people in Lewisville worked at The Mill. It went through a slow period for several years but was now welcoming better times.

After reviewing the job list, a heavy-set security lady, dressed in a blue uniform, and wearing white gloves, directed Mae to take a number. Mae lifted a cardboard number from the hook, and the gloved security lady gave her an application form to complete. "Fill out this application and when you hear your number called, take it to the interviewer," she barked at Mae.

Mae took the application and her cardboard number and sat in the auditorium as instructed, to complete it. She had difficulty completing the employment application because she could not record when, where, and what schools she attended. Aunt Wilma homeschooled her and taught her everything she knows.

When the interviewer called her number, Mae eagerly sprang from her seat and sat in front of his desk. She was looking forward to her interview.

The interviewer took a moment to read Mae's application. He lifted his eyes and said, "I can tell from your application Mae that you're quite smart and pay attention to details. It is unfortunate you have no school records to back up your education, however. The Mill insists that every applicant include their school records with an application to justify their education levels. Applicants used to lie on their applications and claim school credits for grades they never earned. Once that became known, management insisted that school records accompany every application."

"I was taught at home by my Aunt who was a school teacher for many years. She taught me grades one through to grade ten. Does that not qualify me?"

"I'm sorry Mae, my hands are tied. Your level of education is higher than most people I interview, but the rules are the rules. If I make an exception for you, I risk losing my job."

Mae could not understand the reasoning behind the decision. In a firm voice, she said, "I am disappointed and angered by that stupid corporate policy. A fully certified teacher privately tutored me. It is unfair to disqualify me from a job just because I was home-schooled. I know I have a better education than most due to the private tutoring I received. I don't know how The Mill can be so short-sighted."

The interviewer lowered his head. He knew what Mae said was true. There was a long pause before he spoke. "I'm sorry Mae, but I'm powerless to make an exception for you, even though I believe you have sufficient education to do any job that we are looking to fill." The interviewer paused once more and awkwardly stated, "The only job I can offer you is a position on the yarn sorting line. It is the only job The Mill does not demand that the applicant supply proof of education. Even though you are over-qualified, the job is yours if you want it."

"I'm saddened that you cannot qualify me for something better, but I need a job, so I'll take the yarn sorting job."

"Very well Mae. Report to the Line Supervisor in three days. He will be expecting you."

Mae returned to her lonely apartment, threw herself across the bed, and cried. She questioned why she spent all those years with Aunt Wilma getting an education, only to qualify for a menial yarn sorting job.

People who applied for yarn sorting jobs had limited reading and writing skills. It was not a prestigious job. The other Mill workers scorned the line workers. Everyone knew that they were the least educated, and lowest paid. There was little inter-mingling of line sorting people with other employees.

********************

The Line Supervisor introduced Mae to a contraption called a punch clock. Mae had never encountered such a strange device. She recalled how Father decided his work schedule on the farm. Father watched for the sun to peek over the barn's gabled roof which was his signal to leave for work in the fields. Now, a noisy gadget called a punch clock was about to tell her when to start and stop work. Life will be different, she expected.

Mae received an employee number and punch card. She watched how other employees inserted their cards into the clock. Inserting the card into the slot below the clock caused it to belch, which signified permission to enter. Mae was fascinated with the procedure. She allowed others to go ahead of her so she could get a better look.

Mae sorted long skeins of yarns into an assortment of colors and textures. Twenty employees worked on the line with her. No one spoke to Mae. This job is tedious, she thought. I've been on the job for two hours, and already I'm ready to quit.

The Line Supervisor watched the workers like a dog guarding a bone. There were two fifteen-minute breaks a day, one in the morning, and one in the afternoon. Lunch was from noon to one o'clock. Mae could not leave her station on the line without first obtaining permission from the Line Supervisor.

A loud buzzer signaled the beginning of the allowable time away from the line. The break ended when the buzzer sounded calling the workers back to their posts. Those who returned late faced disciplinary action. The line workers were highly regimented. Mae supposed she should be happy with her new job. I wonder when the happiness will start. I hope it's soon, Mae thought.

The skeins of yarns arrived on a long narrow table from a machine that resembled a cannon. The cannon never relented, and it shot out large cannon-sized balls of yarn onto a conveyor belt. They unraveled when they hit the belt like a cascading waterfall tumbling onto the rocks. The fibers scurried down the belt like a river.

Male and female sorters staffed the line. They formed two lines, one on each side of the belt. Only the upper part of their bodies moved, grabbing and sorting the yarns, from early morning until late afternoon. What a miserable way to spend each day, Mae inwardly groaned.

Mae's first day on the job was lonely. At least when she worked at the bookstore, she could talk to Uncle Charlie. Here she had nobody.

On the second day, Mae noticed a young man working at the far end of the line, on the other side. Mae caught him glancing at her several times. She admired his friendly smile and pleasant looking face. She wished something would happen so that they could meet.

Two doors were leading from the main sorting room. One marked, 'Smoking' and the other, 'No Smoking' above the door frame. When the buzzer sounded, Mae watched the smiling young man rush into the 'Smoking' room. Even though she did not smoke,

Mae wanted to meet the young man with the smiling face. She thought it would be nice to meet someone her age. Mae was tired of being lonely all the time. Mae concluded that people are not going to go out of their way to meet her. The onus was on her to take the initiative. Therefore, if she wanted to meet the young man with the smiling face, she would have to follow him into the smoking room.

Mae sauntered into the smoke-filled room trying to look inconspicuous. A toxic blue cloud of smoke filled the air. The room was full of smokers puffing on cigarettes, pipes, and cigars. They had only fifteen minutes to satisfy their habits. They were sucking up tobacco smoke as fast as their lungs would allow them, hoping there might be time to light up again before the buzzer sounded. It was a race against the clock.

She did not want to make herself look too obvious so, she took her time and strolled through the room. There was a pungent odor in the air. It was difficult to see and breathe through the haze of smoke. There was poor ventilation in the room.

Endeavoring to look discreet, Mae sought the smiling face. Her eyes were getting sore and watery, and then she saw him standing alone in a corner lighting one cigarette from another. Mae noticed he smoked Players Cigarettes. She recognized the blue package with the familiar picture of a sailor on it. She inched her way toward him.

The cigarette puffing, smiling face, noticed the pretty lady with the shapely body coming towards him. He recognized her as the new girl on the line. He had been watching her all morning. The line workers were always changing. He regarded this new employee as a change for the better. He saw how well-dressed she was, compared to the other women on the line. She was a cut above the other female workers in his estimation.

Mae went over to where he was standing. "Hi, my name is Mae. I saw you standing here alone, so I came over to introduce myself. I have only been here for two days, and I don't know anybody yet."

"Nice to meet you, Mae. I'm Lester."

"How long have you worked here Lester?"

"Over five years."

"That's a long time doing the same job every day. Don't you get bored?"

"Sometimes."

"Why do you stay?"

"I want to get a Line Supervisor's job. Working on the line was the only job I could get. I am a loyal employee, and I know The Mill will recognize that and promote me to Line Supervisor someday. I have more seniority than anybody else on the line."

"How nice. I wish you luck."

"Thanks, Mae."

Lester was friendly and talkative. The kind of person she was looking to meet to fend off her loneliness. She envisioned, through Lester, reaching more people and becoming less lonely. Her consistent loneliness was making her depressed. She needed to step up her efforts to overcome what was making her so unhappy. Lester seemed like a nice man, and he liked her. She needed someone in her life. Could Lester be the one she wondered?

The buzzer sounded calling everyone back to work. Lester squelched his second cigarette out with his foot on the concrete floor. Mae was sorry that the time had gone by so quickly. She wondered if Lester was thinking the same? Mae returned to her post happier than when she left. The job no longer seemed dull - thanks to her encounter with Lester. Mae was glad she took the first step to talk to him. She doubted if he would have made the first move. She surmised he was not comfortable talking freely to members of the opposite sex.

Mae and Lester met up once more that day at the punch clock. Mae wondered if Lester manipulated his way through the exit line, so they would both come together at the punch clock together?

"Good-night Lester. See you tomorrow."

"Good-night Mae. Have a nice evening. I'll see you tomorrow."

Mae traveled home on the streetcar. Aunt Mary made her a cheese sandwich and left it in the icebox. There was a half-bottle of coke on top of a melting block of ice. Mae ate the food and drank the coke. After supper, she sat at the window and watched Stanley flit from one garbage can to another, looking for supper. Later Mae listened to an outdated version of Amos and Andy on the radio. She turned on the black and white TV, with its round picture tube, to catch the news. She could only find a local station which did not interest her. Mae went to bed early. She had trouble to fall asleep. She laid awake listening to the garbage man dumping the cans and the clip-clopping of his horses' hoofs.

# 6

Lester's parents immigrated from England on a Government Land Development Program. The Federal Government contracted with them to clear five acres of land in Northern Ontario. They could build a house on the cleared land if they wanted. Once completed, the lot and home were theirs. They had five years to fulfill the agreement. They received a small monthly Government Allowance.

Lester's father worked hard clearing the land of large trees and dense undergrowth. He worked every day from early morning until it became too dark to see. He took five years to clear the land and build a modest log cabin on it.

Lester was born in a tent in the frigid wintertime. He was an only child, living in the bush, with no friends for miles around. When he was sixteen years old, his father died when a tree crashed on him. After his father's tragic death, Lester and his mother moved to the city of Lewisville where Lester got a job working on the line at a local cotton mill.

Five years later, Lester's mother died. Lester had no other family. He was alone in the city and did not acquire many social graces growing up in the bush of Northern Ontario, nor where he lived alone in the city. Unlike Mae, he disliked mingling with other people.

The young lady who worked at the other end of the line intrigued him. He thought he would like to get to know her better. She looked and acted differently than the other female workers. Lester thought the new line worker added a touch of class to an otherwise loathsome lot of female workers.

Lester assumed Mae was new to the city because he had never seen her before. Everyone who lived in Lewisville knew their neighbors. It was not a huge city. Most people who worked at The Mill knew someone else who worked there also. The line workers all knew one another except Mae. No other line worker ever talked to her. They all had friends, and Mae was an outsider.

Lester sensed Mae could use a friend. Lester was shy and awkward when in the presence of members of the opposite sex. He thought Mae might be shy also. He wondered if there was a chance she would go on a date with him?

Friday was payday at The Mill. Lester thought he would ask Mae to go to a movie with him on Saturday night.

At the sound of the buzzer, Lester and Mae entered the smoking room and met in their usual corner. Lester showing no emotion, asked Mae to go to a movie with him on Saturday night.

"That would be great Lester. What theatre are we going to, and what movie is playing?"

"We'll go to the theatre on Main Street. There is a war movie playing which I'd like to see."

"A war movie?" Mae asked to make sure she heard right.

"Yes. I hear it is full of blood and killing. It will be a great movie."

"Okay, Lester. I was not expecting you to take me to see a war movie. I suppose I will like it. Anyway, it will be nice to be with you."

Lester arranged with Mae to pick her up at her apartment at six-thirty on Saturday evening. Mae spent all day on Saturday getting prepared for her date. She hoped Lester would not change his mind.

At least tonight, Mae thought, she will have more to do than watching Stanley search for supper before the garbage man and his horse arrived to dump the cans. She washed her hair and rolled it up in curlers. She picked out a dress that Aunt Mary bought for her on their shopping spree. It was a simple cotton print dress. She ironed it and put out a new pair of nylons. She hoped Lester liked how she looked.

She wished she had nail polish and lipstick to wear, but Mae didn't know when she would ever wear it again? The Mill did not allow its female line workers to wear lipstick or nail polish. They were guarding against the colors running into the yarns.

Lester arrived right on time. Mae went downstairs to meet him. Lester had on a dull white tee shirt, baggy pants and worn out shoes. His cigarette package formed a square lump in the breast pocket of his shirt. It looked like he combed his hair with a rake. Mae became concerned that Lester might think she was over-dressed.

"Hi, Mae. It is nice to see you. You look pretty."

"Thank-you Lester. I'm looking forward to watching the movie with you."

The streetcar rattled along the rails for fifteen minutes before it arrived at the theatre. Mae felt out-of-place riding the tram in her fancy clothes. It did not bother Lester that he was the least casually dressed of everybody riding the rails that evening. Mae wondered if he had any other casual clothes to wear.

When they arrived at the theatre, Lester went to the wicket and bought the tickets. They entered the theatre and passed the concession stand where the smell of fresh popcorn permeated the lobby. It reminded Mae how hungry she was. Mae hoped Lester might stop at the concession booth where the hot popcorn was popping inside a glass cabinet. She watched it pop over the pot and fall to the bottom where the attendant scooped it up and dumped it into a tall cardboard container. It looked and smelled delicious which activated her taste buds even more.

"Do you like popcorn Lester?"

"I hate popcorn. It sticks in my teeth."

Sarcastically Mae commented, "That's too bad Lester."

Mae thought she would try another tactic. She asked, "Have you had supper yet Lester?"

"Yes. I opened a large can of pork and beans before leaving."

"Good for you," Mae commented again sarcastically. Mae could not get Lester to grasp she wanted to munch on some popcorn.

The Movie Reel News was playing when they entered the theatre. Mae whispered to Lester, this was her first time in a movie theatre, and she found it very dark.

"I'll go ahead," Lester said. "Take my hand and follow me."

Mae reached out in the darkness for Lester's hand. She found it, and they walked together down the aisle hand in hand. Lester's hand felt nice clasping hers.

Lester spotted two vacant seats in the center of the theatre. To reach them needed disturbing four other people already seated. Lester climbed over bodies on his mission to reach the empty seats. Mae followed behind him, embarrassed at the way he conducted himself. Lester did not even excuse himself to the other movie goers. He needs to learn some manners, she said to herself.

When they reached the seats that Lester hunted down, he put himself into one chair and left Mae standing. Mae was not impressed with his lack of chivalry.

The newsreel finished, and the main feature was about to begin. It started off loud and violent, and it continued that way throughout. Mae did not like the movie. She would have preferred something more romantic, with a better storyline.

Lester thought the movie was great. He asked Mae if she liked it too?

"Some parts I liked better than others," Mae answered diplomatically.

"Good," Lester responded to her uncommitted reply. "We'll have to do it again."

Mae suggested that they go to a different type of movie the next time.

"We'll see," Lester replied.

The streetcar arrived at Mae's stop, and they both exited from the rear door. They started their walk along Pitt Street, to Mae's faded green apartment door. On the way, Stanley appeared from a doorway and approached Lester. He asked if Lester could spare a dime for a cup of coffee?

Lester shouted at Stanley, "Get lost and get a job, you bum."

Mae thought that Lester's action was mean and cruel. "His name is Stanley, Lester. He is a homeless man who hangs out in the neighborhood. He sometimes sleeps in my doorway. He's harmless."

Mae reached into her purse and took out a quarter. "Here you are, Stanley. Get yourself something to eat."

"Thank you, Miss. God bless, you."

"What a waste of money," Lester snarled at Mae.

Lester noticed Mae's look of disapproval. He took her hand in his, and they walked the rest of the way hand in hand. Neither spoke, each enveloped by their thoughts.

Mae's apartment was getting closer. She was wondering what will happen when they arrive at her doorway. Would Lester want to come upstairs? What would she say to him if he did?

She recalled Aunt Wilma's warning that men only wanted one thing from a woman — to get her in bed.

Mae was correct. That's what Lester was hoping would happen. Could he get lucky tonight?

"This is my doorway," Mae said when they arrived at the faded street-level door.

Mae thanked Lester for the pleasant evening and held out her hand to shake his. Lester, surprised at Mae's words and gesture, shook her hand and thanked her for agreeing to go on a date with him. They turned and went their separate ways.

Mae put her key in the latch and opened the downstairs door. She walked up the creaky stairs to her dark empty apartment. Upstairs, Mae pulled the handle which opened the sofa into a bed and threw herself across it, still dressed and reminiscing about her evening with Lester. She enjoyed being with him even though she did not like his choice of movie, and rudeness.

After the awkward handshake, Lester walked back to the streetcar stop. He lived across town. His mother used to own the house he lives in, and Lester continued to live there after her death.

On the streetcar, Lester recalled his evening with Mae. He thought about the abrupt ending at her doorway. Lester was unsure what happened at Mae's door. Was Mae upset with me, he wondered, or was it the way I spoke to the homeless guy?

Lester recalled how Mae looked in her beautiful dress, which accented her stunning body. It made her more attractive than The Mill issued smock he usually saw her wearing. He thought he would like to go on another date with her, assuming he hadn't screwed things up on this date. I will ask her to another movie, Lester thought. I hope she agrees.

On Monday, Mae and Lester met in the smoking room, as usual. Mae thanked Lester for the enjoyable evening on Saturday even though she was not pleased with the way he dressed for their first date, nor how he conducted himself at the theatre when he climbed over the other seated theatre customers without excusing himself.

Lester did not ingratiate himself with Mae when he made his cruel, and lewd remarks to Stanley. Mae thought Lester was crude and self-centered. He was not the person she first thought he was.

In the smoking room on Monday morning, Lester asked Mae if she would like to see another movie next week? Mae's thoughts flashed back to the hours spent alone in her apartment, and how depressed it made her feel. Which is worse, she asked herself, to sit alone crying to myself all weekend, or put up with Lester's ill-mannered behaviors? She quickly concluded it was better to put up with Lester's bad manners than to be alone.

Mae answered Lester, "I'd love to see another movie with you Lester."

"Good. Another great war movie is playing this weekend. We will see that one."

"Okay, Lester."

"I'll pick you up at six thirty on Saturday night, Mae."

Mae knew she would not enjoy seeing another war movie, but she would pretend to like it anyway. She did not want to offend him. Mae knew it was better than the loneliness she would suffer if she stayed home.

Mae and Lester met every day in the smoking room. It made the tedious job of sorting yarns more tolerable. Unlike Lester, Mae was not developing any romantic attraction towards Lester. He was a means to put contrast into her life and protect her from boredom and loneliness - nothing else.

Lester was developing feelings for this young lady. He had no one in his life to love. He thought he might be falling in love with her.

Saturday evening arrived. Mae went downstairs to meet Lester when the doorbell rang. She made sure she ate beforehand. Mae wore a different dress for this date with Lester. She hoped he liked it. It clung tighter to her body than the one she wore a week earlier and had a more revealing neckline.

When Mae opened the downstairs door, Lester's eyes widened, as he greeted her with a big smile and said, "Hi Mae. You look good."

Eying her shapely body, he commented, "I like your dress. It fits you well."

"Thank you, Lester. I am glad you like how I look. I guess I look different than the way you see me dressed for work."

"You sure do," Lester said admiring her up and down.

Mae wanted to return the compliment until she noticed that Lester had on the same tee shirt and baggy pants he wore a week earlier. Even the cigarette package in the shirt pocket looked the same, although she knew it was not because Lester smoked a packet of cigarettes every day. Mae wished he had dressed a little better for her. She suspected he had no other casual clothes to wear.

At the theatre, Lester bought the tickets, bypassed the concession stand, and went straight into the theatre. This time they found two seats on the aisle. Mae was pleased that they did not have to climb over other people to get to their places.

After the movie, Mae reflected that it was no better than the one she saw last week. Excitedly, Lester asked, "Wasn't that a terrific movie Mae?" Not waiting for an answer, he continued, "It was full of shooting and bloodletting."

"I'm glad you enjoyed it," Mae answered dryly.

Afterward, they walked hand in hand to the streetcar stop. Mae thought Lester strode closer to her than he did on their first date.

Mae detested the movie and was not pleased with the way Lester dressed, but she was sorry that the evening was ending. It meant that she would have to return to her lonely apartment and remain there until it was time to meet Charlie and Mary for church and dinner.

As the streetcar rumbled along the tracks, Lester made his move. "I notice that you wore a different dress than last week Mae. It looks terrific on you."

Lester thought that a little flattery now may reap results later at Mae's front door. He wanted no repeat of last week. Lester adored Mae's pretty legs. He wanted to see more of them. He wondered what his chances were?

Mae noticed that Lester was paying more attention to her than last week. They walked toward her front door hand in hand. Mae wondered what to do next. She was not looking forward to returning to her empty apartment and crying herself to sleep like she did most nights.

When they arrived at her door, Lester aggressively asked, "I'd love to have a cup of coffee. Can I come upstairs?"

Mae quickly thought that entertaining Lester would beat sitting alone in her tiny apartment listening and watching for the garbage man and his team of horses.

"That's a nice idea, Lester. I will make coffee when we get up-stairs. You'll be my first guest."

"I'm pleased to be your first guest Mae. Hopefully, there will be more invitations." Mae just smiled at Lester's remark. Thoughts of Wilma telling her that men only wanted one thing from a woman zoomed momentarily into her mind and fleeted away just as fast.

Mae invited Lester to have a seat on the sofa. She went to the stove to boil water for instant coffee and put out a few oatmeal cookies she baked that afternoon. Mae placed a pitcher of milk and a bowl of sugar beside the cookies.

"I'm sorry Lester I don't have a coffee table in front of the sofa. Come into the kitchen and put the milk and sugar in your coffee. Take a cookie while you're there."

"Okay. Thanks, Mae"

Lester walked to the kitchen table where his coffee was waiting. Mae was already at the table fixing hers. Lester stood beside her. She sensed something different about him.

"We can watch the rest of the hockey game with our coffee and cookies."

"I'm all for that," Lester said excitedly.

They both returned to the sofa. Mae turned on the TV. The game was in the third period. There was little time left. Lester was a Toronto Maple Leafs fan. His team was losing, which was not unusual.

Mae and Lester watched The Leafs lose, but Mae was happy to have someone to talk to and wanted Lester to stay longer.

"Would you like some cheese and crackers, Lester?"

"Yes, please."

Mae put out a platter of diced Canadian cheddar cheese and some Ritz crackers. She was happy Lester agreed to stay. They spent the rest of the evening chatting and watching TV. Lester glanced at the clock on the wall and said, "It is getting late Mae. I missed the last streetcar. I'll have to call a cab."

"That's not necessary Lester, you can stay here if you wish. This evening has enabled us to get to know one another. If you stay, we could get to know each other even better."

"I like that idea Mae. There is nothing I would rather do right now than get to know you better. I'll get more comfortable and make myself another cup of coffee."

"Will you make one for me also Lester?" Lester replied, "Of course."

While Lester was making coffee for them, Mae pulled up the handle under the sofa and magically, it turned into a bed. Mae hoped loneliness would escape her tonight.

# 7

The next morning was Sunday. Mae and Lester woke up together. "My aunt and uncle will arrive in a couple of hours to take me to church. I must be ready when they get here, although I'd much rather stay here in bed with you Lester."

"I'd prefer that too Mae."

"Thank you for staying with me last night Lester. I get very lonely living here all alone, especially at night. It was nice to have you beside me. Unfortunately, all good things end. I must get ready for Uncle Charlie and Aunt Mary to pick me up downstairs. You can leave after I am gone. I think it best if we keep the joys of last night to ourselves."

"That's fine Mae. I'll see you tomorrow at work."

"Thanks Lester for your understanding. I enjoyed your company last night. Maybe we can do it again sometime."

"I'd like that Mae."

This morning was better than most mornings. Mae had someone to talk to and make love to overnight. The depressive feelings Mae usually woke up with on Sunday mornings were gone. She felt rejuvenated, thanks to Lester. It would be nice to feel like this every morning, Mae thought.

Mae dreaded the thought of coming back to an empty apartment later. Before leaving, Mae kissed Lester on the cheek and thanked him for staying with her last night. She knew she would miss him when she returned later that afternoon. The apartment will seem empty without him, she sadly thought to herself.

Lester told Mae he would miss her too when she left to meet Mary and Charlie. He enjoyed staying with Mae over-night instead of sleeping alone as he usually did.

Mae regretted having to leave Lester in her bed. It had become a ritual that Uncle Charlie and Aunt Mary picked her up every Sunday at her street-level door, and then off to church and dinner afterward at Mary and Charlie's place. She dared not change that weekly habit fearing questions from Uncle Charlie and Aunt Mary she was not prepared to answer yet. She was sure they would not understand.

"Mae, you look radiant this morning," Charlie remarked as Mae slid into the back seat.

"Thank you, Uncle Charlie. I had a good night's sleep and woke up refreshed."

"It looks like city life agrees with you Mae."

"Yes, it does, Uncle Charlie. It certainly does."

The next morning, in the smoking room, Mae thanked Lester again for staying with her on Saturday night. Lester confided that he felt the same way about her.

Because he lived alone, Lester knew how lonely nights could be. He had nobody in his life either. Spending time together helped Mae and Lester overcome their fears of loneliness. They agreed it was a good arrangement.

Both found it interesting that they both suffered from the same ailment - loneliness. Mae had an idea. She suggested they meet for coffee after work and discuss it further. There was no time in the smoking room to address such an intricate subject. They agreed to meet over coffee that evening.

At the coffee shop, Mae came right to the point. "Lester, we are two lonely people. I believe that we could help each other heal our afflictions. I'd like to deepen our friendship. I am new to the city, and I have no friends, only you. Moreover, it sounds like you could use a friend also. We can help each other. I'd like you as my friend Lester."

"What do you suggest Mae?"

"Let's spend more time with each other instead of just going to a movie together on Saturday nights. We could enjoy each other's company during the week which would spell off the loneliness we are both experiencing. You could visit my place, or we could go to your place. Loneliness is depressing. I like being with you Lester, and it would be fun to do things together, rather than alone."

"I like the idea Mae, but I'm concerned about what your aunt and uncle might think about me spending so much time in your apartment, particularly if I were to stay overnight. I don't want to create problems for you."

"For the time being Lester, it is best they do not know about you. We are just friends, but it may be hard to explain that to them. Besides which, my living arrangements in the apartment are temporary. I must move out soon because Uncle Charlie needs the space to store supplies when school starts up again. We can decide how to tell them after I move. It is none of their business who I invite into my apartment as long as I do not abuse the property and pay the rent on time."

Lester said, "If I'm going to spend more time at your place, I'll need a few things like a razor and some clothes."

"Go home now Lester and pick up what you need, then come back to the apartment. You can hide your stuff behind the sofa to keep Mary from seeing it when she enters the apartment to put ice in the box and empty the pan underneath. Meanwhile, I will go to the apartment and start supper for us."

"It sounds like a good plan Mae, let's make it happen."

Mae was delighted at Lester's quick acceptance to her invitation. No more loneliness, she delightfully thought. Upon exiting the coffee shop, Mae told Lester she would leave the bottom door of the apartment unlocked for him. She told him to regard it as his second home. She would get a key made for him.

Mae wanted to make a nice supper for Lester. On her way home, she bought beer and cigarettes. She knew how much Lester liked to smoke and drink beer.

Mae put the beer in the icebox, and the cigarettes on the table where Lester could see them. Next, she changed out of her Mill issued smock and put on a cute black skirt and a cream-colored blouse. They were clothes that Aunt Mary bought for her on their shopping spree. It was the first time she had worn them.

She prepared supper for two, a first since moving to the city. She hoped it would not be too long before Lester arrived. He will add new life to this otherwise dull apartment, she told herself.

Mae heard Lester open the downstairs door and come upstairs. He arrived with an old suitcase.

"Hi Lester," Mae called out to him. "Hide your stuff behind the sofa and relax. Supper will be ready soon."

"Okay. I'm a little tired," Lester sighed.

Mae motioned towards the cigarette package on the table. "I bought you a package of cigarettes, and there is beer cooling in the icebox."

"Thank you, Mae. You think of everything."

Ten minutes elapsed then Mae called Lester for supper. There was no answer. She glanced toward him and saw he was asleep on the sofa. She called again in a slightly louder voice, "Supper is ready Lester."

Lester jumped. "I'm coming, I'm coming," he repeatedly answered, as he rubbed his eyes and trudged across the floor to where Mae was dishing out supper in the kitchen.

Without waiting for Mae to join him, Lester dove into his food like he was afraid it might jump off the plate before he got to it. He is very ill-mannered, Mae thought. I first noted that at the theatre when Lester climbed over the other people without excusing himself. He was also rude to Stanley. I would be uncomfortable introducing him to Aunt Mary and Uncle Charlie. They are too sophisticated to understand why I'd associate with someone as crude as Lester.

Mae watched Lester devour his supper. She waited until he pushed the last few peas onto his spoon with his thumb, and said, "I'm happy you enjoyed your supper, Lester. We have apple pie for dessert. Would you like a slice?"

"Yes. A big one."

Mae took the pie out of the icebox, cut a large slice, and placed it on a plate which she slid over to Lester. Lester, using both hands, lifted the giant slice of apple pie to his mouth, and ate it like a piece of toast. Mae was awestruck at the way he ate.

When Lester finished eating, Mae told him to rest on the sofa while she cleaned up in the kitchen. After Mae tidied up, she joined Lester on the sofa and they relaxed and watched TV together. Mae was happy the way things were working out. Lester was the answer to warding off her loneliness. Lester, from his viewpoint, felt the same way. They were there for each other. When romantic inclinations arose, they were there for each other in that respect also, although Mae did not encourage sexual encounters. If it happens, it happens, she said to herself. Lester wished it would happen more often. But he too was happy that he found someone to keep him from feeling lonely and unwanted.

Lester always stayed with Mae at her place. They never stayed at Lester's home. Mae did not even know where Lester lived. Lester only returned to his house to pick up the mail and do his laundry. He never asked Mae to go with him. Mae wondered why. She knew he lived on the other side of town. Mae was curious to see where he lived and in what type of house. Mae assumed that one day Lester would take her to see his place. She did not regard it important enough to insist he do it now.

Other than having Lester as a friend, life went on as usual for Mae. She hated her monotonous yarn sorting job, and she still had nothing in common with other workers on the line. She needed something more than a low paying, yarn sorting job, to challenge her.

The other workers all knew one another, both on and off the job. They were not interested in progressing any further than where they were. Most workers regarded their position as an unfortunate interruption to their fun time. They often arrived at work drunk, especially on Monday mornings.

Mae wanted a job more suited to her qualification level. To do that she needed documents to prove her education. The only steady employment was at The Mill. The depression left Lewisville economically scarred, and it was only now recovering, after several years of negative growth. Uncle Charlie tells me I'm lucky to have a job.

# 8

Mae and Lester continued to live together. They kept their relationship secret. Mae recognized that Lester could be rude and possessive. It bothered her at first, but she was powerless to correct his in-grained mannerisms. She learned when Lester got into one of his moods to ignore him and let him vent. Eventually, he would return to his usual self.

Mae was indebted to Lester because he was the sole person in Lewisville who saved her from the acute anxiety and loneliness she experienced after moving to the city. Only one part of Lester remained murky. Mae had yet to see where he lived. Lester never seemed comfortable talking about his home, nor his personal life.

Mae liked having Lester in her life. The thoughts of marriage occasionally entered her mind, but she kept them to herself. Mae was unsure how Lester would react to marriage or a permanent arrangement. She wanted to test him and measure his response.

"Lester, ever since our first meeting, we supported each other, and been available for each other when the need arose, I'm grateful to you for helping me overcome my loneliness. If you had not been there for me, who knows what state of despair might have encompassed me. I want you to continue to be a part of my life."

Lester asked, "What are you getting at?"

"I want us to have a more permanent arrangement, Lester,"

He gave her a strange look.

Mae continued. "We could get married," she stammered.

Lester appeared startled at Mae's suggestion.

Mae resumed, “I’ll have to move out of this apartment soon and find another place to live. I do not want our relationship to change. I like having you in my life. I want to marry you, Lester.”

Lester answered, “You mean a lot to me also Mae, my life would be empty without you. I thought about marriage a few times but thought we should wait until I got the Line Supervisor’s job, then get married. I don’t make enough money now to support both of us.”

“We could live off both salaries like we are doing now, Lester.”

Lester replied, “I believe that a woman’s place is in the home, looking after the house, and tending to her husband’s needs.”

“I understand Lester. After you get the Line Supervisor’s job, I can stop work. Meanwhile, nothing is wrong with me continuing to work until you get the promotion.”

Lester asked, “Where would we live when you give up this apartment?”

“You have a house Lester, even though I’ve never seen it. We could get married and live at your place.”

“My house is old and needs repairs. I don’t have time, or money, to fix it up,” Lester replied.

“I’d still like to see where you live Lester so that we can make a joint decision.”

“Let me think about it,” he answered.

Mae let the discussion rest. She sensed he was not ready yet. She reminded herself that was one of Lester’s weaknesses. He has difficulty making decisions.

The following Sunday at dinner time, Uncle Charlie asked if Mae had made any plans to move out of the apartment? He explained that he would need it soon to store inventory before school reopens.

Mae said that she would look for a place during the week. She thanked him for allowing her to stay at the apartment for an extended period.

“That’s okay Mae. I just wanted to give you a warning so that you don’t get stuck at the last minute with no place to live.”

“Thanks, Uncle Charlie for your concerns.”

Mae still did not want to say anything about Lester to either Aunt Mary or Uncle Charlie. She knew that neither would approve of their living arrangements.

Mae wanted Lester to agree to move into his house, even if he does not want to get married. She believed it would give them time to save money and make plans. It did not matter that his house was in bad shape, they could live there until they could afford something better. Mae suspected that Lester was ashamed of his home, and that was the reason for not letting her see it before now.

The next day, Mae and Lester met in their usual corner of the smoking room. “When you come home tonight Lester, there is something we need to talk about.”

Lester asked, “Why can’t you tell me now?”

“Because we have only a few minutes before the buzzer sounds and that is not enough time to discuss what I have in mind.”

“Oh, okay. I will see you tonight. I hope you have something good to eat.”

“I’ve something special in mind. I want to keep it as a surprise.”

On her way home, Mae splurged and bought two T-bone steaks. She usually would not buy such expensive cuts of meat, but tonight was special. She bought the usual six bottles of beer and cigarettes for Lester.

Lester went to the apartment directly from work. He was sitting on the sofa watching TV when Mae arrived.

Lester grumbled that Mae took too long to get home.

Mae explained that she had to stop and buy T-bone steaks for supper. Lester did not comment. Mae was unsure if Lester knew what T-bone steaks looked like or tasted.

The steaks were tender and delicious. Mae cooked them to perfection in the frying pan on top of the stove. Lester liked his meat well cooked. Mae enjoyed her steak a little on the rare side. She had only one frying pan. Mae could just cook one steak at a time. She prepared Lester’s first.

Lester as usual demolished his dinner before Mae got to the table. He was just finishing the last bottle of beer when she sat down to eat.

“Uncle Charlie told me that I’ll have to move soon and that I should start to look for another place to live. So, Lester, we must make plans.”

“When do you have to move?” Lester asked

"In a month."

Lester asked, "What are your plans?"

"I want to talk to you about that Lester. Whatever plans I make must include you. I like what we have together. I want it to continue. I want to suggest that we move into your place and continue living like we are. We do not need to get married. Living together will save us money. We can combine our salaries and buy a nicer house someday."

"My house needs a lot of repairs. You'll not like to live there."

"Is that why you never invite me to your house, Lester?"

"I guess so," Lester answered sheepishly.

"Lester, we have come a long way together. Nothing will shock me. We can live in your house and save money. With two of us working, it should not take too long."

"Okay. We will go there tomorrow after work. Be prepared - the house does not look nice."

The next day, Mae and Lester rode the streetcar to Lester's place. It took longer than riding to Mae's apartment. After getting off, there was a further two-block walk. Strolling along the street with Lester, Mae thought, that the area looked poor and desolate. There was garbage everywhere, and the neighborhood seemed dumpy and reeked of foul odors. She knew why Lester did not want her to see where he lived.

Half a block away, Lester pointed to his house for Mae to see. Mae believed it was the worst looking house she had ever seen.

Lester opened the front door. Mae noticed the broken doorbell. The screws that once held it in place had become detached from the well-rotted wood frame. The push button dangled at the end of two wires and appeared broken for a long time.

Lester held the door open for Mae. A harsh smell permeated the house. The walls and ceiling needed painting and the linoleum replaced. Lester left his clothes strewn throughout the house where he took them off but was too lazy to hang them up.

Mae told herself that Lester didn't exaggerate when he said the house needed work. Once inside Lester said, "Make yourself at home Mae. I'll make coffee."

While waiting for Lester to make coffee, Mae peered around the house from her vantage point in the kitchen.

What a dump, she thought. It will take a lot of work to fix this place up. It looks like a pig sty.

When Lester re-entered the kitchen, he asked, "What do you think Mae?"

"It needs work, Lester. I'll not like living here under these conditions, even for a short while."

"I know it needs a little tidying up," Lester confessed. "My mother owned it until she died. Then it became mine. I've never had time nor money to fix it up."

Mae commented, "I know that the house needs repairs, but before we move in, we should clean inside first. I will come over after work each night and start. You have a lot of rubbish to throw out. If you help me, the work will get done faster." Lester agreed to help.

Mae commented, "I want us to have a nice clean home Lester until we can afford something better. You have been living as a bachelor for too long."

Relieved Lester sighed, "That's a good plan, Mae. Living with you in a nice clean house will make me happy. I feel closer to you than ever before. We will have a good life together. We'll make this old house come alive."

Mae denoted a change of attitude with Lester after she outlined her plans. She was happy that he was pleased.

Mae wanted to tell Mary and Charlie she was moving in two weeks. She waited until Mary served dessert to make her announcement. "Uncle Charlie and Aunt Mary, I've something to tell you both. I'll be moving in two weeks. There are still a few details to sort out, but you can assume the apartment will be empty in time for the next school term Uncle Charlie."

"That's good Mae. Thank-you for freeing it up early."

Even though most of her time in the apartment triggered loneliness and isolation, Mae told Charlie, "I'm grateful to you Uncle Charlie for letting me stay in the apartment. It helped me to adjust to a new way of life. Thanks also for the on-job training in the bookstore. I'm indebted to both of you for all your help. Perhaps someday I can repay you for everything you have done for me."

Charlie responded, "We are both happy for you Mae."

Turning towards Mary, Mae said, "I want to thank you too, Aunt Mary, for keeping the icebox filled with ice and preparing lunches for me. I'll always remember our shopping fling. You raised my sights to new levels. I'd like to model my life after you."

In a tender voice, Mary said, "You're welcome Mae. You're a fine young lady, and I enjoy spending time with you."

Mae hoped that neither Charlie nor Mary would ask where she was planning to live. She preferred not to have Lester's name introduced just yet.

"You'll always be welcome here," Charlie said. "We like having you join us after church for dinner each Sunday. We hope that can continue."

Mae thought that when she moved in with Lester, that would be the end of church and Sunday dinners with Mary and Charlie. She suspected Lester would be uncomfortable in their company. Mae was doubtful if Lester ever went to church. Two reasons she thought her visits with Uncle Charlie and Aunt Mary would soon end.

To appease both, and avoid having to divulge her relationship with Lester, Mae lied and told Charlie. "I can think of no reason why we cannot maintain this pleasant weekly tradition of church and dinner."

That night Mae told Lester about the conversation with Mary and Charlie announcing her upcoming move.

"I did not say anything to them about you Lester. I did not think the timing was right."

"I prefer not to meet them," was Lester's response. "I don't like meeting people. I would not know what to say to them. I only feel comfortable with you Mae."

"I understand Lester. You won't have to meet them. I feel best when it is just the two of us also Lester. We'll make a good life for ourselves."

"If it is all right with you Lester, I'd still like to go to church on Sundays, and have dinner with Aunt Mary and Uncle Charlie afterward."

"Why?" Lester growled.

"Because that's what I've been doing every Sunday since I arrived here. It has become a tradition."

"What about me? Who will make my breakfast and dinner on Sundays? I want you to stay with me."

Mae was not surprised by Lester's decision, what surprised her, however, was his demanding attitude to keep her all to himself.

"We'll work something out," she told him. Mae did not want to prolong the conversation. Lately, she was experiencing stomach cramps, and she was feeling ill. She was not in any mood to argue.

"I'm not feeling well tonight. I want to go to bed and get a good night's sleep. Tomorrow is a workday."

Lester said, "How about a little lovemaking before you go to sleep?"

"Not tonight Lester. I want to go to bed and rest. I want to feel better tomorrow. I need strength when I work on our house tomorrow. It is a big job."

Lester bellowed, "Oh all right then. I'm leaving. I'll see you tomorrow at work."

Lester slammed the door behind him. Mae listened to him stomp down the stairs. She wondered if he might come back and apologize to her, or at least kiss her. Her hopes crashed when she heard the downstairs door thump closed, followed by the engaging click of the lock.

Before getting into bed, Mae reflected that she usually slept in the nude with Lester. Tonight, was different, however. Lester would not be sharing her bed, and she was not feeling well. She only wanted to be in her warm bed alone.

Mae left the door to the apartment unbolted in case Lester returned to apologize for the way he treated her.

Mae put on a new pair of pajamas she bought when she went shopping with Aunt Mary. She opened her bed, and slid under the blankets, wrapping them tightly around her, and went to sleep.

The next morning, Mae woke up to the sound of footsteps mounting the creaky wooden stairs. She thought it must be Lester coming back to apologize because nobody else had a key to unlock the downstairs door. She gasped when she saw Charlie standing in the doorway.

"Hello, Uncle Charlie. You scared me. It is early Monday morning, and I must get ready for work. Why are you here?"

Mae noted that Charlie looked at her like he did when they met at the train station. He was frightening her. Why is he here, she asked herself?

"I came to see you, Mae. You will be leaving from here soon. I came to say goodbye."

Getting out of bed and clutching her new pajamas tightly around her, Mae said, "I'm not leaving yet, Uncle Charlie, and when I leave I'm staying in Lewisville. Besides, we agreed to continue to attend church together and meet for dinner afterward, like we have every Sunday since my arrival."

With a defiant smirk on his face, Charlie said, "I want to say goodbye in another way, Mae."

"I don't understand Uncle Charlie," Mae said as she grabbed the blanket from the bed and draped it over her.

"First you can start by kissing me."

Charlie approached Mae and pulled her against his body. He brutally pressed his lips against Mae's. She could feel his tongue in her mouth. Mae fought to push Charlie away, and in doing so, her blanket fell to the floor. She was crying uncontrollably.

"Uncle Charlie, please stop," she screamed. "You're a beast. Why are you doing this? What would Aunt Mary think?"

Retreating, Charlie shouted, "What an ungrateful wench you are after all I have done for you."

"Uncle Charlie this is not the way I want to thank you for your favors. Please leave."

"Okay. I'm leaving, but you had better not say anything to anybody about this, especially to your Aunt Mary. If you do, I will make your life miserable. Don't forget that I have a lot of influence in this city. People will believe me over you. I will broadcast around town how you coerced me up to your apartment. I can make you lose your job at The Mill."

Sobbing profusely, Mae said, "You're mean Uncle Charlie. I want you out of my life. Please get out. I don't deserve this."

Charlie retorted, "I want you out of the apartment tonight. I will padlock the door tomorrow." Charlie dashed through the door and thundered down the stairs.

Charlie left Mae standing at the bottom of her bed crying. The blanket, which made her feel good the night before, laid in a heap on the floor. Her new pajama top was missing three buttons that popped off when Charlie tried to rip it off her. Charlie's advances tore her pajama bottoms. She was devastated by what happened. It took several minutes for her to compose herself. She trembled from her ordeal with the one person she least expected would be so mean and violent towards her. She felt dirty and ashamed. She wondered what she should do next. It was clear she could no longer stay in the apartment any longer. When she left, there would be no coming back. What will I do, she cried out in the empty apartment. She thought, if only Lester were here, he would have protected her.

Mae went into the bathroom. She scrubbed her body and put iodine on the scratches that Charlie inflicted. Mae understood this was the end of her living in the upstairs unit. She knew Charlie's threat to padlock the apartment was real. After dressing, she stuffed personal items into Father's old duffle bag and left for work taking the packed bag with her.

As usual, Lester was waiting for her at the punch clock. Mae found it strange that he made no mention about the duffle bag she was toting into work.

"Well, you made it," Lester jeered. "You don't look sick. I don't believe you were sick last night either. You just wanted to get rid of me."

"Believe me, Lester, I was sick last night, and I'm still sick." Mae thought it was best that Lester did not know that Charlie had molested her two hours earlier.

"When we meet at break time I've something to tell you, Lester."

"Okay," Lester said, expressing no curiosity.

Mae had difficulty standing at her station. The cannon never relented shooting out balls of colored yarn. Her body was aching, and she still felt ill. The rules made it clear that she could not leave her post. She was delighted when the buzzer finally sounded. She moved as fast as she could into the smoking room to hijack one of the few chairs available. She dragged it into the corner and sat down. A few minutes later Lester joined her.

"Lester, I told you that I had something to tell you."

"What is it?" Lester inquired.

"I originally wanted to wait a couple of weeks before we moved in together."

"Yeah, I remember," Lester said.

"I changed my mind. I want to move in with you tonight."

Lester was surprised at Mae's sudden change of mind, and the urgency she expressed. He asked, "What changed your mind?"

Mae did not want to tell Lester about her episode with Charlie, and that he would padlock the apartment to prevent her from entering. "I want us to live together in your house now Lester. I can wait no longer. I packed my things into a duffle bag, and it is in my locker. We can leave after work and go to your place tonight and start our new life together."

"Okay with me," Lester answered. Mae was happy to hear Lester's positive response.

The buzzer sounded calling the workers back to the line. Returning to her post this time did not affect Mae negatively like it usually did. She was happy that she was getting away from Charlie and entering a new life with Lester. She thought it proper that she and Lester decided not to get married yet. Mae figured there was enough stuff going on without adding marriage into the mix.

Mae was feeling better. Her upset stomach disappeared. She had no remorse for leaving the apartment, and Charlie behind. She was sorry she could not say goodbye to Aunt Mary. Would she wonder why Mae suddenly disappeared from her life?

# 9

Mae worked hard making Lester's home livable. It reminded her of doing chores on the farm when she was a young girl. Lester helped her with the cleaning at first but gradually withdrew his participation. He felt that cleaning house was women's work. Undeterred, Mae continued to work hard to spruce-up their new home, even if it meant she had to do all the work herself.

In less than two weeks, Mae's diligence paid off. She cleaned and organized the entire house. She even freshened up the walls with fresh paint. She enjoyed that part, as it enabled her to employ her artistic talents again. The trendy colors she chose reflected her natural creative style. It was no longer the dumpy looking house Lester introduced her to only two weeks earlier. Lester even complimented her on how pleasant the house looked. Mae was happy that Lester acknowledged what she had done, but deep-down she doubted if he meant it.

It didn't matter, she thought. She was with Lester and free from the depressive mood swings she went through when alone in the apartment each night. Now I have Lester to care for me, she joyfully thought.

She no longer had to put up with Charlie's groping hands and snide sexual overtones. Lester did not know about Charlie trying to rape her. She thought it best to keep it that way.

One morning before leaving for work, Mae told Lester she still did not feel well. She wanted to see a doctor and discover what was wrong with her. Mae went to a drop-in clinic after work so as not to take too much time off work. Lester went home to wait for her and later she would bring him up-to-date on what the doctor said. She perceived Lester was more concerned that she would not be back in time to make supper for him over what the doctor said was causing her to feel ill.

That evening, Mae went directly to the drop-in clinic. Lester went home to wait for her to come back and make supper for him.

The doctor asked, “How can I help you?”

“I’ve been sick for several mornings in a row. I’m hoping you can make me feel better.”

“Have you had a period this month?” the doctor inquired.

“I’m very irregular. Sometimes I miss a month, and sometimes I have two periods in one month. I never know when I’ll start or end.”

After a quick examination, the doctor told Mae, “Well young lady, it looks like you might be pregnant.”

“Pregnant?” Mae exclaimed. “My fiancé and I are very careful. I had a vaginal ring inserted. How could I possibly be pregnant?”

“No birth control method is foolproof,” the Doctor countered. “To make sure, I’ll order a pregnancy test and send it to the lab. Come back in a week. I’ll have the report back by that time. Meanwhile, I’ll give you something to ease your morning sickness.”

The doctor scribbled out a prescription and handed it to Mae. “This is a free clinic. You can get the prescription filled at the pharmacy down the hall.”

“Thank you, Doctor, for your help.”

Mae was full of emotions. If she was pregnant, how would she ever tell Lester? Because he had no interest in getting married, Mae expected Lester to have even less interest in becoming a father. She hoped that the doctor was wrong and that she was not pregnant. Now was not the time to complicate their life with a new baby.

Lester was waiting at home for Mae to return. He was sitting at a round table in the corner of the kitchen. Lester held a half-empty bottle of beer in one hand and a lit cigarette in the other. Mae noted Lester was putting on weight. He was shirtless, legs spread wide apart, wearing only a pair of underwear briefs. Strewn across the kitchen table were old newspapers, crumbled chocolate bar wrappers, unpaid bills, and empty beer bottles.

“I thought you would never get home,” he sneered at Mae. “I’m starving.”

Mae realized Lester changed significantly from when they first met in the smoking room on her second day of work. He had become very possessive and demanding.

She reminded herself that Lester rescued her from the depths of loneliness and depression. I can put up with his change of attitude towards me. She thought it was far better than living by herself with nobody to talk to, night after night. Lester did not inquire how Mae made out at the clinic. She was glad he didn't.

A week later, Mae returned to the clinic. She was full of anxieties over what the doctor might tell her.

The waiting room was full. The receptionist told her the doctor was running about thirty minutes behind schedule. Sitting in a waiting room full of strangers, Mae reflected on how she would break the news to Lester if she were pregnant. She hoped he would be happy but doubted he would be. What would she do, and where would she go, if he made her leave? Lester held all the cards. It was his house, and they lived common law. He had no official obligation to her. She hoped he had a moral obligation.

The nurse called her name and led Mae down a hallway into a small examining room.

"Hello Mae," the doctor said as she entered the room.

"Hello, Doctor. I'm nervous. I hope you have good news for me and tell me I'm not pregnant."

"I cannot do that Mae. Your tests returned positive. You're pregnant."

"Oh my God," Mae exclaimed. She gathered herself together as best she could, and said to the doctor, "We can barely make ends meet on two salaries. I don't know how we'll manage with a new baby. How will we grapple with the added expenses on one meager salary?"

The doctor told Mae he foresaw no complications and that she could expect a healthy pregnancy and deliver a healthy baby. He suggested she engage a gynecologist to watch over her pregnancy. Mae told him that was not financially possible.

He suggested she apply to the Charity Hospital where she can deliver her baby at no cost. He told her they would also offer pre-natal, and post-natal care. Mae thanked the doctor for the information and left the clinic filled with concern.

That night Mae sat at the kitchen table with Lester. She opened the conversation with, “As you know Lester I’ve consulted with the walk-in clinic doctor twice.”

“Yes, I know.”

“There is a reason for that.”

“I know that too. You had an upset stomach. It did not sound important. I wondered why you went to the clinic for something so trivial. I presumed there was nothing wrong, and the pills you came home with would fix whatever it was that was making you sick.”

“Well as it turns out Lester, it is more serious than just having an upset stomach which a few pills can cure.”

“Then what’s your problem?” Lester demanded.

“We are going to have a baby.”

Lester’s jaw dropped. He turned pale and stared at Mae in disbelief. After a few seconds of silence, he blurted out, “How did that happen?”

“You know how it happened Lester. You were the major contributor.”

Lester roared back, “It’s your fault. You probably took the ring out to trap me into marrying you.”

“That’s not true Lester. The fact remains we’ll have a baby, and we should be happy about that.”

“We cannot afford a baby, and I’m not happy,” Lester snapped. “I don’t like kids.”

“You’ll like our baby, Lester. I know you will. I’m certain you’ll come to love your child.”

“I doubt it,” Lester scoffed.

Lester’s reaction startled Mae. That’s something else I must work on, she thought. Lester has developed such a negative attitude about things.

Mae worried he might have trouble with fatherhood. She feared if he got angry enough, he would throw her, and her unborn child out of his house, and out of his life. She needed to prevent that from happening.

“When the baby is born, I want us to be married, Lester. I don’t want the baby to be born out-of-wedlock. Please do that for us Lester and our child. It is the right thing to do.”

Lester said that he had no use for churches and therefore a church wedding was out of the question.

Mae suggested they use a Justice of the Peace. "We can get married at the City Hall. We can go there tomorrow and reserve a time for a Justice of the Peace to marry us. It is less expensive than a formal wedding. We can arrange for an afternoon appointment sometime next week. That way we'll only lose a few hours from work."

Lester was not happy at the prospect of getting married. It was a significant commitment. It was difficult for him to make a life-long decision – like marriage.

Mae was adamant she and Lester would marry before their baby was born. On their lunch hour the next day, they went to City Hall to arrange for a civil marriage. The City Clerk told them to return on Wednesday, at one o'clock. "A Justice of the Peace will marry you at that time," she said.

The wedding day arrived. Even though Mae hoped her wedding day would be different, she was excited that she and Lester were about to become man and wife.

Mae and Lester went to work as usual and asked the Line Supervisor for permission to leave early, explaining that they were getting married. The supervisor granted their request.

When they arrived at City Hall, several other couples were in the room waiting to get married. The appointments were running an hour late. Lester grumbled the whole time they were there.

Mae responded, "Oh Lester be quiet. It's your wedding day. Be happy."

The ceremony lasted fifteen minutes. Lester and Mae returned home on the streetcar to start their married life together.

Mae was looking forward to when their baby would be born. She estimated motherhood would occur in six months. A baby bump was showing. She was not sure how happy Lester was about becoming a father, however.

Mae's pregnancy was not going as smooth as the doctor intimated it would. The medication prescribed for her morning sickness did not work. She was sick every morning. Lester was unsympathetic.

Lester continually reminded Mae he did not want children and accused her of tricking him into fatherhood. He retreated away from Mae and into a self-imposed moody exile. Mae could not understand his reactions and hoped he would soon come to accept and love his new offspring.

# *TRANSITIONS*

*Just when the caterpillar thought its life was over - it became a butterfly.*

# 10

Mae continued working throughout most of her pregnancy. She stopped three weeks before her due date.

She had strange feelings. Her back was aching more than usual. Her feet had swollen to where they looked like over-blown balloons. She was tired but could not sleep. She needed to pee every few minutes. The baby's foot was sticking into her ribs, making breathing difficult. Mae concluded that the time had come to go to the hospital and get the baby out of there.

She phoned The Mill and left a message with the Line Supervisor to ask Lester to call her on his break. When he called, he told her to go to the hospital on her own. He explained that he could not afford to take time off. They needed every penny. Lester assured her she would be okay on her own.

Lester signified he had no intention of showing up at the hospital that night. Mae was disappointed but understood that Lester needed someone to tell him what to do next. She did not grasp that trait when they first met, but only after they lived together.

Mae was in no mood to goad him into visiting her at the hospital that night. She was not comfortable and thought it best that she handles things by herself. It was always a hassle when Lester got involved. She was confident he would show up before their baby was born.

Mae understood why Lester did not want to take time off work to sit with her at the hospital while Mae was prepping for delivery. Mae was still concerned about where they would get the money to support a new baby. Before she got pregnant, the lack of money flowing into the house was an issue for her and Lester. Now

Lester was the only one bringing home a paycheck, and they had a baby to feed and clothe. Contrary to Mae's concerns, Lester did not think there would be any problem with three people living off his small salary.

Mae knew that the lack of money would make it tough and it could be a struggle to make ends meet. She hoped that Lester would allow her to return to work after the baby was born, although she doubted he would. He was too proud to let his wife go out to work.

Mae rode the streetcar to the hospital, her big belly showing that a baby was soon to be born. It was not a pleasant journey. She was thankful the tram was almost empty, she flopped down on a seat near the front. Her body was aching from head to toe. The tram's wheels, rolling against the steel rails, seemed louder, and bumpier than usual.

The streetcar stopped in front of the publicly funded hospital for expectant mothers. To qualify for the hospital's free services, mothers had to live at, or below, the poverty level.

Mae entered the reception area and filled out the registration papers. She was happy she took the doctor's advice and preregistered. It saved a lot of time.

Mae's bed was on the second floor, in a large ward filled with other expectant mothers. Busy, and understaffed, there was little time available for individual attention.

Mae listened to the sounds of scampering nurses, and busy doctors, tending to other patients in the ward. Soon, she hoped, it will be my turn.

There were ten beds in the ward. Five against each wall. Only a flimsy curtain separated them. Nurses hopped from one bed to the other checking on patients and wheeling them to and from the delivery rooms.

After a long wait, a nurse finally arrived to examine Mae. She pulled the curtain around the foot of the bed. In her haste, she forgot to reopen it when she left.

Alone, and full of anxiety, Mae's only view was a three-sided, faded, white curtain. Her world for the moment.

Elsewhere in the ward, Mae heard the moaning of other expectant mothers. She knew in a short while she would sound like that too.

Mae wished Lester could be with her for support. Giving birth is more difficult than she expected.

Most husbands would be at their wife's bedside when they were about to give birth to their first child - not Lester, she fumed. Mae felt that Lester was mean and inconsiderate. He was not the same pleasant young man, with the smiling face, she first met in the smoking room at The Mill. Lester's behavior changed when Mae told him he was to become a father. He was a different person now. Mae thought it strange how his personality and attitude changed so abruptly. She hoped his peculiar approach to values and responsibilities would not be a problem for them.

There were lots of people milling around in the ward and still, Mae felt alone. A feeling she used to experience and dreaded when she lived above the bookstore until Lester entered her life and rescued her. She wondered what happened to that kind and caring man?

Mae let her thoughts wander about her life with Lester. She recalled that Lester had no formal education growing up in the bush. Thanks to Wilma's proficient schooling, she was far more adept at reading and writing than Lester. My job at the bookstore improved my general knowledge skills. Poor Lester. He does not know what is happening outside his simple task of sorting yarns day after day at The Mill. In that respect, she regarded him like everybody else on the line. There was no desire to move from their everyday mundane job of sorting yarns at a minimal wage to something better.

The economy in Lewisville was showing signs of improving. Mae hoped that it would improve enough to enable Lester to find a better job. That would benefit the entire family, including the unborn child she was carrying inside of her.

The yarn sorters were the lowest paid of all the workers at The Mill and not entitled to fringe benefits as the other workers were.

Lester was not as ambitious as Mae was. It would not be easy on Mae's part, to convince him to change his job. He keeps holding out for a Line Supervisor's job which Mae did not believe would ever materialize.

Mae understood that she had more immediate things to concern herself with now over her concern for Lester. She was about to give birth to her first child.

There was a strong smell of ether throughout the hospital. The walls were white once upon a time. The toll of time had turned them a brownish yellow. A bevy of nurses walked past the foot of her bed. None ever stopped to ask her how she was doing, or if there was anything she needed. No one cared that her curtain remained closed and she was all alone.

Hours went by, and as she expected, still no sign of Lester. Mae figured that Lester by this time was asleep at the kitchen table after having smoked a half package of cigarettes and guzzled down four, or more, bottles of beer.

Her labor pains were coming more often. She tried to make herself comfortable. Finally, a nurse opened the curtain and started prepping her for the most significant event of her life.

Mae gave birth the following day to a baby boy. As she feared would happen, Lester never showed up.

Mae remembered in the delivery room, two nurses and a Doctor coaching Mae through the birth of her first child. She recalled the Doctor asking her, "What is the name of the child?"

She answered, "I don't have a name yet. My husband and I could not come up with one."

"You had nine months to decide," the doctor said sarcastically. "I'm busy and have no time to wait for you to decide on a name. You must give me one now."

Mae thought for a moment. The name Ronald leaped into her mind. I always liked the name Ronnie, she mused. Before losing her thoughts in the excitement of the moment, Mae shouted, "His name is Ronald - Ronnie for short."

Mae and Ronnie bonded together alone without Lester present to share those precious moments. The next morning, a nurse told Mae that Lester phoned to say he will stop by on his way to work.

An hour later Lester arrived at Mae's bedside. Lester saw his son for the first time. Mae introduced Ronnie to his father by asking Lester to hold his newborn son.

Lester did not want to pick Ronnie up claiming he did not feel ready to do so yet. He preferred to wait until Mae and the baby came home.

Mae could not believe Lester's hard-hearted attitude. She told Lester, "This is your son Lester. I don't understand your lack of love and compassion."

In a loud voice, to ensure Lester heard, Mae looked down at Ronnie and said, "Ronnie you'll have to wait to meet your father. He's afraid you'll embarrass him."

Lester wanted to change the subject. He asked Mae, "When are you coming home?"

Mae replied, "We will be home in a day or so. Please be patient Lester."

Lester grunted, "It's getting late, I have to leave for work." After spending ten minutes with Mae and his new-born son, Lester left the hospital and his wife and son.

Mae had difficulty understanding his selfish attitude. She held Ronnie close to her breast and said, "Ronnie I promise to do everything in my power to make sure you don't grow up like your father. I promise always to protect you and keep you from harm. I want only the best for you, and I will do everything possible to help you reach all your goals. I promise you, as God is my witness."

Mae and Ronnie remained in the hospital for five more days. On the last day, a social worker spoke with Mae and told her that the hospital could provide her with some clothes to take Ronnie home in if she wished. Mae was happy with the offer of free clothes.

The worker told Mae she was eligible to receive a monthly Government Family Allowance until Ronnie was sixteen years old. She handed Mae an information packet explaining the Mother's Allowance Programme. In it was the allotment for the first month. Mae was not expecting to receive any financial support. It came as a pleasant surprise.

Pointing to the envelope, the worker told Mae that some mothers use the money to take their baby home in a taxi, rather than on a packed, germ-filled, streetcar.

"Thank you," Mae replied. "I'll speak with my husband before deciding."

Mae wondered where Lester was. Once more he left Mae alone to decide. Whatever decision she made about taking Ronnie home on the streetcar, or in a taxi, Mae knew Lester would not agree with it. Mae pondered taking Ronnie home in a cab and took the advice of the social worker. She decided it would be safer than traveling on the streetcar.

As Mae expected, Lester was furious when he heard that she brought Ronnie home in a taxi, regardless that she paid the fare from her unexpected Mother's Allowance.

"You're not to make decisions like that without my permission," Lester bellowed at Mae "Do you think money grows on trees?"

Mae retorted back to Lester, "I decided to bring Ronnie home in a taxi for his own safety Lester. You were nowhere in sight to help me decide. Be thankful Lester I brought home a healthy baby."

Lester continued ranting. "I hope you did not tell anybody that you accepted free baby clothes. What will people think?"

"Lester, you're so caught up in what people think. Who cares what people think? People don't care. They have enough to worry about in their lives. The hospital gave out clothes to help new parents. It was a gesture of kindness from the hospital. Try to understand, Lester."

Regardless of Mae's attempt to explain, Lester continued to rant, "In future, don't accept anything from anybody. Do I make myself clear? I don't want to give people the idea that we are poor."

"But we are poor," Mae exclaimed. "Wishing we were not, does not make us rich. We must bring more money into the house. If you will not let me go back to work, it is up to you to make it happen."

Lester shouted, "Shut your mouth. I do not want to hear you talk like that. I bring money home every week. It is up to you to spend it wisely."

Lester's loud voice frightened Ronnie and made him cry. Mae picked him up from his cradle and held him close. She told Lester she had no more time to argue with him. "I have a baby to look after now. That's my priority."

Lester roared back, "I'm your priority. I will not allow that baby to replace me. I'm in charge here and don't forget it." Lester stormed out of the room leaving Mae alone to comfort Ronnie.

# 11

Everything in Lester's home looked old and decrepit. He lived in a run-down, crime infested, neighborhood.

Lester paid no attention to keeping the house in good repair. His yarn sorting job did not pay enough money for the upkeep of his home. Rather than sell the house, and move to something he could better afford, he did nothing. Lester could not understand that by not keeping his house in good order, it was decreasing in value.

Mae did her best to keep the house clean and respectable, but Lester did not co-operate. Mae decided that Lester was a slob. All the household facilities were outdated, and most did not work. The roof leaked, and hot water from the tap seldom occurred.

Mae warmed Ronnie's bath water on an old, second-hand, wood stove. It also heated the house in wintertime and cooked meals. Mae substituted towels for diapers. There was not enough money to allow Mae's family to live otherwise.

Black stove pipes zigged and zagged throughout the four small rooms. Sometimes they over-heated and glowed red. Mae worried when that happened because they became a fire hazard.

Ronnie spent his early life lying in a cradle, on the floor, near the stove. It was the warmest spot in the house. On frosty winter nights, Mae slept in a chair beside the stove with Ronnie, to make sure the fire did not go out.

Mae bought cheap clothes at a nearby second-hand store. She often had to redesign or repair them before wearing. She did not mind because she liked designing new clothes, especially for Ronnie.

Mother used to tell Mae she was artistic. Recently Mae realized that Mother was right, she did have some creative talent.

Maybe, she thought, she could apply her talent to generate added revenue. Designing clothes to generate added revenue would be fun, instead of always doing it as a day to day necessity.

When Ronnie out-grew the cradle, he moved into a bed, in another room. Mae bought a used bed and mattress for him. The lack of money was a significant obstacle to living a good, safe, and healthy life.

Lester continued to ignore Mae and Ronnie. He rarely referred to Ronnie by name. He physically and verbally abused Mae when he got drunk, which was often. It was not a pleasant atmosphere to live in and raise a child. Mae did not know how much longer she could continue to live in such unbearable conditions.

Mae was fearful that her loneliness, brought on by Lester ignoring her and Ronnie, would drive her into a depression like she experienced in the apartment. She needed to keep active to avoid sinking to that level. Sewing and designing clothes for Ronnie to wear was good therapy and saved her from having to buy new expensive clothes. Ronnie was growing fast and always needed something to wear. Mae made clothes for Ronnie from remnants she bought at a nearby second-hand clothes store.

Despite the money she saved sewing and designing Ronnie's clothes, there was still a shortage. Mae thought about placing an advertisement on store bulletin boards to do some outside sewing and design work. She asked Lester for permission to do so. He refused her request saying, it looked too much like a charity request.

The only time Mae and Lester talked to each other was to argue over money. Lester refused to bury his pride and let Mae look for a job. It was a struggle to pay the monthly heat, light, and power bills and buy food.

Not ready to concede Mae returned to suggesting she hire a babysitter for Ronnie and go out to work. She reminded Lester she could get her old job back again at The Mill.

As he often did, Lester rejected Mae's suggestion that she go out to work to improve their financial well-being. Mae was becoming increasingly frustrated at Lester's short-sightedness. Mae told Lester that his foolish pride affected his judgment and that he should bury his ego for the good of his family.

"Shut up bitch," he screamed at her. Mae ignored Lester's disrespectful remark. It was not the first time he talked to her like that.

Mae continued trying to knock sense into Lester's head and reminded him of their dire financial situation.

Lester, in a demeaning sounding voice, told Mae, "No. A woman's place is in the home to do housework for her family only— not for other families."

Mae refused to let Lester have his way. The lack of money concerned her. She knew action needed implementing, to prepare for Ronnie's future. "Lester, think about when Ronnie starts school next year. That will create more expenses. We should put plans in place now to prepare for those future costs. It will be impossible to provide for future needs if we continue like we are at present."

Lester retorted, "I'll worry about it when the time comes. We will find a way. We always do."

"I don't know how we'll make it on your small salary," Mae said. "You keep putting this matter off to sometime in the future. The problem will not go away by itself. I do not know why you cannot understand that Lester. You make me mad when you refuse to recognize the obvious."

"Watch your mouth when you talk to me," Lester shouted. "I deserve more respect."

"Lester, I'll not go back on the promise I made to Ronnie. He will have a better life than what he has now. I made it my goal to fulfill that promise. You, nor anybody else, can take that dream away from me."

Lester threw his hands skyward signifying that he no longer wanted to discuss the subject. Mae was not prepared to quit yet. She was determined to make him understand. "Lester, life would be so much easier for us if we had a little more money coming in."

"No," Lester yelled. "You're not going to work. Your place is at home to look after me, and the kid, and that's final."

"But Lester, we can't afford the luxury to let me stay at home. You simply do not bring home enough money to allow it. We need to prepare ourselves now." Mae was getting angry at Lester's stubborn attitude. She reminded him if he gave up drinking beer, and smoking cigarettes - they would have more money to spend on food and other essentials.

Lester glared at her. He launched his arm above his head and took a vicious swipe aimed at her head. The back of his hand landed squarely in the middle of her face. Dazed, and partially unconscious, she fell to the floor. Straddling her limp body, Lester grabbed her hair, pulled back her head, and forced her to look at him. Mae saw fire and hatred in Lester's eyes. She tried to avoid his fast descending fist, aimed at the left side of her face. She could not move fast enough. Lester's massive fist plowed into the side of her head. She fell to the floor and tried to squirm away from the steel-toed work boot coming at her. She could not get away fast enough. Lester's heavy foot crashed into her ribs. Everything went black. When she woke up, she was on the floor. Lester was standing over her. She knew if she did not move he would hit her again. She ached from head to toe.

Looking up at Lester she pleaded, "Please Lester, don't hit me anymore. I'm sorry that I upset you with what I said. I'll never talk like that again to you — I promise."

Mae saw the hateful look on Lester's face looking down at her sprawled on the floor. Fearful that he was about to kick her again, she crawled on her hands and knees to the other side of the room. Ronnie witnessed Lester's fury. He was afraid that Lester might hurt him also. He sat terrified and sobbing in the corner of the kitchen. Mae put her arm around Ronnie and held him close. Her pain was excruciating. She blacked out for a second time while holding Ronnie.

Mae did not know how long she had been unconscious. When she awoke, Ronnie was laying at her feet. He looked at his mother with big sad eyes. She could see he was frightened. Mae pulled him closer, "It is okay Ronnie. Mommy loves you and will protect you."

Mae touched the side of her face. It hurt so much. Her eye was swollen shut. She could not breathe through her nose. It was full of blood. In a muffled voice, to keep Ronnie from hearing, Mae said, "The son-of-a-bitch broke my nose." She felt a stinging pain in her side. "I think he broke some ribs also. It hurts to breathe."

Mae heard Lester stumbling around in the next room. "He's probably drunk," she said to herself. "That's what Lester does when things don't go his way. He drinks hoping to make problems go away. Ronnie and I are not safe. We need to get away from here."

Mae reached for the phone on the wall above her head. She gently lifted the receiver off the hook. Mae did not want Lester to hear her. She dialed zero. She was relieved when she heard the female operator's voice say, "Operator, how can I help you?"

Mae whispered into the phone, "My husband just beat me up. He is still here. I am with my small son. We need help."

"Are you at home on Hadley Street now?"

"Yes."

"Help is on its way," the operator said.

A few minutes later Mae heard thumping at the door. She heard Lester go to the door. When he opened it, she heard a loud commanding voice say, "Put your hands behind your back."

Mae and Ronnie remained crouched on the floor in the kitchen. Within seconds of the police arresting Lester, and taking him away, an official looking lady entered the kitchen and sat beside Mae and Ronnie on the floor.

"Hello Mae," she said in a tender voice. "My name is Charlotte. I am a social worker. I am here to help you and keep you safe. You and your son must leave at once. I'll take both of you to a shelter where you'll be safe, and your wounds tended to."

Charlotte waved her arm, and two paramedics entered the kitchen pushing a stretcher. One of them asked, "Are you able to stand up?"

"I think so," Mae answered.

"We'll help you."

Two paramedics helped Mae onto the stretcher. They strapped her down and wheeled her to the waiting ambulance. The police had taken Lester away.

Charlotte took Ronnie's hand in hers. They followed Mae's stretcher to the ambulance. She asked Ronnie, "Do you want to ride in the ambulance with Mommy?" Ronnie answered, "Yes please."

The paramedics rolled the stretcher into the ambulance. Charlotte lifted Ronnie into the ambulance and followed in behind him. "Would you like to lay down beside your Mother?" Charlotte asked.

Ronnie nodded his head signifying that he would. Charlotte helped him onto the stretcher. She wrapped him in a warm blanket beside Mae. He was a frightened little boy.

Charlotte leaned over to speak with Mae. "I'll follow behind the ambulance and meet you at the shelter. I'm here to look after both of you."

Mae asked, "Where is my husband?"

Charlotte answered, "He is no longer on the scene. He will not hurt you, or Ronnie, anymore. Relax Mae."

"Thank you for your help Charlotte."

The ambulance took Mae and Ronnie to a three-story, red brick building. There were no markings on the building to show what type of facility it was. The paramedics wheeled them through full double doors, onto an elevator, and up to the second floor. Charlotte stayed with them the whole time.

The paramedics wheeled Mae and Ronnie into a small room, which Mae thought resembled a hospital room, but on further inspection figured out that it was not. The bed looked like it belonged in a hospital, but that was all. Charlotte told Ronnie to step down from the stretcher.

The two paramedics, one on each side, grasped the sheet and with a mighty heave, lifted Mae onto the bed. Within minutes a doctor was tending to her wounds.

Charlotte gave Ronnie juice, cookies, and toys to play with, while the doctor looked after Mae.

The doctor and two assistants bandaged Mae's wounds. Mae asked, "Is this a hospital?"

The doctor smiled and said, "It looks like it, doesn't it? This facility is a battered women's shelter. For the safety of the residents, which you and your son have become, there is no public recognition of its location. Women and children are here to protect them from abusive husbands, boyfriends, and pimps. No adult male residents reside here, only women and children."

"I never knew that such a place existed," Mae told the Doctor.

"That's good. It means that the safeguards in place are working."

The doctor continued talking, "You have two broken ribs Mae, which I taped up. That is all I can do for broken ribs. You will be in pain for a while. I have bandaged up the wound on the side of your face also. The staff will help you to wash and change the dressings. I have prescribed some pain medication. You might need it when the freezing comes out, which I injected into the side of your nose when I reset it."

"Thank you, Doctor, for patching me up. What a wonderful and caring place."

The doctor smiled and said, "I'll look in on you in a day or two. The staff will keep me informed of your progress."

Charlotte said, "Mae, I'll wheel you and Ronnie to your room. I want you both to sleep. You have been through a lot."

"That sounds wonderful Charlotte. I am grateful for everything you have done for Ronnie and me. It is more than anybody has ever done for us."

"We're not finished yet, Mae. I'll help you change your life – for the better." Charlotte pushed the bed down a long hall with Mae and Ronnie on board. She turned into a well-lit, pleasant looking room. She pushed the rear end of the bed against the back wall. Ronnie's was already set up for him. She lifted Ronnie from Mae's bed and stood him on the floor.

"You'll sleep in that bed over there tonight Ronnie. I have nice warm pajamas for you. There's a bathroom over there," pointing to a door in the corner. "Take your clothes off and put on your new pajamas. Don't forget to pee."

"Okay," Ronnie said as he walked to the bathroom door.

While Ronnie was getting ready for bed, Charlotte spoke to Mae, "I want you and Ronnie to get some sleep. It is past Ronnie's bedtime. He looks tired – and so do you."

"I'm tired and quite sore, Charlotte, but I know Ronnie and I are safe here. We'll sleep well tonight."

"There is someone here all night if you need anything. Just push this button." Charlotte pointed to an electronic button that looked like a doorbell at the end of a coiled telephone cord. "Someone will be looking in on you and Ronnie during the night."

Pointing to the door where Ronnie was changing, Charlotte said, "You know where the bathroom is. It is only a few feet away. If you are too sore and unable to get out of bed, or if Ronnie needs attention, just push the button. Breakfast is between eight and ten o'clock in the morning. The dining room is at the end of the hall to your left. I'll talk to you more after breakfast tomorrow."

At that moment, Ronnie came out of the bathroom sporting his new pajamas. He stood at the side of Mae's bed and said, "Good night Mommy. I'll be here to look after you."

It was all Mae could do to keep from crying. She had to stay strong for Ronnie's sake. She told Ronnie, "Thank-you Ronnie for looking after me."

Ronnie leaned over to receive his goodnight kiss from Mae. He jumped into his new bed and Charlotte wrapped him in a warm blanket, kissed him on his forehead, and said, "Go to sleep Ronnie. Mommy is right beside you in the other bed."

"I know. Mommy hurts, but I'll look after her."

"I know you will," Charlotte whispered confidently in his ear. "Good night Ronnie."

Charlotte switched off the overhead light when she exited the room and said, "Good night, Mae."

"Goodnight Charlotte. Thanks for everything."

Ronnie soon fell asleep under the warm blanket in the comfortable bed. Mae peaked over at him and silently wished him a good sleep, assuring him that things will get better.

# 12

Mae did not sleep well. Her body was aching from Lester's beating the night before. She swallowed two pain pills the doctor gave her. They only partially worked. She looked over at Ronnie. He was still sleeping soundly. It's great he's able to sleep, she said to herself, and thankfully Lester only directed his fury at me and not at Ronnie. He has been through so much in his young life. I wish I could make his life better as I promised him I would.

Mae let her thoughts ramble. I've nothing to show for my life to this point. How can I make a better life for Ronnie when I've no quality of life myself? I must change my life around — but how?

Mae glanced around the room. A double pedestal chest of drawers sat directly in front of her. It had a mirror attached. Mae sat up in her bed to see herself in the mirror. She was aghast when she saw the blood-soaked bandages covering her swollen face and eyes. She gasped and said out loud, Oh, my God, I look awful.

A large bandage stretched across her face. She had two black eyes, swollen, to where they looked almost shut. The dense swellings distorted her face. Dry blood rested on her lower lip. Continuing to look at herself in the mirror, Mae said, Lester, you mean bastard, how could you do this?

Beige colored drapes hung from the window. Through the slit, Mae could see it was getting light outside. She didn't know what time it was or where she was - only that she and Ronnie were safe in a women's shelter somewhere in Lewisville. Mae had a lot of questions to ask Charlotte when they met after breakfast. She was looking forward to the meeting and getting answers.

Mae returned her swollen head to the pillow and stared at the ceiling wondering what will happen next.

Ronnie woke up a few minutes later. The first thing he did was check to see that Mae was still there. He said good morning to Mae and asked if she was feeling any better.

Ronnie told his mother he was worried about her last night.

"It is okay Ronnie. We are safe now. Come over here and lay beside me."

Ronnie got up and leaped into the bed with Mae. "I love you, Mommy," he said.

Mae kissed him on the forehead and said, "I love you too Ronnie. More than anything else in the world."

They laid embraced in each other's arms for a long time, happy that they were safe, and together.

A soft knock sounded at the door, and it cracked open. A lady dressed in a pink nurse's outfit put the upper part of her body through the door and said, "Good morning Mae, good morning Ronnie. How are both of you this morning?"

"We're Okay," Mae answered from the bed where she and Ronnie were still lying.

"I'm one of the resident assistants," the pleasant lady said. "Breakfast will be served in an hour. When you and Ronnie are ready to eat, come and join the other residents in the dining room for some breakfast." Before leaving the worker went to the window, opened the drapes, and adjusted the blinds to let the sunlight flow into the room.

Mae and Ronnie got up together. Ronnie went into the bathroom first. After a few moments, he came out and told Mae, "The bathroom looks funny Mommy. It's got a lot of stuff in it that I never saw before."

"I'm not sure what you're talking about Ronnie. Let's explore together."

Ronnie pointed to the large white porcelain tub and the strange contraption on the wall above it. "What are those?" he asked.

"That's where you take a bath. Like you do at home in the metal tub." Mae pointed to the two taps hanging over the end of the tub. "One tap gives hot water the other cold. We do not need to heat the water on the stove anymore, and that funny thing on the wall up there is a shower. You stand underneath it, and it sprays warm water on you. You don't have to sit in the metal tub and have me pour the water over you."

"Wow," Ronnie exclaimed. "Can I try it now?"

"Of course, Ronnie. You go first. I will go in the tub after you finish your shower. I cannot take a shower because of the bandages on my face. Mommy has never washed in a big tub or stood under a shower either. It is the first time for both of us."

Ronnie frolicked in the warm shower. It was a new and glorious experience for him. Mae too was pleased for Ronnie. Mae recalled that he has not had many happy moments in his life. She wanted to change that for him. She hoped she could.

Mae had difficulty getting in and out of the tub. She only filled it part way with water. She reminded herself not to let the bandages get wet.

Ronnie and Mae had only the clothes they arrived with at the shelter, and Mae's were severely bloodstained. She wanted to get clean clothes for her and Ronnie to wear. Meanwhile, she would wear the housecoat hanging behind the door when they went for breakfast.

The dining room held a dozen or more tables each set for four people. The room was half full of other women and children eating breakfast. Mae and Ronnie sat at an empty table. A smiling attendant said, "Good morning," and handed Mae a menu. Noticing Mae's bandaged faced, she asked, "Are you able to eat and drink on your own, or will you need some help?"

Attempting to smile Mae, answered, "Thank you, I'll try it on my own first. If I run into trouble, I'll tell you."

"Very well," said the attendant. "Don't hesitate to call if you need help."

Mae ordered corn flakes with milk for herself and toast with peanut butter for Ronnie. The bandages prevented Mae from opening her mouth fully. The milk dripped down her chin. It took a while, but she ate everything without asking for help. Ronnie loved his toast and peanut butter. It was a rare treat for him.

The attendant returned to the table, picked up the dirty dishes, and placed them on a tray. She said, "I spoke with Charlotte a few minutes ago. She asked me to tell you to wait here for her. She'll be here in a few minutes."

In a soft and caring voice, the attendant turned to Ronnie and said, "Some other children live here also. They are in the playroom. Would you like to join them while Mommy and Charlotte talk?"

Ronnie looked over at Mae, "Can I Mommy?"

"Go and have fun, Ronnie. You deserve it."

"Please don't go away and leave me here Mommy."

"I'll never leave you," Mae assured him.

Mae watched the attendant take Ronnie out of the dining room. Mae thought, Ronnie and her were so bonded she missed him when he was not beside her.

Charlotte arrived five minutes later. She was of medium height, with dark auburn colored hair that covered her ears. She had a stern look that said, *'You had better not mess with me.'* She impressed Mae as a, take charge individual. She wore flat-heeled shoes. Her navy-blue, mid-calf length uniform, designated authority. Her nails were unpainted and cut short. She wore no lipstick or make-up. Her authoritarian sounding voice commanded attention. Mae estimated her to be about forty years old.

"Hi, Mae." Charlotte chirped. "Your face looks better this morning. The swelling has gone down from last night. That's a sign your healing."

Charlotte did not allow Mae any time to feel sorry for herself. She had an agenda, and now was the time to implement it. "This is the first day of the rest of your life Mae. What are your plans for the future?"

Mae gave Charlotte a blank look through her swollen eyes and muttered. "I don't know. I have no plans."

"That is the first thing to work on," Charlotte said in a firm voice.

Mae asked herself if this was the same soft-spoken lady who escorted her and Ronnie out of Lester's home last night and brought them to this safe place? I am seeing the authoritative side of Charlotte now. What a difference.

"You need a plan," Charlotte instructed. "You cannot depend on Lester. He has done nothing for you, except hurt you. You need only to look in the mirror for proof. Stay away from him at all costs. If not, your life will never improve, and you'll become a regular visitor to this shelter."

"Where is Lester now?" Mae inquired.

"He spent the night in jail, charged with domestic violence. He is going before a magistrate this morning. There is a restraining order pending against him. He cannot come within one hundred yards of you. That will prevent a reoccurrence of what happened last night. Documents will arrive here for you to sign this afternoon. When I receive them, I will go over them with you. They will spell out the terms of the restraining order, and what you need to do if Lester does not comply."

Charlotte continued, "Let's talk about Ronnie instead of Lester. You must register him for school which will be starting in a few months. He will need clothes, shoes, books, and pencils. All that stuff requires money. Where will you get money from Mae?"

"I don't know. I have no job. I can try getting back my old job at The Mill."

"That's the last place you want to work. Lester works there. Remember you will have a restraining order issued against him. Besides, why would you, with all your intelligence, apply for a dead-end job like that anyway? You can do better. There is no opportunity for advancement working on the line sorting yarns. Get a job with potential," Charlotte commanded.

Charlotte continued to prod Mae, "How will you get a job with future growth possibilities Mae?"

Mae was becoming increasingly frustrated at Charlotte's line of questioning, principally because she could not answer her prying questions. "I don't know Charlotte. I've no skills," Mae stated.

"Therein lies the solution Mae. You must acquire skills upon which to build a career." Charlotte asked, "Where were you educated?"

Mae explained how Aunt Wilma, a retired one-room school teacher, taught her from grade one through to grade ten. It took five years.

Charlotte asked, "What are you good at?"

"I like to design and sew clothes. When I was a young girl, I liked drawing pictures of vegetables on the sides of canned tins of produce. I sewed and designed most of Ronnie's clothes and made a housecoat for my Aunt Wilma."

With a stern look on her face, Charlotte leaned on the table and peered into Mae's swollen eyes, "You need to investigate enrolling in an art school. I detect an artistic talent. The University has an excellent, undergraduate, fashion design program. Classes are available for night students. You have the brains to further what your Aunt Wilma taught you. She did an excellent job. Too good to waste on menial jobs like sorting yarns. Build on your strengths, Mae."

Charlotte continued, "First things first, however, your priority now is to return to good health. Your second one is to get a job. If you decide on a design career, for example, look for a job where you can get on the job training. There is no reason you can't look for a job, while you're recovering."

"That sounds good to me," Mae said in an excited voice. "Where do I start?"

"You need to let potential employers know that you're available for work. Prepare a résumé showing education and work experience. I'll help you put one together."

Charlotte said, "You and Ronnie can stay at the shelter until you become financially independent. There are strings attached, however. First, you must actively seek employment and report your job seeking activities to me every day. Second, you must actively look for a place for you and Ronnie to live. You can stay here for up to two years. I expect Mae you will be gone long before that. We are here to help you turn your life around. The onus is on you to take advantage of this opportunity."

"There is one other important condition."

In a cautious tone of voice, Mae asked, "What's that Charlotte?"

"If you want to succeed in life you must have an education. If not, your desire to make a better life for you and Ronnie will only be a dream. You must go back and finish high school. You have only two years left. There is a general education course offered by the shelter. The school is on the third floor. If you stay here, you must attend classes every day, two hours in the morning, and two hours in the afternoon, Monday to Friday. You will aim to finish the last two years of high school. That will almost guarantee you entrance to the University Design Course. The shelter will certify your education level. Are you in agreement to better your chances of success?”

“I am — I am,” Mae repeatedly said to ensure Charlotte understood. Mae was excited at the prospect of completing high school, receiving a certificate, and enrolling into the University Fashion Design Curriculum.

Charlotte concluded, “Alright, we have a plan. Now we need to get you down to the infirmary and have those bandages changed. You and Ronnie will also need fresh clothes to wear.”

# 13

The next two weeks were hectic. Charlotte and Mae got together every day to measure Mae's progress.

With Charlotte's help, Mae registered Ronnie for school. He would start in three months.

The restraining documents arrived for Mae to review and sign. Charlotte helped her to understand the legal language. Charlotte emphasized that if Lester violated the court order, she was not to hesitate to call the police.

Mae considered the Fashion Design course offered by the University. "It is costly," she told Charlotte. "I don't have that kind of money. I'm broke."

Charlotte said, "You're not to concern yourself about that Mae. The course is offered free to shelter residents."

"That's wonderful news Charlotte. Thank-you for telling me. I'll enroll at once."

"Do you remember what I told you in the dining room, Mae?" Not waiting for an answer, Charlotte continued, "I told you that we are here to help you change your life. This opportunity to further your education, and help you get a job, can be life-changing for you, Mae."

The University accepted Mae's application to the Design School course. The winter semester was starting in two months. Mae's wounds were healing nicely, and she was furthering her education through the adult education classes on the third floor. Mae was pleased with the progress she was making.

After a month, her wounds healed, and she dispensed with the bandages. There were a few scars, but she covered them up with make-up. The shelter's beauty counselor showed her how to do it.

"It is time for you to make things happen," Charlotte told her. "You need to look for work. Before doing so, however, you must prepare a résumé. We'll start to work on it tomorrow."

"Thanks, Charlotte. I never prepared a résumé before. Thanks for offering to help me." Mae and Charlotte worked together for a week putting together a well-formulated résumé. At the end of the week Charlotte said, "Alright Mae, this is a good-looking, and well-detailed résumé. Make it work for you,".

"I will," Mae said. "Tomorrow I'll start actively looking for a job."

"That's great Mae. I wish you luck. You have a good positive attitude, keep it and remember to stay positive amid turmoil. There is a job out there for you. Do not fear rejection. The more times you hear the word, 'No,' the closer you are moving to hearing the word, 'Yes.' It's a game of numbers."

"That's good advice Charlotte. I'll remember that."

The next morning Mae awoke early and had breakfast with Ronnie. Ronnie had made friends with the other kids. He participated in the sports activities program offered by the shelter.

"Ronnie this is the start of our new life," Mae told him in an upbeat tone of voice. "The day you were born, I promised you a better life. Today is my first attempt to make good on that promise."

Mae noted that Ronnie did not grasp the importance of what she was telling him. He wanted to be with his friends rather than listen to Mae. Ronnie is still too young to understand, Mae concluded. Someday he'll understand though.

As Mae was leaving the shelter, she met Charlotte.

"Do you have your résumés with you?" Charlotte asked.

"Yes, I do Charlotte."

"Make sure you give one to everybody you talk to."

"I will, Charlotte," Mae said.

Armed with her résumés, Mae went from one shop to another. She did not approach any establishment she felt unqualified for or uncomfortable with - like Charlie's Bookstore. Mae noticed how much the downtown core had changed. Several stores were out of business, closed and boarded up. Those that were still open were void of customers.

Going door to door and rejected by every potential employer is less than encouraging, Mae thought. She remembered Charlotte telling her to remain positive. I'll stay optimistic, Mae told herself. I will go up one side of the street, and down the other, looking for prospective employers. Mae trudged both sides of the road with dismal results. She left a copy of her résumé with each shop owner she spoke to, regardless if they needed help or not. Mae told them, to keep her résumé on file for future reference, just as Charlotte coached her to do.

It was getting late, and the shop owners were closing for the day. Mae was disappointed that she did not have better results from her day-long efforts. Dejected, she returned to the shelter.

The first person she met was Charlotte, who wanted to know how she made out. "Not very well," Mae answered. "Nobody had any openings."

Charlotte told her to work smarter, and not harder. She recommended that Mae only apply to establishments like clothing apparel, dress shops, art supply stores, needle shops, and artistic based establishments. Charlotte also told her not to confine her search to establishments on Pitt Street. "Broaden your field," she directed Mae.

Mae did not understand how to source out such businesses. Charlotte suggested that the phone book was an excellent place to start. That night, after Ronnie went to bed, Mae scoured the yellow pages seeking businesses that might use her talents. The next day, armed with addresses of prospective employers gathered from the yellow pages, she set out once more to look for a job. She returned to the shelter just as discouraged as she did the night before. Charlotte told her not to give up. "You never know when, or where, an opportunity will strike. Nothing will happen if you don't take steps to make it happen."

Mae diligently kept knocking on doors and mailing out résumés. She learned first-hand how scarce jobs were.

One evening when Mae and Ronnie were having supper, Charlotte joined them at the table. "Mae, I received a phone call from a lady who owns a dress shop on Main Street where you dropped off one of your résumés. She is interested in speaking with you. I told her I'd give you the message, and have you call her tomorrow."

Mae could not believe her ears. After all the résumés she mailed out, and doors she knocked on. Finally, one of them generated action.

"Thank you, Charlotte. I'll call her first thing tomorrow morning, and let you know how I made out."

"Before you do that Mae, stop by my office and we'll do some role-playing to make sure that you get an appointment."

The next morning after breakfast, Mae went to Charlotte's office to receive coaching, and do role-playing. An hour later, Charlotte said, "You're ready Mae. Go for it, and good luck. Keep me informed."

"Thanks, Charlotte, I will."

Mae used the phone in one of the shelter's interview rooms to ensure quiet and confidentiality. She dialed the number that Charlotte gave her. The lady's name was Jane Marsh. "Hello Ms. Marsh, my name is Mae. I'm returning your call from yesterday. I mailed my résumé to you last week, and I understand you'd like to discuss it further with me. I'm available anytime today, or would tomorrow be more convenient for you?"

"Thank you for calling Mae. I read your résumé with interest. I need someone in the shop to help me, and you appear to have the qualifications I'm looking for. I'd like to have a chat with you, can you stop by the shop this afternoon, say around two o'clock?"

"I certainly can Ms. Marsh. I'll look forward to meeting you."

Mae hung up the phone and galloped to Charlotte's office to relay the good news.

Mae reasoned before entering the upscale dress shop that a job in a dress shop would fit in well with her fashion design course. Could this be the, 'Yes' Charlotte spoke about? Mae hoped it would be.

Mae entered the shop and introduced herself to the well-dressed, friendly looking lady inside.

"Hi, my name is Mae. Are you Jane Marsh?"

"I am," she responded. "Thanks for coming in Mae. I am the owner of this shop. Please call me Jane."

"Thank you, Jane. Please call me Mae."

Jane invited Mae to enter her office. Mae noticed a copy of her résumé on Jane's desk. "Give me a moment Mae while I review your résumé one more time."

"Take your time Jane, and feel free to ask me any questions."

Jane was a stylish middle-aged lady. Mae estimated she was about fifteen years older than her. She was shorter than Mae and wore a chic up-sweep hair-style. Her facial makeup was soft and well applied. Her light red manicured nails matched her silk scarf and full skirt. She looked eloquent and debonair. A perfect image for an upscale dress shop owner.

"Thank you for preparing such a detailed résumé, Mae. It shows you pay attention to details. I was looking for someone with that strength. I also noticed that you worked on Pitt Street at Charlie's Bookstore. Does that mean you have shop experience?"

"That's right," Mae replied in an assertive voice as Charlotte told her to do. Seeking common ground for discussion, Mae asked Jane, "Do you know Charlie?"

"Not very well. Charlie is older than I and has been in business a long time. He walks in different circles than I do." Mae was relieved Jane did not know Charlie well. It reduced the chance that Charlie would gossip about her as he threatened to do on that terrible morning.

The job entailed labeling dresses and keeping the racks neat and tidy. It was not a difficult job, and Jane predicted Mae would learn fast. It was a permanent job from Monday to Friday. The duties also included aiding customers when they came into the shop.

"That is what I am looking for," Mae responded with a radiant smile.

Jane asked, "When can you start?"

"Monday morning," Mae responded with enthusiasm.

"Monday is fine," Jane said. Jane and Mae discussed salary details. Jane offered her a salary which was higher than what Lester was earning at The Mill.

"When you become proficient at the job, I will review your salary," Jane said. "When you no longer need supervision, you'll be eligible for a raise. I estimate you should qualify for a review in three months. Is that okay Mae?"

"That's fine Jane. I'll work hard to warrant your approval."

Jane continued, "I noticed you have enrolled in the University Fashion Design Course offered by the University. It is an excellent course. Working in The Dress Shop will give you, hands-on experience." Jane said, "We are the only lady's fashion store in town. The market in Lewisville has changed, and not for the better, unfortunately. I must find new markets, or I will fail like the other shops did. I need you to learn the business quickly, so I can free myself to search out new markets. Your enrollment in the design course could be beneficial for both of us Mae."

"I'm grateful for the opportunity Jane. I promise to work hard and learn the business as fast as I can."

"I know you will Mae. I can tell by your attitude and enthusiasm." In a soft voice that invited people to listen, Jane said, "You have told me all about you Mae. Allow me to highlight a few things about me."

"I'd love to hear more about you Jane," Mae said to her imitating Jane's soft voice. "I'm a widow," Jane said. "My husband was an executive at The Mill, and I was his secretary. About ten years ago he got cancer and could no longer work, so I quit my job to stay home and care for him. Cancer eventually took over his whole body, and he died five years ago. He left me a large inheritance. I used some of it to open this dress shop, three years ago."

Glancing around the shop, Mae said, "I'm sorry for your loss Jane, but your husband's legacy surrounds you. You carry beautiful designer clothes."

"These dresses are all made from fabrics produced at The Mill."

"How interesting," Mae said. "You have a built-in supply of high-quality fabrics."

"Up until a few months ago, that was the case. The Mill no longer weaves fabrics in Lewisville because it is cheaper to produce them in Asia. The Mill only produces yarns in Lewisville now. It has had a devastating effect on the local economy. My costs have increased substantially."

"I noticed the boarded-up shops," Mae said.

Jane elaborated on the Lewisville economy, "People have been laid off from The Mill, and they don't have money to buy expensive designer dresses. I have experienced a downturn in business over the last six months. I still have a few personal resources I can plow into the business, but they will expire in short order if sales don't improve. I am looking to secure other markets outside Lewisville."

"How is that going so far?" Mae inquired.

"Not well," Jane responded in a sad tone.

Jane continued showing Mae through the shop filled with beautiful dresses at prices Mae could not afford. Mae noted that the entire time she was with Jane, no customers entered the shop.

"I'll look forward to starting work Monday morning Jane."

"I'll look forward to seeing you, Mae. Have a pleasant evening."

"Thanks, Jane. See you on Monday."

Mae floated out of the shop, elated at what she had carried out. She walked to the streetcar stop at the end of the street. Out of the corner of her eye, Mae saw someone approaching her. She turned her head to look. It was Lester.

"Lester, you're not supposed to be near me. I have a restraining order against you. You cannot be within one hundred yards of me. I could have you arrested."

"I know you could Mae, but you won't. I love you too much, and you know it."

"That's the first time you ever told me that you loved me, Lester. There were times I longed to hear you say those words - instead, you shouted insults at me, and beat me up."

Lester replied in a rude tone, "I always thought you knew that I loved you, Mae. I did not think I had to tell you. After you left, I realized how much I missed you. My life is empty without you."

"You were so cruel to me Lester. You beat me up and broke my nose. Is that love?"

"You made me do it, Mae. You constantly accused me of not making enough money. I told you I earned plenty of money. You never believed me."

"I'm not going to argue with you here on the street Lester," Mae answered back in the same demeaning tone that Lester used.

Lester continued to talk, "Please come back home to me," he pleaded. "I'm sorry for everything that I did and said to you. I have learned my lesson. I promise to behave myself around you and Ronnie."

Mae glanced down the street and felt relieved when she saw the streetcar approaching. "Here comes my streetcar. Do not follow me. My life is about to change, and it does not include you, Lester."

"Please think about what I said, Mae. I can change and become anything you want me to be. I want us to be a happy family."

"I have to think about that Lester. Nothing will happen until your restraining order is lifted." Mae got on the streetcar, dropped her fare into the box, and took a seat by the window. She looked outside as the tram pulled away. Lester was standing at the curb, blowing kisses to her.

Mae wondered how that chance meeting with Lester happened? Her day was going well until Lester surprised her at the streetcar stop. He seemed to have changed his ways, but Lester had lied to Mae so often, that she didn't know whether to believe him or not. She felt sorry for him but unsure why. Without me in his life he has nobody. He must be lonely she presumed. She knew that loneliness was a terrible thing and could lead to other severe problems.

The shelter was on the outskirts of town which meant Mae had to take three streetcars to get back. While rumbling along the steel rails aboard the noisy tram, Mae reminisced about the series of events that led to her getting a job at The Dress Shop.

Last week, Mae armed herself with a purse full of résumés and no idea what they would do for her. They opened the door to a potential new life-changing opportunity at The Dress Shop. She could hardly wait for Monday to arrive when she would start on her new career path. She knew Charlotte would be happy for her.

As Mae expected, Charlotte was waiting for her when she returned to the shelter. She asked, "Are you as happy as you look Mae?"

Mae ran towards her and threw her arms around her. "Oh Charlotte, things could not have gone better. Thanks for all the coaching and advice you provided. The résumé and role-playing worked. It all came together for me."

Mae related the details of her day to Charlotte. She told her about Jane, and what a lovely lady she was. "I start work on Monday," Mae told Charlotte.

Charlotte was happy that Mae's starting date was so soon. Charlotte said, "There is a young, good-looking man, sitting in your room reading a book. Tell him the good news you told me. I am happy for you Mae. Congratulations."

Mae thought it was unwise to tell Charlotte about her encounter with Lester. She decided not to tell Ronnie either. She wanted the mood to remain positive.

Ronnie was happy to see Mae when she walked into the room. Mae hugged him and said, "I have good news to share with you, Ronnie."

"That's good Mommy. What is it?"

Mae told him about her new job at The Dress Shop. Ronne was pleased to hear of his mother's success. "We are about to make a new life for ourselves Ronnie."

"Thanks, Mommy. I love you, and I will help you make a new life for us. I'll work hard in school to make you proud of me."

"I know you will Ronnie, and I'll work hard to make you proud of me too."

Changing the subject, Mae asked Ronnie, "Are you hungry Ronnie? I know I am. Do you want to get something to eat?"

"Yes, please Mommy, I'm starving."

Hand in hand, Ronnie and Mae skipped down the corridor and into the dining room.

That night, after tucking Ronnie into bed, Mae laid awake thinking about the life unfolding in front of her. Her thoughts wandered to her encounter with Lester. She thought if she was ever to take Lester back into her life, things must be different. Mae concluded, there was no point of even thinking about Lester coming back into her life. He'll never change.

Mae closed her eyes and went to sleep.

# 14

Monday morning arrived. The sun's rays were peeking through the slit in the drapes.

Mae decided it was too early to get up. She glanced over to Ronnie. He was still asleep.

Her mind was working over-time. She had a fantastic event happen on Friday. Today was Monday, and Mae wondered what new experiences this day would bring?

She pulled the covers up higher thinking more about the life-changing incidents that happened on Friday. She was pleased she did not give up when things looked so bleak. Under Charlotte's tutelage, she learned to persevere. Had she quit, the interview with Jane would not have occurred.

Today begins a new chapter in my life, she told herself. She reminded herself that she must remain strong, and resourceful. Her success was key to fulfilling all her dreams.

Mae pondered her encounter with Lester on Friday. She was not ready to meet him yet, and even if she were, the restraining order would keep her from seeing him.

Mae wanted to tell Lester to get lost when he approached her on Friday, but for some reason she couldn't. He still had power over her. She told herself she must remain strong, and independent, and reject his advances. Otherwise, she figured, he would drag her down to his level which she did not want to let happen.

Enough of those negative thoughts, Mae told herself. She had a new life to pursue. She had to get on with it, and it starts today.

Mae jumped out of bed and slid over to Ronnie. He was still asleep. She softly whispered in his ear to wake up. A new day was on its way. Ronnie took his time to wake up. It was still early for him.

Ronnie kissed Mae and said, "Good morning Mommy. I will miss you today. Will you be gone all day?"

"Yes, I will Ronnie, but starting next week, we'll leave together. I'll go to work, and you'll go to school."

"That will be good Mommy. I want to be smart like you."

"You're a smart boy already Ronnie. If you work hard at school, you will become even smarter than Mommy. In the meantime, stay here at the shelter with the other children. I will see you when I get back tonight."

"Okay, Mommy. I hope your first day is not too hard for you. I will miss you."

"Thanks, Ronnie. Let's have breakfast before I leave."

*********************

Mae arrived at The Dress Shop before Jane. She waited at the front door for Jane to arrive. She appeared ten minutes later. "Good morning Mae," Jane said in an joyful voice. "You're early. Welcome to The Dress Shop. I'm looking forward to working with you Mae."

"So am I Jane. I'm excited."

Jane used her key to open the door. She motioned Mae to enter before her. Above the door was a small bell that gave off a friendly jingle each time the door opened. Jane flicked on a light switch by the front door. Unlike the dangling lightbulbs in Charlie's Bookstore, the indirect lighting in The Dress Shop was soft and glowing. It enhanced the beauty of the dresses waiting for rich ladies to buy. Wall to wall deep red carpet covered the floor. It sparkled compared to the pieces of well-walked-on linoleum in Charlie's Bookstore. Jane employed a maintenance service to keep the shop clean. It looked beautiful.

Sometime over the weekend, Jane set up a desk in the rear of the store for Mae to sit at during the day. Jane's office occupied the front corner of the shop. The set-up looked impressive to customers when they entered the shop. Mae could readily see that Jane had a flair for style.

"I'll enjoy learning from you, Jane."

"I'm glad to have you on board Mae. I think we have a lot in common. We'll learn from each other."

Jane reviewed Mae's responsibilities with her. On her first day, Mae noted that few customers entered the shop. Those that did were browsers only and bought nothing. Mae concluded that Jane needed help to bring customers into the shop. It was in Mae's best interest to ensure that Jane prosper. She wondered how Jane would feel if she gave her some feedback from information and techniques learned through her Design Course studies?

Jane spent hours in her office pouring over wholesaler catalogs. Later in the afternoon, Jane asked Mae how she was doing after her first day?

"It was fine Jane. I thought I'd be busier, however," Mae answered.

"I wish you were busier Mae. Business is slow. I hope things turn around soon. I've spent most of the day looking through catalogs of beautiful dress designs. The problem is we are in a depressed area. There are not enough people in Lewisville who can afford to buy these dresses."

"That's too bad Jane. We need to come up with another way to increase business for us."

"Bless you, Mae. Your first day on the job and already you are assuming a management role. Very commendable. We'll get along fine together."

"I believe so too. Your success will become my success, Jane."

"That's a great attitude, Mae."

At closing time, Jane and Mae closed the shop and left together. Mae rode the streetcar back to the shelter where she met Charlotte at the front door. "Hi Charlotte," Mae greeted her in a cheery voice.

"I need to speak with you privately," Charlotte responded in a sober tone.

Mae's happy mood changed, and she said, "Okay Charlotte, by the tone of your voice it sounds like you have something serious to discuss."

"I do," Charlotte answered. "Step into my office where we can talk."

Charlotte led Mae into her office and closed the door. It was not the usual friendly, smiling, and good-humored Charlotte that Mae knew. Once again Mae met Charlotte, the boss lady, with something serious to discuss. Mae first saw that side of Charlotte on the morning after she arrived at the shelter.

"The shelter received a phone call from Lester," Charlotte informed Mae.

Mae asked, "How did he get the number?"

"I'm not sure because it is unlisted," Charlotte answered. "He was probably stocking you when you were dropping off your résumés. He probably coerced somebody to give him a copy." Charlotte continued, "Of course, the shelter phone number was on the résumé. I presume that's how he got it."

"That bastard," Mae exclaimed. "Will I ever be free of him?"

"I understand your frustration, Mae. The good thing is that he does not know where you live, only your phone number. Then again, if he's capable of getting the phone number, he'll figure out where you're living."

"What do we do now Charlotte?"

"We have no choice, Mae. We must move up our plans to find you another place to live. The shelter's location cannot be compromised."

"That's regrettable Charlotte. I thought I'd have a little more time to get Ronnie set up in school, and me more established at my new job. However, I'll not put you, or this facility in jeopardy Charlotte. I'll find a new place to live."

"That's the only solution, Mae. I'll help you any way I can to get you and Ronnie settled somewhere else."

"Charlotte, I appreciate your help. I'll tell Ronnie about the change in plans."

Amidst looking through the newspapers to find an apartment, getting Ronnie registered into school, working every day at The Dress Shop, and attending the design school classes, Mae was active and busy. She had no time to worry about Lester's antics.

Mae thought perhaps she should have divulged to Charlotte that Lester spoke to her at the streetcar stop. If she had, things might not have escalated to where she must move away from the safety of the shelter.

That damn Lester, she said to herself. He affects my life, even when he's not a part of it.

One day when both Mae and Jane were working in The Dress Shop, the bell above the door tingled. Both Jane and Mae looked up expecting to see a lady entering the shop. Instead, it was a man. It was Lester. "Lester, what are you doing here?" Mae demanded.

"Hi, Mae. I'm here to see you."

"Get out Lester. I have a restraining order against you. If you don't leave at once, I'll call the police."

"The restraining order expired yesterday. I can speak to you anytime I want - like now."

"I don't care Lester. I don't want to talk with you. Now please leave."

"Alright, Mae but I'll be back. You cannot avoid me forever." Lester left the shop and Mae heaved a sigh of relief.

Jane overheard the conversation between Mae and Lester. "Mae, it is none of my business to pry into your personal life, but if you would like to talk, I'm an excellent listener."

"I know you are Jane. I'll bring you up-to-date on the circumstances which led to that encounter with Lester, my estranged husband. You have a right to know as my boss and the owner of this business."

Mae poured out to Jane all the miserable details she and Ronnie had to sustain under Lester's dominance. She told Jane of Lester's violent attack on her which led her and Ronnie to take up residence at the shelter. Jane gasped at several points in Mae's deliverance of the events.

Jane said, "I don't know what I can do to protect you from Lester's tyranny Mae. I'll not allow him to set foot inside this shop another time. I'll keep my eyes open for a new apartment for you, in a safe area. You and Ronnie must watch out for each other."

"Thanks, Jane. I like my job here, and I like working with you. You have become a good friend, and a person I trust."

To illustrate that trust, Mae thought it was a proper time to bring Jane up-to-date on her design activities.

"Changing the subject away from Lester to something more positive Jane, I want you to know that my success is dependent on you, and the success of The Dress Shop. The fashion design course has creatively inspired me. Would you mind if I share some of my ideas with you?"

"Nothing would please me more Mae. I need all the help I can get. Thank you for your loyalty and dedication. I'm fortunate to have you working with me."

On her way back to the shelter, Lester appeared at the streetcar stop again. He was lurking there watching for Mae to arrive.

"Lester, please leave me alone," Mae hollered at him. "You have caused me enough grief already."

"I just need to speak with you for a few minutes," Lester told Mae. "We can talk over coffee at the café across the street."

Mae thought about Lester's proposal. Perhaps if I listen to what he wants to tell me, he'll leave me alone, she thought.

"Alright Lester, but only for a few minutes. I should not be talking to you at all."

"Just a couple of minutes," Lester said.

They crossed the street to the café. Lester directed Mae to a small round table in the back. They sat on two red plastic seated stools facing each other. "What do you want to tell me, Lester? Please be quick. I must get home for Ronnie."

"Mae, I've changed from how I used to be. I am sorry for the way I treated you and Ronnie. That will never happen again, I promise. The house is no longer in the same filthy condition that it once was. It has had a complete make-over, from the top of the roof to the cellar. It took a year to get it in shape." Lester continued, "I've installed modern furniture and appliances, a new floor, and new windows. The old icebox is gone and replaced by a modern refrigerator, and the roof doesn't leak anymore."

"Where did you get the money to do all that stuff, Lester?"

"I went to the bank and took out a loan. I gave up smoking and drinking. The money I'm saving goes to pay down the loan."

"That's very commendable Lester. What are your plans for the future?"

"I've two major plans. The first is to get a better paying job. I think they will offer me the Line Supervisor's job any day now. The second thing is, I want you, and Ronnie, to move back home with me. I want us to start over and be a happy, loving family. What do you think Mae?"

"I don't know what to think Lester. Stop coming on to me so strong. It is too much to think about right now."

"I understand," Lester replied. "I have a suggestion."

"What's that, Lester?"

"Why don't you and Ronnie stop by on Saturday and see for yourselves, then decide?"

"More than just the house has to have changed Lester. You must show me that you are agreeable to change also. That's important. More important than living in a renovated house. Improvements to the house are secondary."

"I've changed for the better Mae. You'll see."

"Alright, Lester. Ronnie and I will drop by on Saturday afternoon for a short visit. Understand, no promises."

"Fine Mae, I'll look forward to welcoming both of you on Saturday."

"Before I leave, you must promise me one thing, Lester."

"I'll do anything for you Mae."

"Please do not phone me, and don't try to find out where I live."

"I'll not contact you, Mae, I promise. I'll see you on Saturday."

Mae wanted to ensure that Lester did not contact the shelter again. She uttered a confirming request, "The next time we talk will be at your place on Saturday afternoon. Agreed Lester?"

"Agreed," Lester said, holding out his hand to help Mae off the stool.

Mae decided not to say anything to Charlotte about her encounter with Lester. "She would not approve," Mae supposed.

That night, before Ronnie went to sleep, Mae sat on the end of his bed and said, "Guess what Ronnie."

"What?" Ronnie inquired.

"I spoke with Lester this afternoon," Ronnie said nothing. The look on his face told Mae everything. She could see he was not pleased. Mae went ahead anyway to tell Ronnie about the improvements to the old house. "Lester told me he has fixed up the old house to make it nice. He wants us to move back in with him."

Ronnie commented, "Are you sure Mommy that you want to go back to him?"

"He has promised to be nice to us Ronnie. He has invited us to the house on Saturday to see the changes he made."

"Are you sure Mommy we should do that? Lester scares me."

"I'm not sure what the right thing to do is Ronnie. I have not decided yet what we should do. I only agreed to see the new house on Saturday. You and I will speak afterward. We will decide what is best for us, not what is best for Lester. He'll not be part of our conversation."

"Okay, Mommy. If you stay with me, I'll do what you think is best."

"Okay, Ronnie. You go to sleep now. It is getting late."

"Goodnight Mommy."

The following morning was Friday. Mae told Jane about her encounter with Lester. Jane warned her to be careful because men like Lester can be devious. She urged her to decide based on facts, and not on emotions. Mae promised she would heed Jane's words. "I wish you good luck tomorrow," Jane said. "You and Ronnie have an arduous task ahead."

Mae could not eat her dinner that evening. Her mind was on her upcoming meeting with Lester. She knew Ronnie had concerns, but he trusted her to make the right decision. A daunting task. If Lester has changed like he says he has, there is a chance we could become a family again, Mae surmised. It was something she always wanted but never had. Mae wondered, if Lester was being truthful when he said he had changed? I'm not sure, she answered to herself.

Mae and Ronnie left for Lester's in the afternoon. After the long streetcar ride, they walked the two blocks to Lester's place. Mae noticed the house was an attractive light grey color. It needed paint the last time she saw it. The new roof sparkled in the sunlight. It no longer looked like the dilapidated old house it once was. Based on its curbside appearance, Lester's house was now one of the nicer looking homes on the street. Very different from the first time she viewed it.

Mae's thoughts went back to when she and Lester first met. Lester's charms clouded her mind. She thought, had I only evaluated things as they were, instead of how I wanted them to be. It was the worst mistake I made in my life. She told herself, I must take care not to make that mistake again. She needed to remain strong for Ronnie's sake.

Ronnie and Mae mounted the concrete steps leading to the front door. A new doorbell had replaced the broken one. Mae pressed the doorbell, and from inside the house, the sound of musical chimes announced their arrival. A few seconds later, Lester came to the door. He was clean-shaven, and his thinning hair neatly combed across his head. Lester had on a fresh pair of slacks, a stylish open-collared blue shirt, and polished leather shoes instead of the steel-toed work boots he usually wore. He looks good, Mae thought.

In a jovial voice, Lester welcomed Mae and Ronnie. "Hi, you two. Come on in, I've brewed a fresh pot of coffee for you Mae, and juice is in the fridge for you Ronnie."

Mae and Ronnie entered the kitchen with Lester. It looked nothing like the old kitchen. The light pastel colors of beige and brown on the walls, coupled with the new fluorescent lighting, made the kitchen brighter than before. Where old, broken, and out-of-date furniture used to be, was new modern furniture. Light colored hardwood flooring replaced the worn-out linoleum. The table was clear of rubbish and covered with a red checkered tablecloth. What a difference, Mae thought. Lester has worked hard to fix this place up.

Lester motioned to Ronnie. "I've got something to show you. Follow me."

Lester led Ronnie into his former bedroom. Mae followed close behind.

"Do you remember what your old bedroom looked like Ronnie?"

"Yes, I do Lester," Ronnie replied politely.

Lester threw open the door and said, "This is your new room, Ronnie."

Ronnie could not believe the transformation his room underwent. It looked nothing like his former room. The old lumpy bed with the protruding springs was gone. In its place was a new brass bed and deep captain's mattress. The walls were light blue and the ceiling white. "Look in the corner Ronnie," Lester invited.

Ronnie looked where Lester pointed. Against the wall was a double pedestal desk and beside it was a snappy looking goose-necked floor lamp. Lester placed a full-size blotter, a lined pad of paper, and some pens and pencils on top of the desk.

Lester said, "Your mother tells me that you started school. I figured you might need a quiet place to study and do homework. That's your new desk to work on Ronnie."

"Thanks, Lester. It will be better than laying across the bed to do homework."

Lester chuckled. "Yes, I guess that's true Ronnie. In the corner is a new built-in closet. I put a few things in there that I thought you might enjoy." Ronnie opened the closet door and discovered new sports clothes, a basketball, and hockey stick. "They are nice Lester. Thank you."

Motioning to Mae, Lester said, "Let's have some coffee. I have juice for you, Ronnie."

They all sat together around a new chrome kitchen set. Mae was impressed with the improvements Lester made. Lester turned to Ronnie, and said, "I've invited you and your mother to move back in here with me. What do you think about that Ronnie?"

Mae interjected in an assertive voice and said, "Lester, stop bullying Ronnie and bribing him with new toys and furniture. Ronnie and I will decide what we want to do. Don't use Ronnie to gain favors from me."

"I'm sorry Mae. I did not mean to put you in an uncomfortable position. Please forgive me."

"I forgive you this time Lester. There will be no forgiveness if you do it again though."

Ronnie looked at his mother in astonishment. He was pleased to see how strong she had become. Mae too surprised herself at how well she stood up to Lester. A few years ago, she could never have talked to Lester like that. Mae had become stronger, more self-sufficient and no longer dependent on Lester for support. She had become the stronger of the two.

When she finished her coffee, Mae turned to Lester and said, "We have to leave now Lester. You have done an excellent job fixing up the house. Ronnie and I will talk together. I will speak with you next week and give you our decision. Meanwhile, please don't try to contact me."

"Okay, Mae. I hope that your answer is positive. I promise not to contact you."

At supper time, Mae asked Ronnie, “Well Ronnie, what do you think of moving back with Lester?”

“I still don’t like Lester because he hurt you, Mommy. If we go back to Lester, I hope he does not hurt you again like he did the last time, and I hope he does not hurt me either.”

Mae could see the fear within Ronnie. Mae could plainly see if Ronnie had a choice, he would not want to have anything to do with Lester.

Ronnie told Mae, “Mommy if you decide to go back to Lester, I’ll go with you and do whatever you decide.” Mae could discern from Ronnie’s tone he would not be content living under the same roof with Lester.

“Okay, Ronnie. We have arrived at a final decision. We will not go back to Lester. You and I will make it on our own. We don’t need Lester.”

Ronnie’s facial expression changed from gloominess to happiness. He jumped up from his place at the table, flew over to Mae, and threw his arms around her. “Thank you, Mommy, thank you; thank you.”

Mae knew she made the right decision.

# 15

On Monday morning Mae phoned The Mill and left a message with the Line Supervisor to have Lester call her. Lester called at break time. They planned to meet that night at his place.

Mae wondered how Lester would react when she told him she and Ronnie would not be moving back with him. Because he went to such efforts to fix up his old house hoping to entice her and Ronnie back with him, Mae did not expect him to be happy. At first, she thought about writing a note telling him she and Ronnie would not be moving back and slip it under his door. She abandoned that idea thinking it was rude and cowardly. It was not her nature to be so cold. That was how Lester would react. She did not want to sink to his level. The thought of making a phone call crossed her mind. She thought that was as bad as slipping a note under the door. After evaluating all possibilities, Mae concluded, that the only proper way to do it was to tell Lester face to face.

Before telling Lester, Mae spoke to Jane and described Ronnie's opposition to moving back with Lester.

"Ronnie is a smart boy," Jane told Mae. "He figured that no matter how beautiful Lester made the house look, his temper remained unchecked. He feared for his Mom's safety and his own, knowing both of you could again become victims of Lester's wrath. As hard as it will be to tell Lester tonight Mae, you and Ronnie made the right decision," Jane reassured her.

That evening, Mae rang Lester's fancy doorbell. Lester came to the door right away. "Hi Mae, it is good to see you," Lester threw the door open wide and cheerily welcomed her. He invited her into the kitchen. Lester had fresh coffee brewing. Mae told Lester, "The coffee smells good, Lester.

"I made it just for you Mae. I know how much you like fresh coffee," Lester said.

After Lester poured coffee for them, they both sat down together at the table. Mae opened the conversation. She was nervous, not knowing what Lester's reaction would be. She hoped her nervousness did not show.

"Lester, you and I have shared some good times together. We have also shared times that were not so good. The road was often rocky. As I told you many times, Lester, I want to give Ronnie a better life. You do not share the same deep conviction as I do. That's been a problem ever since he was born."

"But I am not like that anymore Mae," Lester pleaded.

Mae ignored Lester's comment and continued talking. "You and I have grown apart Lester. The lack of money has been a major obstacle. You lack ambition, while I am full of ambition. Working on the line will never generate enough money to meet our needs. Your stubborn insistence to not allow me to go out to work only aggravates the problem."

Mae could tell Lester was inwardly seething at her comments. He never heard her speak so forcefully to him, and he did not know how to react to it. Lester had no comeback to Mae's accusations, which agitated him even more. He knew what Mae said was true.

Mae continued, "Money and ambition are not the only issues that concern me, Lester. Our lifestyles are going in opposite directions. I am furthering my education at the University and hope someday to open a designer dress shop. I want to travel and see the world. I want to have friends who respect me. I do not want to be alone. You know Lester how loneliness affects me. You rescued me from that when we first met. Those were good days, and then everything changed when Ronnie was born."

Lester, in a weepy and pleading tone, exclaimed, "I'm just asking for another chance Mae. We can make it work. I've changed."

"I'm sorry Lester, but Ronnie and I don't think you have changed enough. I suggest that we stay friends and work on renewing our association gradually. Who knows what the future will bring? Meanwhile, Ronnie and I want to live separately from you."

Lester's demeanor abruptly changed. Mae could see the rage rising within him. He pounded the table and shouted. "You're so ungrateful and inconsiderate of my feelings Mae. After all the time, work, and expense I put in to fix this place up for you, and this is the thanks I receive?"

Mae's mind flashed back to her encounter with Charlie. Lester was using the same derogatory words that Charlie used. Mae was scared and quickly moved away from the table when Lester shouted. She had seen this happen before. She knew how fast Lester could lose control. Lester got up from his chair and lunged towards Mae. His fist landed squarely on her jaw. She heard it crack. Lester followed her across the kitchen and grabbed her hair. Mae saw the all too familiar fist coming at her again. She ducked and received a glancing blow on the side of her head. Mae knew things would get worse. She reached for the phone and dialed zero hoping the operator would not take too long to come onto the line. Mae let the receiver dangle and ran towards the front door. She could not open it before Lester caught her and pounded his fist into the side of her face. She fell to the floor. Lester walked away shouting obscenities at her.

Mae crawled into the bedroom and hid in the closet amongst the toys that Lester intended for Ronnie. She hoped the phone operator heard her screams, and Lester did not hang up the receiver and disconnect the line. I'll just stay in the closet until it is safe to come out, Mae reasoned. I hope Lester doesn't come looking for me.

The police arrived within minutes. They handcuffed Lester and escorted him to the back seat of a waiting squad car and drove away. Mae peeked from the closet, and a police officer told her it was safe to come out and that Lester was on his way to jail. When the Officer saw the extent of Mae's wounds, he called for an ambulance to take her to the hospital. X-rays showed Mae suffered a broken jaw bone. The healing process would take four to six weeks. When Mae exited from surgery, a nurse told her she would have to remain in the hospital for at least a week.

The police contacted Charlotte as Mae asked.

Charlotte came to the hospital and told Mae, "You are not to worry about Ronnie, Mae. The shelter will look after him until you return."

Mae thought that Charlotte would scold her for not telling her about meeting with Lester. Charlotte never raised the subject. She was only concerned with Mae's wellbeing.

Charlotte also informed Jane of Mae's circumstances and told her Mae would be absent from work for a week. Jane went at once to the hospital after hearing of Mae's misfortune. Jane assured Mae her job would be waiting for her when she was well enough to return.

Two days after her surgery a lawyer from the District Attorney's Office came to meet with Mae in the hospital. He told her that Lester is in jail pending trial. He asked Mae if she wanted to press charges.

"Yes, I do," Mae adamantly responded. The prosecutor took down the details he needed to go to trial. He asked Mae if she was agreeable to testify against Lester. She said she was.

After her recovery period in the hospital, Mae returned to work at The Dress Shop. The business had not improved during her absence.

A month later, Mae attended Lester's trial. Two armed guards ushered him into the courtroom, one on each side. He wore a prison-issued, black and white jumpsuit, and his chains created a loud clanging noise when he walked. Two guards, one on each side of Lester, brought him into the courtroom and escorted him to the prisoner's box. They stood beside him throughout the trial.

He made fleeting glances toward Mae. He's trying to intimidate me, Mae thought. I know him so well.

When called to testify, Mae told the court how mean and cruel Lester was to her and Ronnie over the years. The defense attorney made her go into graphic details about his most recent attack on her.

The judge found Lester guilty of assault and sentenced him to ten years in prison. Because this was Lester's second offense, he would not be eligible for parole. The same two officers who guarded him throughout the trial escorted him out of the courtroom through a side door. Lester did not turn to look at Mae on the way out.

"I'm glad that's over with," Mae told the prosecutor, "It was difficult testifying with Lester only a few yards away from me. I am still afraid of him."

The prosecutor commented, "It is over with Mae. Lester can't hurt or intimidate you any longer."

"Yes. I hope so. After Lester serves his sentence, I trust he will leave prison a better person than when he entered. He has ten years to work on it."

After the trial, Mae returned to The Dress Shop to bring Jane up-to-date on the results. Jane was genuinely happy for Mae. "Now you and Ronnie can get on with your lives, without Lester hindering you."

"Thank you, Jane." Mae no longer wanted to keep talking about Lester. She much preferred to talk about something more positive.

"Jane, I have some ideas I would like to share with you in the next few days, but right now I want to go to the shelter and give Ronnie the news about Lester. He has been anxious for me these last few weeks."

"Take as much time as you need Mae. Call me if there is anything I can do for you. Like Ronnie, I've been worried about you also."

"Thanks, Jane. I feel things are about to change, for the better."

Mae was at the shelter to greet Ronnie when he returned from school. He was delighted to see her. Mae explained everything that happened at the courthouse and that he need not fear Lester any longer. "Lester won't be around anymore to hurt us, Ronnie."

"That's good Mommy. I like it better when it's just you and me."

"I do too Ronnie."

Mae wanted to speak with Charlotte before she left for the evening. She found her in her office. Mae gently knocked on Charlotte's door. Charlotte raised her head and smiled at Mae.

"Mae, I'm so happy to see you. Come in and tell me everything that happened today in court." Mae related the details to Charlotte.

Charlotte said, "Now that Lester is no longer a threat to revealing the location of the shelter you can delay moving from the shelter if you wish. As you know, you can stay here for up to two years."

"Thanks, Charlotte, but Ronnie and I are prepared to move out of the shelter as planned. I think it best to keep those plans in place. It will enable Ronnie and me to start our new life together earlier."

"That's a wise idea, Mae. The sooner you get on with your life, the better. The shelter and I will always be here if you need us."

"Charlotte, you and the shelter were here for Ronnie and me when we needed you the most. I'll always remember what you did for us - I promise."

Charlotte asked, "Have you found a place to live Mae?"

"Not yet. I've been searching through the papers looking for something we can afford, but I've not come up with anything yet."

Charlotte calmly said, "Lester's place is available."

"But I don't know what my rights are regarding Ronnie and me living there while Lester is in jail."

"You have every right to live there Mae. You're still married to Lester, and under the law, you may live there as long as you pay the taxes."

"That's good to know Charlotte. That is what we will do then."

"Good luck with everything," Charlotte said.

# *CHANGES*

When all else fails
- return to the drawing board.

# 16

The next day Mae went to work at The Dress Shop. She told Jane she and Ronnie planned to move into Lester's place. Jane was happy that something good evolved from a horrific situation.

"Now you and Ronnie can get on with the rest of your life," Jane confidently told her.

Mae and Ronnie left the confines of the shelter and moved into Lester's house. It took time for them to expel the evil memories the house held. Eventually, time mended the unhealthy thoughts and replaced them with good ones.

Ronnie progressed well in school, and Mae continued her studies at the University polishing her skills. Mae and Ronnie were making a new life for themselves without Lester.

Mae freshened up the appearance of the house with fresh paint, redesigned the kitchen, and modernized the bathroom to her and Ronnie's liking. It became Mae and Ronnie's home. Lester's name rarely came up in conversation.

Business at the dress shop did not fare too well during Mae and Ronnie's transition to their new lifestyle. The economy in Lewisville remained stagnant. The Dress Shop had its regular clientele, but client traffic into the shop was declining. Jane was concerned that she could not stay in business too much longer if sales did not improve.

Mae told Jane, "You are a good and caring friend Jane. I am grateful for everything you have done for me. I am concerned however about you, Jane. How are you doing?"

"I've some personal concerns," Jane confessed. "I'm concerned about the lack of business. Lewisville cannot sustain a dress shop of this caliber. People in Lewisville have no money. I have spent hours trying to come up with a solution to my dilemma. I still do not have a solution, and I'm beginning to worry."

Mae commented, "I've been concerned about the lack of business also Jane. I am not blind, and I can see how few customers we have. They take one look at the prices and leave."

Mae looked Jane squarely in her face and said, "Jane I have put together some contemporary designs. I think they may be right for a changing marketplace. Would you like to see them?

"I'd be happy to look at your designs, Mae."

"Good," Mae answered excitedly, "I'll bring some sketches in tomorrow for you to look at."

Mae was pleased that Jane agreed to view some of her work. Mae rushed home after work to choose sketches she thought would be proper for her discussion with Jane the next day.

The next morning, with her sketchbook, tucked firmly under her arm, Mae left for work at The Dress Shop. She was eager to share her ideas with Jane.

Mae got to the shop before Jane. She opened the door with her key, put on a pot of coffee, and waited for Jane to appear, which she did a few minutes later.

"Good morning Jane," Mae called out to her.

"Good morning Mae," Jane responded. "You're here early."

"I'm anxious to show you my sketches. I hope you like them. We can look at them together over coffee."

"That's an excellent idea, Mae. Bring your sketchbook and coffee into my office. We can drink coffee and work together."

Jane adored Mae's designs. "I never dreamed you had such a talent Mae. Where did you learn these inspiring design styles and techniques? They don't teach you that at the Design School."

"I've always liked designing things, especially clothes," Mae answered. "Through necessity, I designed and sewed most of Ronnie's clothes for him. Occasionally, I designed a few things for myself. I designed and created a distinctive housecoat for Wilma."

Mae continued, "Charlotte encouraged me to enroll in the University School of Design course where I am honing my skills. It is a five-year course, and I will graduate next year with a 'Fashion Designer' designation. The course teaches me how to build and promote my design skills."

Mae continued talking to Jane. "I was thinking how we could improve business for The Dress Shop. These sketches are only a small sample of my designs. Whenever I have an idea, I grab my sketchbook and record it before it vanishes out of my head."

Jane asked, "What do you have in mind for The Dress Shop Mae? Women who live in Lewisville still cannot afford your elegant, expensive designer dresses, Mae. The problem will remain unsolved."

Mae expected Jane's question. "Jane, you spend many hours every day pouring through catalogs, looking for dresses to buy and hang up in the shop, where they stay because nobody can afford to buy them."

Mae directed Jane to the neatly hung dresses on the racks. "What if we created a catalog of unique designer dresses, and offered them to retailers across the USA and Canada?" Mae gestured to the stack of well-thumbed through books and magazines on the floor beside Jane's desk. "There is nothing special about the dresses in those catalogs. I believe that I can design dresses just as good, or even better. Our focus would be to get our catalogs into the hands of international couturiers, and entice them to show, and market, our creations to their buyers. The only thing we would have to do is to focus on producing a well-put-together, high-end, catalog for them to show to their rich clients, and wholesalers."

Jane's eyes widened. "Mae not only are you a creative designer, but you're also an astute business person. Your idea could work."

"I believe so too Jane. But it will not happen by itself. It will need a lot of work and planning. First, we need a manufacturing and distribution company to make it work. I suggest Jane, you speak to some of your executive contacts at The Mill and float the idea by them. If they are interested, we can set up a meeting to discuss it further. If they are not interested, we will look for other manufacturers who will be interested. It would be easier, however, to do business with The Mill who can distribute dresses right here from their Lewisville facilities."

Mae said, "One thing more Jane, instead of spending time thumbing through catalogs every day, let's seek out organizations who can produce attractive catalogs, and periodicals, to illustrate our designs. The printing business has fallen on tough times just like every other business. I think there are printers and lithographers in the Lewisville area, who would be happy to work with us and produce high-end catalogs. You are well-known and respected in Lewisville, Jane. You could search-out qualified printers and lithographers through your many contacts."

"I'll get on it right away," Jane answered. "You certainly are a take-charge person Mae. I'm so glad to have you working with me."

"I'm happy to work alongside you too Jane. This job allows me to let my creative juices flow. I have some contemporary designs in mind for varying markets and demographics. It will be fun, and hopefully profitable."

Mae gleefully jumped to her feet, raised her half-empty coffee cup, and clicked it against Jane's, shouting, "Here's to new markets."

Mae thought, could this be my first step to giving Ronnie a better life than he was born into?

That night after supper Mae sketched several designs that flowed into her mind. Mae worked long into the night after Ronnie had gone to sleep. She did that every night for a week.

Meanwhile, Jane was cultivating contacts at The Mill and spreading the word she was looking for creative lithographers, photographers, and modeling agencies. She spent a lot of time trying to raise interest at The Mill of becoming a manufacturing and distribution agent for high-end designer dresses.

A week later Jane told Mae, "I spoke to George Smith yesterday. George is the Vice-President of Marketing at The Mill. I ran your idea by him of using The Dress Shop as a design center and incorporating The Mill as the manufacturing and distribution agent. He thought the idea had merit and wants to discuss it further with us."

"That's wonderful news, Jane. My portfolio is ready. We can meet anytime."

"I've arranged a meeting in two weeks with George at The Mill. He is a very busy man. That was the earliest date he had available."

"That's great Jane. I will be ready."

At supper time, Mae expounded to Ronnie the possibility of her and Jane working with The Mill. Ronnie was old enough now to understand the value, and importance, of his mother and Jane partnering with The Mill.

"I like my job Ronnie, and I want us to continue living in Lewisville. I want to give you a better life, as I promised you I would. I hope Jane and I succeed, and we can find new avenues to market my designs."

Ronnie said, "Mother, I know how hard you work as a single Mom. Thank-you for everything you do. I am very proud of you."

"And I'm proud of you too Ronnie. You are in high school now. Where have all the years gone? Your report cards show that you are an excellent student. You came first in your class again last semester."

"Thank you, Mother. I hope always to make you proud of me. By-the-way, there is a meet-the-teacher night next week Mother. I know you have little time on your hands but, I would like you to meet my teacher. Do you think you could find time in your busy schedule to come to my school and meet him?"

"I'll make sure I have time Ronnie. I would be pleased to have you introduce him to me. I have never been to your school before."

"Oh, thank you, Mother," Ronnie replied with glee. "His name is Mr. Arvin. I like him, and I think you'll like him also."

"I'm sure I will Ronnie."

A week later, Mae went with Ronnie to his high school to meet his teacher. It gave her a diversion from the hectic days at The Dress Shop preparing for her all-important meeting at The Mill.

She wanted to stay in tune with Ronnie's progress and school activities, but she was busy at the Dress shop and admitted she didn't pay as much attention to Ronnie as she would like to.

Ronnie was doing well in school, despite his dysfunctional home life when he was a child. Mae was thankful that was no longer an issue.

Mr. Arvin, Ronnie's homeroom teacher, told Mae that Ronnie was a bright and intelligent young man. He warned her however of a potential looming future problem for Ronnie. He explained that pupils of Ronnie's intelligence, have trouble in school because they become bored with the curriculum and explore other areas to satisfy their inquisitive thirsts. Sometimes they choose socially unacceptable activities and get into trouble.

Mae politely listened to Mr. Arvin articulate his thoughts regarding intellectually gifted students. She was confident Ronnie would do nothing that was socially unacceptable. He had too many other things to occupy him - like becoming proficient at schoolwork, she told herself.

On the drive home from his, meet-the-teacher event, Mae commented to Ronnie, "Thanks Ronnie for taking me to your school. Your teachers all hold you in high regard. I do too, and I am proud of what you have accomplished, under trying circumstances at times."

Mae assured Ronnie, "Lester is out of our lives now Ronnie. You need not worry about him hampering your progress. Continue to learn as much as you can. A good education will provide you a good life, providing you don't allow negative things to get in the way and hamper your success."

Mae was confident Ronnie knew right from wrong and would always be a good student.

I don't need to worry about Ronnie, Mae assured herself. I can concentrate on my career-building fashion designer business, knowing that he is progressing well in school.

********************

Mae and Jane drove to The Mill together in Jane's car. They parked in the visitor's parking lot and walked to the entrance of, The Executive Offices. They were in a separate building away from where Mae worked on the sorting line with Lester. Mae was unaware of a separate building housing the Executive Offices.

They walked up the concrete steps to the brass handled, double door entrance. It smacked of authority.

Mae remarked to Jane, "This looks nothing like the entrance where I had to punch a clock to record my comings and goings when I worked on the line sorting yarns."

Jane smiled. "With any luck Mae, you'll become more familiar with this entrance than you ever did with the punch clock entrance."

Mae and Jane entered the lobby where a smiling, well-dressed, professional-looking receptionist greeted them, "Can I help you, ladies?"

Jane responded, "My name is Jane Marsh. I have an appointment with Mr. George Smith."

The receptionist replied, "He's expecting you. Have a seat. I'll tell him you're here."

After a few minutes, George walked into the reception area. He had a pleasant smile and shook Jane's hand. They exchanged pleasantries.

"George, I want you to meet Mae, my new associate. She's the talented lady I talked to you about."

George and Mae shook hands. "It is nice to meet you, Mae. Jane has spoken highly of you."

"Good to meet you too George. I hope I can live up to everything Jane has told you about me. It is a long fall from the high pedestal she placed me on."

George smiled at Mae's quick, and witty, response.

George was a tall, good-looking, middle-aged, distinguished corporate executive, with a hint of grey hair grasping at his temples. His fingernails were neatly clipped and manicured.

He wore a navy blue well-tailored suit, a starched white shirt, and a blue silk tie to complement it. His shoes gleamed to a mirror-like finish.

Good looking, well-dressed men, command attention, Mae thought. That certainly applies to George. He oozes attention-seeking qualities.

George ushered Jane and Mae down a marble-floored hallway. He held open the heavy oak door to his office and invited both to precede him into his well-appointed office. He followed them into his luxurious office and sat in a high-backed black leather chair behind a double pedestal, beautiful mahogany desk. Mae and Jane sat in two luxurious black leather armchairs in front of his desk. George's office, like him, resonated power and authority.

Jane opened the conversation. "As you know George, the economic outlook for Lewisville has been in decline for several years. The Mill has suffered a decline in revenues, as has my shop. Mae is about to become a graduate fashion designer from the University

Design School. She came up with an idea to market her fashions using The Dress Shop as the designer wholesaler, and The Mill as the manufacturing distributor. We wanted to run the idea by you and invite you to look at Mae's design portfolio."

On cue, Mae opened her portfolio and placed it in front of George. He had no alternative but to look at it. Jane and Mae remained silent while he thumbed through detailed sketches of Mae's delightful, forward-thinking, contemporary designs.

"I'm impressed," George said after looking at Mae's exquisite couturier style designs.

Jane asked, "Do you think our idea has merit, George?"

"I certainly do. The Mill has been looking for new markets. The North American market for weaved fabric is demanding, but the cost to produce it in this marketplace makes us uncompetitive. The Mill only produces yarns in Lewisville which go to Asia for weaving into fabric."

George said, "Our Asian partners could produce your designer dresses Mae, and bulk-ship them to The Mill for distribution throughout North America. That solution would benefit everyone and enhance the economic status of Lewisville. I will need agreement from our fabric producer in Hong Kong, but that should be a mere formality. I'll run the idea by them in a few days."

George turned and addressed Mae directly, "I can see that you have put a lot of thought into this Mae. Not only are you an excellent designer you also have a good feel for consumer trends as well."

George closed Mae's portfolio and jointly addressed Jane and Mae. "Your proposal is well-timed ladies. Leave it with me for a week. I'll discuss it with our Hong Kong producers, and if they are agreeable to proceed, I'll take it up with our President who will make the final decision."

Looking at Mae, George asked, "Can I keep your portfolio Mae?"

"Of course. I put it together for you to use however you want George."

George responded, "When the President views this presentation I believe he too will be impressed."

Jane and Mae shook hands with George and thanked him for the time spent with them, and cordially left. In the parking lot, Mae turned to Jane and said, "I think that went well, Jane. How do you think it went?"

"I think it went okay Mae. George liked your designs and your business sense. I admire those qualities in you too."

"Thank you, Jane, for that vote of confidence."

Mae was curious to know more about George. "Does he live in Lewisville Jane? How long has he worked at The Mill and how did you get to know him so well?"

Jane answered, "George lives in an upscale part of Lewisville not far from where I live. My late husband hired him to work at The Mill about fifteen years ago. George is well-known and respected throughout the world in the garment producing industry."

Jane continued talking about George, "When my husband was still alive, we often had George and his wife, over to our place for dinner. His wife died about ten years ago. A few years later, my husband got sick and died also. George and I remained good friends, but that's all."

At supper time that evening, Mae told Ronnie about her and Jane's visit to The Mill. Ronnie understood the world of business.

Ronnie was excited and happy for his mother. "I hope it all works out for you Mom. It will be fun to have a fashion designer for a mother."

# 17

Before meeting with Jane and Mae, the two Mill executives conferred between themselves. Both agreed that if the deal to partner with The Dress Shop had any chance, it was vital that Mae remained as the cornerstone of the operation. In typical executive thinking, they agreed Jane was a good shopkeeper, but that was all she was.

Mae brought unique, designer and marketing skills to the table. Without an assurance of those skills, the prospective deal would be of little value to The Mill. The two executives needed Mae to become a fifty-fifty partner of The Dress Shop and hold a seat on The Mill's Board of Directors. They did not want to chance losing her talents to another organization. "She could be The Mill's savior, preventing it from closing its Lewisville operations," the President told George.

George warned The President that Jane might not be willing to give away half of her business to Mae. The President adamantly replied, "Then we walk away from the deal."

"Understood," George said. "I'll phone Jane and set-up an appointment for us to meet at The Dress Shop."

"Hello Jane, this is George speaking. The President wants a tour of The Dress Shop facilities. I want to see them also. Can we meet next Wednesday at your place?"

Jane confirmed the appointment, walked to the back of the shop, to tell Mae the exciting news.

"That is wonderful," Mae said. "Now we have to work hard to get ready for the meeting."

"Tell me what you want me to do, Mae. You're better at this than I am."

Mae smiled and said, "We need to anticipate questions, and be ready with answers for every possible question that may arise." Mae remembered Charlotte's technique and suggested she and Jane role-play before the meeting.

"First, we must anticipate questions that may be asked and have answers prepared. These two executives have done this before. It is important that you and I are singing from the same song sheet, and we both communicate the same views and comments. I suggest we come back to the shop tonight to prepare ourselves. We only have one chance to get it right."

"You think of everything Mae. You are a real take charge person. I cannot believe that you started your life as a simple farm girl."

"I got where I am Jane because I had good people help me move from a life otherwise destined for failure, to a life of opportunity. My Aunt Wilma, Charlotte, and you are the principle motivators in my life."

"Thanks, Mae. Do not forget to take credit for the sacrifices you made to reach this point in your life. You bravely stepped out of a dead-end world, into one that put you where you are today. Your artistic skills, coupled with your strong determination to succeed, have put you on the threshold of success."

"Thank-you Jane," Mae replied modestly. "We will walk the road of success together, Jane."

At the meeting, George spoke first. "Mr. President, I want to introduce you to Jane and Mae."

Everyone shook hands. Mae and Jane conducted a tour of The Dress Shop for the two executives like they rehearsed. Both executives were impressed with the layout and Jane's beautiful inventory of dresses. They were equally impressed with Mae's sketches strategically posted throughout the shop to attract favorable attention from the two business suiters.

An hour later the President said, "I've seen enough. Now is time to talk business. How about we discuss it over lunch at the Lewisville Club? We can talk in private without arousing suspicions."

Mae had never been to The Lewisville Club. The exclusive membership consisted of Lewisville business owners and corporate executives. Mae never expected to qualify for membership.

Jane closed the shop for the rest of the day. All four traveled to the Club in George's Cadillac. The President sat in the front seat. Jane and Mae sat in the luxurious leather upholstered rear seat. It was the first time for Mae to ride in a Cadillac, let alone one so luxurious.

Over lunch, the four principles struck a deal. It stipulated, Mae, to be the Executive Dress Designer under a private label, Jane the liaison officer between retailers in Canada and the USA, and George, the Production Executive. All agreed to have the dresses produced in Hong Kong and shipped to the Lewisville Distribution Center, for furtherance to retailers in North America. Mae would occupy a seat on The Mill's Board of Directors.

The two executives insisted that Mae and Jane form a fifty-fifty joint venture. Jane was delighted with that proposal. Like the two Mill executives, she realized that Mae was the ticket to her success. Without Mae's designs, The Dress Shop would fail. The arrangement locked-in Mae's association with Jane and The Dress Shop, despite Jane having to give up half of her business to Mae.

Under the agreement, The Dress Shop name would disappear, and a new company formed. All parties agreed in principle and shook hands to seal the deal.

The next day Jane asked, "What name will we give our new company Mae?"

Mae replied, "I suggest that we incorporate both our names since we'll be joint owners."

"Do you have something in mind?" Jane asked.

Mae suggested the name, 'Jamae,' because it incorporates both names. J-A for Jane, and M-A-E for Mae.

She told Jane, "It makes a simple sew-in nametag. We can use it for branding in catalogs, promotions, and public relations. Jamae Fashions can be our new corporate name."

"Mae, you're brilliant. What a terrific sounding name for our new venture. Welcome to Jamae Fashions, Partner."

In short order, a 'Jamae Fashions' sign, replaced, 'The Dress Shop' sign, on the outside of the building. Eventually, the lawyers assembled all the pieces to fulfill the conditions of the agreement, including the production company in Hong Kong.

Business for Jamae Fashions flourished. Jamae dresses started making a name for themselves in North America. Their markets included Montreal, Toronto, and New York. Requests for samples came from, New York, Los Angeles, and even Paris.

Mae became a member of The Lewisville Club where she developed a rapport with prominent community inspired individuals. She, Jane, and George often met at The Club for lunch. It was an ideal place to conduct business in private. Mae was comfortable in her new role as business owner, corporate executive, and community leader. Sought after by the local media, and a prominent member of the Lewisville business community, Mae basked in her new-found status and popularity.

Jamae Fashions brought new life into The Mill and Lewisville. The extensive distribution center employed locals from Lewisville, and surrounding areas, causing the overall economy to flourish again. Local shop owners looked to her for advice and inspiration. She was in demand as a keynote speaker by various charitable organizations.

The unrelenting demand for her up-scale fashions kept Mae busy creating innovative designs. She arrived at Jamae Fashions early every morning and returned most nights after preparing supper for Ronnie. When she got home, usually late at night, Ronnie was asleep.

As Mae's popularity and business grew, both consumed a lot of Mae's time until she had little time for anything else. Most times Ronnie was alone and only saw his mother in the mornings before she left for work. He was lonely in the evenings but did not want to tell Mae because he was the reason she worked so hard. Mae assumed, because Ronnie was so smart and doing so well at school, there was no need for concern.

# 18

One night Mae came home late and found Ronnie bent over the kitchen table. There was something different about him. On further examination, she noticed he had two black eyes and a swollen lip. Blood on his forehead indicated earlier bleeding. "Ronnie, what on earth happened to you."

"I'm sorry Mother. I got into a fight at school today."

"Why," Mae asked.

"A school bully accused me of having no guts. He said I would be nothing if I did not have a rich mother to look after me. He kept pushing and shoving me. I got mad and punched him back. That is how the fight started. We were both sent to the Principal's office and expelled for three days. When I return, you must come with me and meet with the Principal. I am not proud of myself."

"Let's get you cleaned up and tend to those cuts and bruises. We'll talk about this more tomorrow." Mae could tell that Ronnie was genuinely sorry and embarrassed.

The next morning, she called Jane at home and told her she would not be at Jamae for the next three days. She explained the trouble that Ronnie met with at school. Jane was sympathetic and told Mae to take as much time as she needed. "Ronnie is your priority right now," she said.

After a sleepless night, Mae rose the next morning and sat in the kitchen waiting for Ronnie to wake up. Meanwhile, she asked herself, what precipitated the altercation between Ronnie and the school bully? Why was he not in the library reading or studying? I always thought Ronnie was too smart to get himself into trouble like that.

Ronnie walked into the kitchen. "Good morning Ronnie," she greeted him. "Your face is looking better this morning. How are you feeling?"

"Better, thank-you Mother, but I am still ashamed for disappointing you. I did not want you to come home last night and see how I looked. Unlike other nights when I long for you to come home."

"There is no need to apologize Ronnie. I laid awake most of the night thinking about your situation. I figured out where the problem originated – it's me. I am the reason for your problems, Ronnie."

Ronnie did not comment and intently listened to his mother speaking.

Mae continued, "Mr. Arvin, your former homeroom teacher, warned me three years ago that something like this could happen. I dismissed it at the time, and never reconsidered that you might be bored with your school curriculum and need other outlets to challenge you."

Ronnie continued to remain silent. He looked at her intently and hung on to her every word.

"I'm guilty on another front too Ronnie. I put work, and other people's concerns before you, Ronnie. I am truly sorry for leaving you alone every evening while I went about solving problems for other people and Jamae Fashions. I had my priorities all wrong, for which I deeply apologize Ronnie. I should have known better."

Mae confessed, "I went through a period of loneliness before you were born. It led to other problems. I should have realized that due to my absence you were subject to what I too previously experienced. I am guilty Ronnie and ask your forgiveness. I promise that will never happen again. I will be home every night - starting tonight. The one person who means the most to me, I neglected. I should have known better."

"Thank-you Mother. I did not want to tell you how lonely I was. I hated when you left me alone each night. I did not want to say anything because everything you do, you do to make a better life for me. My life does not get better however when you're not here with me."

Mae scolded herself saying, "How could I be so stupid, Ronnie?"

Ronnie continued, "I get lonely at school also. I finish my assignments long before the other kids. I have no homework because I finish it at school when the teacher is explaining the assignments to my classmates. I do not need extra tutoring as my classmates do so my teachers ignore me. That makes me different, and therefore my friends ignore me too. That is how the fight started. I wanted my classmates to like me."

"I understand Ronnie. You wanted to send a message to your classmates that you were not a sissy because you are smart, but you are just like them, and therefore they should like you. Am I right Ronnie?"

"Yes, you're exactly right Mother."

Ronnie and Mae spent the rest of the day together. She saw her maturing son in a different light. She reminded herself that he is no longer a little boy and in three years he will be attending University. These are challenging times for him, and he needs me for support, but I was not there for him. That will change, she told herself.

The next day Mae and Ronnie sat before the School Principal. Ronnie was nervous. He was uncertain what his mother would say, about his unacceptable behavior.

The Principal reminded Mae that Ronnie's behavior was not in keeping with school expectations, and if it happens again, permanent expulsion would be the result. He told Ronnie he was a brilliant student and did not need to prove himself worthy by fighting. Ronnie remained silent throughout the tongue lashing.

Up to this point, the Principal controlled the conversation. Mae, from experience, knew when to talk and when to listen. Now, it was her time to speak.

When the principal finished critiquing Ronnie, Mae said, "Sir, Ronnie was wrong to fight with another student. It is my fault Ronnie finds himself in this predicament," Mae categorically stated.

"Ronnie and I have spoken and effective immediately I will be getting more involved in Ronnie's life at home and school. This situation will not happen again. Ronnie, as well as the other students, need to be challenged more than they are at present."

In awe at Mae's straight-forward approach, the Principal said, "I commend you as a forward-thinking responsible parent. Most parents blame the school for their child's shortcomings. You recognize there is a problem that needs a solution. A rare quality in parents these days."

Mae asked the Principal, "With your permission, can Ronnie go back to his class now?"

"Indeed. Come with me, Ronnie. I'll walk you to your classroom and tell your teacher everything is okay." Turning to Mae, he said, "Give me a few minutes. We can talk when I return."

Mae wished Ronnie a good day and assured him she would be at home to greet him after school.

The Principal returned to continue talking with Mae after delivering Ronnie to his class.

"I know you have some ideas to share with me," the Principal told Mae. "I detected your desire not to discuss them in front of Ronnie. We can talk in confidence now. I'm interested in hearing what you have to say."

"Sir, with all due respect, you have a situation which needs fixing. While I appreciate your viewpoint and agree that schools must set and support high academic standards, it is not enough. A rounded education means students need to incorporate extra-curricular activities into their school life, where they can hook-up with other students with similar interests. I believe the school needs to involve parents more than it does. Had I known Ronnie's academic concerns earlier, I would have taken steps to help him overcome his social difficulties with the other students. Had Ronnie, and the other student, had an opportunity to vent their frustrations in a gym, or on a running track, or maybe participate in some other activity outside the classroom, the fight between them may not have occurred."

The Principal was awestruck by Mae's views and comments. Mae continued, "The reason students fight with each other is that they have no other way to compete. Ronnie has become bored with school. I suspect he is not the only bored student in school either. The school needs to explore ways to corral the energy of all students, gifted and otherwise. An individual with rounded skills stands a better chance of succeeding in life. My own life is a perfect example."

The Principal knew of Mae's social and business prominence. He knew nothing about her abusive life on the farm and the time spent being home-schooled by Wilma.

"Your points are well taken. What extra-curricular activities do you have in mind?"

Mae expected the question. She replied, "A schoolyard big enough to encompass a football field, a running track, and a sand pit for field events. Indoor activities could include a well-equipped gymnasium, a drama theatre, and a well-stocked library."

"I agree with everything you are suggesting, but we don't have the funding to provide facilities as you propose."

Mae asked, "If funding was not an issue, would you support my suggestions?"

"Indeed, I would," the Principal answered enthusiastically.

"Alright," Mae said. "Assume the funding will be in place."

"Thank you for your generosity," he replied. "To best implement your ideas, you should become a member of the Parent Teachers Association, commonly known as the PTA."

Mae agreed she would.

********************

Daydreaming over a cup of coffee, Mae recalled the Principal enticing her to join the PTA. After joining, Mae helped to set up a foundation to fund the purchase of a section of land near the school to develop into an outdoor sports facility. She anonymously funded the seed money to start the project. No other schools in the region had facilities like Ronnie's school. The Principal, a few PTA members, and the school board were the only ones aware of Mae's financial involvement. She asked them to keep her participation confidential to avoid others treating Ronnie differently, although she suspected he knew about her financial commitment.

Mae let her thoughts ramble back to those days on the PTA.

I see you at every meeting I remembered the PTA Chairman saying. You have a good knowledge of how the PTA functions. You are the kind of parent we like as a board member. There is an opening coming up. Would you be interested in letting your name stand?

I accepted, saying, nothing would please me more. I recall my election to the PTA Board of Directors. I remained as a board member for two years until appointed President. Ronnie's school ranked first under my leadership. I remember the accolades we garnered.

Ronnie's school achieved the highest academic standards in the region, and its' sports programs were second-to-none. It became the model other school boards set out to attain.

At the end of my first term, I remember the Principal telling me how happy he was with the new directions the school had taken. He thanked me for my insight, knowledge, and dedication. Never in the school's history had it had such a vibrant Board of Directors. I was pleased to be a part of it.

Those were memorable days where I felt close to Ronnie, helping him and his fellow students' mold their lives for the future. Aunt Wilma taught me the value of a rounded education.

Mae continued daydreaming, Ronnie was pleased with my involvement. I remember him thanking me for all the work I did to make his school one of the best in the Province. I told Ronnie I was proud of him too. He was an excellent student and a good sport. He was an inspiration to students and teachers alike. I told him he was destined for extraordinary things in life.

Throughout high school, Ronnie was a straight 'A' student. In later years he was highly respected and liked by students and teachers. He excelled in school sports. He particularly enjoyed playing football.

After my life-changing meeting in the Principal's office, I paid more attention to Ronnie's needs and less to my own. It's hard to believe Ronnie is now in University studying to become a Doctor. He will be graduating in two years.

Watching over Ronnie and Jamae Fashions was enough for Mae to handle. She discovered that involvement in other activities served only to feed her ego. She refused to let anything come between Ronnie's or Jamae's progress after that.

Ronnie was attending McGill University, in Montreal. He came back to Lewisville on weekends.

# 19

Ronnie rode the train every Friday night from Montreal to Lewisville to visit his mother. Mae looked forward to spending weekends with him. Mae expressed to Ronnie how happy she was with her new-found freedom and success.

Ronnie commented, “I’m happy for you Mother. You withstood the worst of Lester’s wrath. Now you can be yourself without having to deal with his hostile actions and comments.”

“I hope to help make you as successful as you can be Ronnie. That has never changed from day one. I don’t want you to grow up and become like Lester.”

“You have attained that goal Mother. The best thing that Lester bestowed upon me was to instill a burning desire never to become like him. I want to be like you Mother, community-oriented and respected. Contrary to Lester, sitting in the county jail as we speak.”

Ronnie continued with his adoring comments, “I’ll always be grateful for the sacrifices you made to ensure that I obtained a good education. I will be graduating next year from medical school. I’ve only you to thank for that Mother.”

“You don’t need to thank me, Ronnie. Lester too was my inspiration to ensure that I did everything possible to provide you with a good education. I did not want you to sort yarns at The Mill like your father.”

Mae never liked driving Ronnie back to the train station on Sunday nights. They stood on the station platform watching for the train to approach in the distance, knowing that when it pulled into the station, that was the end of their time together for another week. It was a sad time for both. Mae remained on the platform and watched it travel down the rails until she could see it no more. She was always the only person left standing on the platform. Mae would meander back to her car, sad and alone again. She drove slowly back to Lester's house, put the key in the lock and opened the door. Darkness and silence greeted her every Sunday night.

Entering Lester's house Mae reflected, Ronnie is off to university and Lester is in prison. I am sad and lonely. I don't even have Lester to argue with anymore.

Looking around the house, and all alone, Mae said aloud, I returned to Lester's house and all his stuff. Nothing here is mine. I live in a house full of bad memories.

*********************

Jamae Fashions took up all of Mae's time. There was no room left at the end of each day for personal enjoyment. Years had passed since testifying at Lester's trial. She was still living in his house.

Ronnie continued to excel at university. He was in his last year of medicine. He would soon graduate. Mae bragged about his accomplishments at every opportunity.

After Lester's imprisonment, Mae fell into a routine. She met with Jane every morning at Jamae Fashions. They had coffee together before starting work. Not only were they business partners, but they also shared a close friendship. They enjoyed being in each other's company. They knew each other for a long time.

One morning Mae drove to Jamae Fashions and met Jane like she always did. "Something is happening with our production contact in Hong Kong," Jane said.

"What do you mean Jane? I am not that close to the production end of our business. I leave that to you and George."

"Our deliveries from Hong Kong are arriving late. Our clients are complaining and turning to the competition to obtain product to display in their shops."

"That's not good news," Mae said emphatically.

"I've spoken to George about the problem, but he's at a loss to explain it."

"I'm sure you and George will solve the production dilemma," Mae commented. "Right now, I must get to work on the designs for the Spring Catalog."

"Good idea Mae. We have enough problems with distribution without adding marketing problems into the mix."

Mae laughed and retreated to her Design Center at the rear of the shop. I like working back here, Mae thought. It is the place where I get my inspirations.

Mae did not want to work in the front office area where Jane had customers, photographers, graphic designers, and lithographers coming and going all day long. Mae told herself, there is too much going on out there for my liking. I need seclusion to do my job. I marvel at how Jane keeps everything in order. She has so much going on at the same time.

Mae did not hear Jane coming towards her despite the clacking of her high heeled shoes. Mae jumped when she spoke. "I have a meeting at The Mill Mae. I hope to get our delivery problems resolved."

"Okay, Jane. I hope to get these designs finished for the Spring Catalogue. Good luck trying to identify our delivery problems."

"Thanks, Mae. Good luck to you too," Jane said turning to go back down the hallway.

Mae was uncertain how long she was alone in the Design Center when she heard the doorbell jingle. Someone was walking down the corridor towards her. Mae looked up from her easel and saw a tall man standing in the doorway.

"Hello, Mae. My name is John. My last name is not important. You don't know who I am, but I know you. I am an agent for The Canadian Security Intelligence Service, known as CSIS." He gave Mae one of his business cards.

In a caustic voice, Mae asked, "How can I help you?"

"Before anything else, I need to present you with my credentials."

"That's an innovative idea," Mae said sarcastically. "What business have you got with me anyway?"

John presented a Canadian Government, sealed and certified, pictured, official identification document proving that he was a CSIS agent. Mae scrutinized his credentials. She asked, "How do I know this stuff you're showing me is not fake?"

"It is an excellent question, Mae. Your misgivings show a powerful tendency not to accept everything at face value. I'm not surprised by your questioning my credentials. I was told you would."

"Who told you that?"

"Another positive trait," he said smiling. "I'm not at liberty to divulge that information. Even if I did, there is still no reason for you to believe me. I've got a better plan."

"I'm getting a little suspicious of you. What is your plan? And it had better be good, or I'm calling the police."

"My superiors in Ottawa, the nation's capital, are seeking your help regarding a serious international matter."

"Why me?" Mae inquired.

John ignored her question and continued to speak. "There is a Canadian Government plane sitting on the tarmac at the Lewisville airport. A uniformed Federal Officer is sitting in an unmarked car across the street. I am leaving you now. You will never see me again. I only ask that you go to the airport in your car and show some identification at the security office. They will be expecting you. The officer in the car across the street will follow you to the airport. At the airport, you'll be subject to a security clearance. You'll be escorted to a waiting plane and flown to Rockland Airport, the high-security government airport in Ottawa."

"It all sounds very intriguing," Mae said.

"You'll be flown back to Lewisville in time for dinner tonight. Can I advise my superiors that you're agreeable to help in this top security investigation?"

"Since you put it that way, I suppose so."

"Very well Mae. I will tell them to expect you. Thank you for your cooperation. It was nice meeting you."

Mae locked the front door when she left and drove to the Lewisville airport. She saw the black, Ford Victoria, in her rear-view mirror. At the airport, everything went exactly as the CSIS agent said it would. Mae was comfortable that all actions and procedures were legitimate. The principal question was, what's this all about?

Mae was soon on the government plane winging her way to Ottawa. It was a short flight.

Mae thought, other than a pilot and co-pilot, I'm the only passenger. I told no one what I was doing. If I go missing, nobody in Lewisville will know where to look for me. I should have made George, or Jane, aware of what was happening. Things happened so fast. Were they rushed purposely to keep me from informing anybody what was happening? Oh well, it's too late now. This cloak and dagger business is intriguing, however.

Upon arrival at the Ottawa airport, a limo whisked Mae to the CSIS headquarters. On arrival, a security officer escorted her into a small interviewing room.

After a few minutes, a large burly man, sporting a thick black beard, entered the room. "Hi Mae, my name is Boris, the Chief of Espionage and Sabotage. I am also the Canadian Interpol representative, the international police organization headquartered in Lyon, France. Thank you for agreeing to speak with me."

In a demanding voice, Mae asked, "I want to know what this is all about before I say anything else."

"Very well Mae, I will get right to the point. Mae, you're a designer of high-end dresses marketed through Jamae Fashions. Correct?"

"Yes, that's right," Mae answered.

"Your dresses are being used to smuggle drugs into Canada. The origin is your production company in Hong Kong. Some of the Hong Kong employees are sewing drugs into the pleats and hems of your dresses. The Hong Kong authorities know of the illegal operation. We believe there is an underground organization at The Mill in Lewisville monitoring shipments and forwarding the information to people in Montreal."

Mae interjected. "For your information, we are presently experiencing distribution problems."

"I know the reason," Boris said. "Someone in Montreal is removing the drugs, repackaging them, and selling them on the black market. We don't know where this is taking place other than it is happening somewhere in Montreal. Consequently, delayed shipments are causing problems between you and your clients.

"We want to know from the shipping manifest when shipments depart from Hong Kong and follow them to Montreal.

When we solve the illicit drug trafficking problem, I guarantee you, Jamae will no longer have delivery problems, Mae."

Mae answered, "My partner Jane is in a better position to help you. I only design the dresses. She deals with the retailers who buy our dresses. She knows every retail consignment."

"Therein lies the problem," Boris replied. "She is involved with too many people. You Mae, on the other hand, work by yourself in a secluded area of Jamae Fashions. You are in a better position to help us. I guarantee you will not be at any personal risk."

Boris gave Mae a chance to digest what he just said before continuing.

"There is one other thing," Boris said. "If you agree to serve your country and accept this assignment, you can not reveal your involvement to anybody, including family and business associates."

"Okay. I will agree to help Boris. What's next?"

"Sign this confidence document. It stipulates you are under oath and you will divulge nothing. It also stipulates if you receive information about this case, you will inform me at once. Inscribed is your unique identification code. You agree never to use your name when contacting us, only your code number. Are you okay with that Mae?"

"Yes."

Boris pushed a wordy, official-looking document in front of Mae. She glanced at it and signed the agreement.

"Thank you for your service, Mae. The officer standing outside the door will drive you to the airport. Your cooperation is appreciated."

They shook hands, and Mae left for the Rockland Airport to return to Lewisville.

This guy Boris doesn't fool around, Mae thought.

# 20

The economy of Lewisville was thriving. Many of the previously boarded-up shops on Pitt Street reopened, and new shops and restaurants established themselves in the revitalized, dynamic downtown area of Lewisville. Business was booming. People were moving back to the city. The Mill remained the largest employer but no longer the only one. Other manufacturing businesses started up adding to the economy of Lewisville.

A housing shortage hampered Mae from finding a suitable residence. Although she was not happy, she had no choice but to live in Lester's house until she found a place of her own.

Business at Jamae Fashions prospered. Jamae clients still experienced late deliveries, however. Mae wondered if CSIS was making any progress in their investigations.

Jane, Mae, and George, regularly met at The Club. After one of their meetings, Jane and George left early to attend another meeting at The Mill. The club kept a rack of neatly folded newspapers on hand for its' members. Mae stayed behind to finish her wine after Jane and George left. She scanned through newspaper advertisements looking for a suitable place to live.

Mae desperately wanted to move out of Lester's house. There were too many memories. It was different when Ronnie was living with her, but now he is gone. Old memories reminded Mae of those dreadful days in the house with Lester.

Mae had trouble sleeping at night, and the worrisome feelings of loneliness were returning to haunt her. If it continued, Mae risked sinking into a depressive state which she wanted to avoid at all costs. She needed to move from that ghastly house and find another place to live - the sooner, the better. Mae searched through the newspaper ads but as usual, found nothing to her liking. She was becoming discouraged. Mae was refolding the newspaper to replace it on the rack when she noticed an elderly lady sipping tea in the corner of the lounge, wearing one of Mae's designs. The nicely dressed lady saw Mae looking at her. They both paused. Mae was the first to speak.

"Aunt Mary," she exclaimed.

"Mae," was the equally enthusiastic response.

Pulling up a plush upholstered chair, Mae said, "It has been so long. How are you?"

"Fine," Mary answered.

Mae resumed, "I often thought of contacting you Aunt Mary, but dismissed the idea fearing you may not want to speak to me. I had no way of knowing what Charlie told you about me."

"You should have called Mae. I lost contact with you. I often wished we could have reconnected."

Mae wanted to change the subject of who should have called who. She told Mary, "I read Charlie's obituary. I'm sorry Aunt Mary."

"Thanks, Mae, but I was relieved when Charlie died. He was not a nice man. I lived under his harsh rule for too long. I never dared to walk away from him. Charlie provided me with a lavish lifestyle which I did not want to give up, and he knew it. My life with him was miserable, however. He was abusive and self-centered. He belittled me in front of others, and he never hesitated to tell me how stupid I was. He said I was lucky to be married to a rich man like him. After a while, I believed him, and put up with his abusive ways."

"I'm sorry Aunt Mary. I had no idea."

"Nobody knew Mae. It was my ugly secret. When you disappeared Mae, I knew that something terrible happened. I suspected Charlie was the cause for your sudden exit from our lives. Am I right?"

"You're right Aunt Mary. Charlie used his key to enter my apartment early one morning and sexually attacked me. When I declined his advances, he told me to leave. Uncle Charlie gave me until five o'clock that evening to get out. He threatened to padlock the door and spread rumors about me around town if I said anything to anybody about what he tried to do. I was planning on moving anyway, but not in that manner."

Mary intervened, “I wanted to warn you about Charlie’s womanizing tendencies, but I was afraid that he might learn that I told you. If Charlie found out that I told you things about him, who knows what he would have done to me. He had such a violent temper.”

Those days were not good days and revisiting them served no purpose for Mae. With a smile on her face, Mae said, “I’ve got a confession to make Aunt Mary.”

“What is it, Mae?”

“My boyfriend Lester lived in the apartment with me. We used to hide his clothes and shaving stuff behind the sofa. I did not want to raise your suspicions when you entered the apartment to stock the icebox.”

“Oh Mae, men are not that crafty. I saw where he stuffed his things behind the sofa. He also left the toilet seat up.” Mae covered her mouth and laughed. “I guess we were too young and infatuated with each other to remember to put the seat down. That’s funny.”

“Is Lester still in your life Mae?”

“Indirectly. Problems developed after we got married. Lester became very possessive like Charlie was of you Aunt Mary. He verbally abused me and beat me up. He was lazy and had no ambition. We were like oil and water after we got married.”

“Where is he now?”

“In prison for assault.”

“I’m sorry Mae. You had your problems also. Unlike Lester however, you’re ambitious Mae. I see you on TV, read about you in the newspapers, and listen to your interviews on the radio. You are a leading citizen of Lewisville. Very different from the shy little girl I first met at the train station long ago.”

Mary was enjoying her conversation with Mae. “I love your dress designs, Mae. I’m wearing one of them now.”

“It looks good on you Mary.”

“Where are you living now Mae?”

“In Lester’s house, but I want to move. I am not comfortable living there. I am lonely, which will lead to other complications if I do not find another place to live soon. I am desperately looking, but no success so far.”

“I know a place, Mae.”

"Where Aunt Mary?"

"My place. I still live in that big up-town house by myself. I am lonely most of the time, especially in the evenings. I wish I had somebody to talk to at night. I am ninety years old, and not able to get around like I used to. I have trouble managing the stairs these days. The upstairs part of the house is dormant. You're welcome to it if you want it, Mae. You can move in anytime. We can keep each other from feeling lonely."

"That could work Mary. I am glad I mentioned it to you. I would love to stay with you in your lovely home. Other than Ronnie, you are my only family member. I would not have even known about you had it not been for Aunt Wilma. Father never talked about family. Had I stayed on the farm we may never have met."

Mary answered, "Even though I never met you, I knew about you. I often asked Charlie to visit the farm, but he always refused. He did not get along with his brother too well. It is a shame that families break up over such petty things. I don't think Charlie, nor your father, knew the real reason they did not like each other."

Mae said, "It does not matter now Aunt Mary. You and I will always be friends and live life to its fullest."

"I agree," Mary said smiling gleefully. "I am happy we reconnected today. Can we go to church together like we used to Mae? It will be nice to start cooking Sunday dinners again. I do not have anyone to cook for anymore. I miss cooking a big Sunday dinner like I used to."

"Me too Aunt Mary. I can hardly wait to tell Ronnie about meeting up with you again and of my new living arrangements. He is studying at McGill in Montreal. He comes home every weekend. You will like him, Aunt Mary. He is my pride and joy. He's studying to become a Doctor."

"I'll look forward to meeting him, Mae."

Mae phoned Ronnie that evening to tell him the good news about moving in with Aunt Mary.

"What a terrific arrangement Mother. Getting out of Lester's old house will be good for you. There are too many unpleasant memories buried in there. When are you planning to move Mother?"

"Next Saturday. When you come home for the weekend, I will meet you at the station on Friday night as usual and stay at

Lester's place. The next day, Saturday, we will take my two suitcases to Aunt Mary's place. Everything I own will fit into two suitcases. The other stuff belongs to Lester. We will drop off the suitcases at Mary's place on Saturday morning, and the three of us will go to one of Lewisville's new restaurants for brunch. I've got a taste for pancakes. There is a new pancake restaurant on Pitt Street I would like to try. I know Mary likes pancakes because she often makes them for herself at home."

"As usual Mother, you have everything planned. I'm looking forward to spending the weekend helping you to make a better life for yourself."

Mae agreed with Ronnie. She too was looking forward to having him watch a new chapter in her life unfold.

Ronnie arrived on the train on Friday night. As usual, Mae was at the station to meet him. They traveled for the last time to Lester's home. Ronnie noticed the two suitcases standing by the door when he entered.

"It looks like you're anxious to leave Mother."

"I've never been more anxious about anything, Ronnie. Since moving to Lewisville, twenty-four years ago, I always had to answer to somebody else. My life was not my own. This house is the last reminder of my wretched past life with Lester. Tomorrow I will not only be rid of Lester but also his house where he held us hostage and abused me."

Mae and Ronnie spent the rest of the evening bringing each other up-to-date on their activities over the past week. Mae was alone every evening during the week. She looked forward to the weekends when Ronnie visited with her.

Ronnie told his mother he was happy to be in her company also.

After supper, Mae phoned Mary and outlined her plans for the following day. She asked Mary if she liked pancakes. "I love pancakes," was her jubilant reply.

"Good," Mae said. "Pancakes it is."

"That's fine Mae. I'm looking forward to meeting Ronnie and eating pancakes with both of you."

The next morning, Mae turned the key of Lester's house for the last time. She put her two suitcases in the trunk of her car, and with Ronnie in the front seat beside her, they set out for Aunt Mary's place. She peeked one last time at Lester's house in the rear-view mirror. A sense of relief enveloped her.

Mae introduced Ronnie to Aunt Mary. "My, you are a handsome young man Ronnie," Mary commented, "You have your mother's good looks." Ronnie blushed and said, "Thank you, Aunt Mary."

Access to her new home was at the top of a curved, luxurious, thick carpeted, staircase. Mae occupied the entire upstairs of Aunt Mary's house. It was formerly the maid's quarters. Mary's home was in prestigious up-town Lewisville. "Wow," Ronnie commented. "I've never seen such a gorgeous house. You'll be very comfortable here Mother."

Bright sunlight flowed through the two large dormer windows. A hallway to the right of the stairs led to two well-furnished bedrooms. To the left were a kitchen and dining room. Mae put her two suitcases in one of the bedrooms.

At the restaurant, everybody ordered pancakes. They were delicious. Mae was happy that everything was falling into place and tranquility was returning to her life. She was pleased to have Aunt Mary back in her life and proud of Ronnie for his accomplishments. He was well on his way to earning his medical doctor's degree. She did not know what his plans were after graduation, however.

After everyone had their fill of pancakes, they returned to Mary's place. Mary was slow getting in and out of the car. Ronnie took her arm and guided her up the front steps. "You're such a thoughtful young man Ronnie. Thank you for caring for an old lady." Ronnie smiled.

Mae got Aunt Mary settled back at home then she and Ronnie mounted the plush carpeted staircase to Mae's new digs. Sweeping her arm in an all-encompassing manner, Mae said, "This will be ideal for me. Don't you think so, Ronnie?"

"It is perfect Mother. I am happy you are out of Lester's house. It will be even better when you sell the house and furniture. The sooner you free yourself of his memories, the better."

"I agree with you, Ronnie. I'll work on it right away."

A few days later, Mae phoned the prison to make an appointment to visit Lester. The voice on the other end of the phone said, "Please identify yourself, and state your reason for visiting the inmate."

Mae told the jailer who she was and that she needed to speak to her husband, Lester. She explained that she needed directions from Lester on the disposal of his house and furniture. Mae made an appointment to visit Lester in two weeks, on a Wednesday.

The prison spokesman said, "For your information, Madam, all visitors meeting with inmates are subject to a bag, purse, and a full body search."

Mae commented, "I was not expecting to undergo a body search. However, I'll do whatever the rules require me to do."

"That's fine Madam," the voice on the other end of the line curtly announced and abruptly disconnected the line. Mae hung-up the phone on her end thinking that prison life was indeed different. She wondered, how prisoners can become socially acceptable when treated in such a harsh, and disrespectful manner? Mae thought that detention facilities had a responsibility to instill social values to prisoners which, when they return to society, would enable them to become law-abiding citizens. By the manner and tone of the jailer she spoke with, nothing seemed farther from the truth.

Mae expected her visit to the prison and visiting with Lester after a lengthy period of non-communication, would be revealing. She had a week to prepare herself for a detailed security check and dreaded body search.

Putting aside the results of the negative phone call, Mae focused her thoughts on the positive happenings in her life. She thought about her renewed relationship with Aunt Mary, her new living arrangements, the success of Jamae Fashions, the departure of Lester from her life, and Ronnie's upcoming graduation. I have a lot going for me, Mae reminded herself. I must remember to focus on the positive things in my life and cast out the negative feelings which arise within me from time to time.

The next night, while sipping tea with Mary, they heard sirens screaming in the distance.

"That's unusual," Mary commented. "It is always quiet around here. I have never heard that much noise in all the years I have lived here. There must be a big accident on the highway."

"Perhaps," Mae answered.

Mae doubted there was an accident on the highway because the sounds came from the other direction. The screeching sirens continued to wail.

"I hope I can get to sleep with all that noise going on," Mary said.

"I'm sure you will Aunt Mary." Endeavoring to put Mary at ease, Mae said, "The noise is bound to stop soon. I am sure it is nothing serious. We'll hear about it on the news in the morning."

"Alright, Mae. I am getting tired. I'm off to bed now."

"Okay, Aunt Mary. Have a good sleep. I'll see you tomorrow."

After making sure Mary got to bed okay, Mae mounted the stairs to her quarters. She had a few design modifications to work on before retiring for the night. Mae went to the dormer window to draw the shade. Through the window, she saw giant flames and plumes of smoke in the distance. She wondered what was happening. The fire and smoke came from the direction of the screeching sirens that Mae and Mary heard earlier. She closed the shades, and with her sketchbook in hand, became engrossed in her work. When finished, she turned out the light, snuggled under the satin sheets, and went to sleep. The noise outside had finally stopped.

The next morning, the clock radio let her know it was time to get up. The news was all about the prison riots that took place the night before. It never entered Mae's mind what effect the commotion at the prison might have had on Lester. She hardly ever thought of him anymore.

After showering and dressing, Mae cooked bacon and eggs for herself. Mary was still in bed, as she usually was when Mae went downstairs. Mae slipped out of the house and drove to the Design Center. Jane arrived shortly after her.

Jane asked, "Did you hear the ruckus last night Mae?"

"I did. I heard about it on the radio this morning. I understand there was trouble at the jail."

"More than just trouble Mae. A full-scale riot involving about two hundred prisoners. They are under lock-down now. The large fire destroyed half the prison. Some prisoners and guards died in the melee."

Mae was surprised at the severity of the riot. "I had no idea things were that bad," she told Jane. "How did it start?"

"I heard that there was a fight and it escalated from there."

"I never heard a thing about it," Mae said. "I suppose I'll hear more about it when I visit Lester next week."

"Probably," Jane conceded.

Jane and Mae went about the business of Jamae Fashions. The townsfolk of Lewisville at first talked a lot about the riots but talk subsided after a few days. Harm only befell prisoners, after all, no big deal was the general attitude of Lewisville folks. Mae assumed, people were too busy with their own lives to worry about the lives of a few low-life criminals.

Two days later, two policemen entered the Jamae premises. Jane was at a meeting with George. Mae was alone in the Design Center. "Good afternoon Madam," one of the officers said.

Smiling, Mae responded, "Good afternoon gentlemen." She remained smiling and jokingly stated, "I doubt you're here to try on dresses. How can I help you?"

The officers did not react to Mae's attempt to joke about their presence in a sea of ladies' dresses. They remained stern and stone-faced.

One of the officers asked, "Is your husband incarcerated at the Lewisville Detention Center, Madam?"

"He is." Mae answered, "What is this all about?"

"We regret to inform you, Madam, that your husband died in the recent prison altercations. Please contact the Warden right away, and he will provide you with more details. Here is his phone number."

The officer handed Mae a business card with the Warden's name and phone number inscribed.

"Is there anything further we can do for you, Madam?"

"I don't think so," Mae answered in a trembling voice.

"Alright, Madam. Please call the Warden right away. He is eager to get this matter closed. He has a lot of urgent matters to take care of since the riots."

Mae needed to talk to somebody. Suddenly she realized there were few people in her life she could confide in, despite her popularity. Mae phoned George's private number. She knew he was meeting with Jane. They were her only close friends.

"George Smith here," George answered the phone.

"Hello George," Mae said in a somber voice.

"Mae, you sound different. Are you okay?"

"No. I just received some disturbing news. Lester is dead. It happened during the prison riots. I need to speak to somebody. You and Jane are the only two people I can talk to."

In a sympathetic tone, George said, "Jane and I are on our way, expect us in fifteen minutes. Sit tight Mae."

Mae spilled out the saga of events to Jane and George. "I'm so confused," Mae stated to her two best friends, "I don't know where to turn to next. I am no longer in control of things. I depend on the actions of others. I have not felt like this since I was a small girl. Damn you, Lester. Will I ever get you out of my life?"

Jane pulled up a chair close to Mae. She sat down and held Mae's hand. George stood on Mae's other side with his hand resting on her shoulder. Mae could feel the soothing power of their caring friendship. Their silence spoke volumes. George was the first to speak. "Mae, you can rely on Jane and me to help you get through this challenging time. That's what friends are for."

He added, "Do you want me to call Ronnie for you?"

"No," Mae answered through her tears. "I don't want to upset him. He has a lot on his plate right now. I'll tell him after I meet with the Warden."

"Okay, Mae. It is best that you set the schedule for yourself. I suggest that you close the shop, go home, and relax. Jane and I will stay in touch."

"Okay, George. I'm feeling better thanks to both of you – my two best friends."

Jane asked, "Are you okay to drive, Mae?"

"Yes. I am fine now. Thank you, both, for helping me."

Mary was surprised to see Mae home so early. She asked, "Are you okay Mae?"

"I'm okay Aunt Mary. I received upsetting news and needed a little time to sort things out in my head. My new home is a good place to do that."

Mae related to Mary the series of events that led to her learning about Lester's death from the two police officers. In a calm voice, Mary said, "Be brave, Mae. Time tends to ease our anxieties."

The following day, Mae called the Prison Warden. He asked, "Can you come in now Madam?"

Eager to conclude things, Mae answered, "I can be there in twenty minutes."

At the prison, Mae went through an intense security interrogation and bag check. She did not have to go through the feared body search because she was not meeting with an inmate. She saw the gruesome devastation to the prison complex. The guards, all dressed in full riot gear, patrolled the burnt-out interior. Mae experienced nothing like it in her life before. She wondered what initiated such violence and destruction.

The Warden was shorter than Mae. He sported a thin pencil mustache. The buttons on his shirt toiled to remain fastened. He wore a blue, official looking uniform with a gold star over his heart.

"Step into my office," he ordered Mae like she was one of his internees. "Let me get right to the point. I am busy and can only give you a few minutes of my time. Lester was the reason we had problems here a few nights ago. He started a fight with another inmate in the cafeteria. They knew each other from elsewhere. They got into an altercation. One thing led to another, and within seconds the whole cafeteria erupted into a chaotic situation. The other inmates did not trust Lester. A recipe for disaster in a prison environment."

Mae asked, "How did Lester die?"

"Initially they stabbed him with a homemade pointed object, then the furniture was set ablaze, and Lester's body burned beyond recognition. We had to use dental records to identify him."

Mae inquired what more she had to do to bring this matter to a conclusion. It was plain to see that the Warden was a man of little patience.

"You will need to make the funeral arrangements," the Warden instructed Mae.

Mae said, "I'll advise the Lewisville Funeral Home when I get back to town. They will take it from there."

"Okay," the Warden conceded. "Please tell them to advise me as soon as possible. I want to get this matter out of the way quickly. I've loads of other more important things to take care of."

Mae was surprised at the Warden's, 'so what' attitude. He had no empathy for Lester, or for Mae. He was doing a job.

When Ronnie arrived on Friday night, Mae told him what happened to Lester. “Mother, please don’t feel sorry for Lester. He got what he deserved.”

“I guess so Ronnie. It still came as a shock. His death has hindered me from getting on with my life. His death means I must sell his house and its contents and find somewhere to deposit the proceeds. It is still Lester’s house, but there is no one else alive except me to look after it. Lester is still haunting me, even from his grave.”

Mae placed ‘For Sale’ advertisements in the local newspapers for Lester’s house. She contacted Charlotte and donated the furniture to The Shelter.

Lester’s house sold quickly due to the recent renovations. There was still a housing shortage in Lewisville, and Mae received top dollar when it sold. Lester had no heirs. As Lester’s wife, all proceeds went to Mae.

Mae did not need the money. She figured if she kept the money it would remind her of Lester. “It is about time Lester did some good with his life. The proceeds should be used to help others.”

Through the Jamae lawyers, Mae set up a Charitable Community Foundation with the proceeds from the sale of Lester’s house. With Jane’s permission, she named the foundation, The Jamae Fashion Foundation. Mae was the sole administrator of the Foundation. All payments needed Mae’s approval before disbursement.

# 21

The delivery problems from Hong Kong subsided. Jane remarked, "I've no idea what occurred to correct the problem. I'm glad that things have returned to normal, however. We have little control over production. That bothers me somewhat."

Mae did not comment. She knew the problem. Members of the Montreal underworld used Jamae dresses to import drugs from Hong Kong to Montreal illegally. She was happy when the authorities resolved the matter. Mae thought that someday Boris might give her the details, then again, she thought, he may decide not to tell her anything. It was Mae's secret per the signed confidential agreement, not to divulge any information.

Mae noticed a turndown in business. She wondered why. She concluded it had nothing to do with the delivery problems from Hong Kong, but from younger women who did not want to wear the fancy dresses, Jamae produced.

Women were becoming more prominent in the workforce, and they were trending towards slimmer pantsuits and blouses. Jamae dresses are inappropriate for office work. Working women demand a more business-like attire. Mae decided that she should heed the signs for simpler fabrics, and slimmer designs, to satisfy the demands of a new generation of younger, working women. Mae calculated that if Jamae did not conform to desires of a changing demographic, Jamae would risk losing market share to other, more forward thinking, designers.

Mae ran her thoughts by Jane. As her partner, Jane would have to approve any design changes.

Jane agreed with her partner's market assessment and that Mae should design garments for a new generation of clients.

Like Mae, Jane concurred with Mae's views of a changing trend in women's fashions driven by an increase of more women in the workplace. Women no longer stayed at home to look after husbands and children like they once did. Jane said, "You're right Mae. We should react now, rather than later."

"I'll start this morning to research and work on a new line."

"Clever idea, Mae. Even if our suspicions of a changing market don't materialize, it is wise to have backup designs for the future. We cannot assume that the demand for our dresses will continue forever. We work in a fickle industry, where a change in the weather can affect what people wear."

"I agree, Jane."

Mae's workload doubled overnight. She became engulfed designing dresses for two markets, an old and a new. Regardless of her increased workload, Mae continued to meet with Jane for coffee each morning. They often discussed municipal politics.

It concerned Jane that crime had increased in Lewisville. Jane said, "When Lewisville was a small town there was hardly any crime. People would leave their doors open without fear of unwanted intruders. That's out of the question now. Not a day goes by without hearing of illegal drug activity. These days drug trafficking is a major problem in Lewisville, which was unheard of when Lewisville was a medium sized village."

Mae replied, "That's the problem a small municipality like Lewisville faces when it has a growth explosion." Naïvely Jane asked, "How did that happen?"

Mae laughed. "Whether you realize it or not Jane, you're one of the major growth contributors in Lewisville. Before the expansion of The Dress Shop to Jamae Fashions, Lewisville was a one-industry town where everyone was employed by one employer — The Mill. Lewisville has grown since those early days."

"I forgot about that. I guess I'm too preoccupied with other things," Jane said.

Mae suspected that Jane might be losing interest in Jamae Fashions. It was getting too big for her. She was having a tough time adjusting to the pace of business.

********************

Aunt Mary liked having Mae living with her. Mae also enjoyed having Mary around. They kept each other company. Mary had no other living relatives. She managed to out-live all her friends in Lewisville. Mary and Charlie had no children. Mary regarded Mae as her adopted daughter.

Mae attended church every Sunday with Mary. After church, Mary rejoiced at the opportunity to prepare a big dinner, even though there were only two people to eat it. There was never a shortage of food.

One morning when Mae and Jane were conversing over coffee, the phone rang. They gave each other a questioning stare. Jane murmured, "Who can that be this early in the morning? Customers never phone at this hour."

Mae answered the phone. It was George.

"Hello, Mae. I must meet with you and Jane, urgently. Can we meet at The Club?"

"When George?"

"Now," George replied.

Mae placed her hand over the receiver and spoke to Jane.

"It's George, Jane. He wants to meet us at The Club. Are you available to meet now?"

"Oh, I suppose so. There is always a crisis looming. I'm tired of all this stuff. Tell George I will come also."

Mae returned to the phone. "We can both make it George. We'll leave right now."

Mae could see that Jane was in a grumpy mood. She told Jane, "Let's go in my car. It will save you from having to drive." Hoping to put Jane in a better mood, Mae added, "I'll enjoy your company. We can finish our conversation on the way."

George sat at a table in a remote corner of the lounge. There were no other Club Members present at that early hour. George ordered breakfast of tea and crumpets for everyone. When the food arrived, George spoke. "Our Hong Kong production company won't renew our contract. They gave me two reasons for their decision.

"First, our business has subsided to the point that it is no longer profitable for them to produce Jamae Dresses. We must find a new facility. Due to our decreasing volume, that could be difficult. Costs will increase.

"The second piece of sad news is that Jamae Fashions is rumored to be running an illicit drug scheme. I don't know where the rumor stemmed from, but it is widespread in the industry. That can hurt us. We must quell it right away."

Jane was still in a testy mood. George's news did nothing to enhance her temperament.

"I'm sixty years old," Jane said. "I'm too old to be going through all this stuff. I'm of a mind to sell my shares in Jamae Fashions, put my feet up, and get out of this rat race."

George and Mae at first thought Jane was joking.

"I'm serious," Jane assured them both.

Attempting to spin a little optimism into the conversation George said, "I'm prepared to go to Hong Kong to look for another producer. I'll source the drug rumors while I'm there and put them to rest."

Mae said, "Good idea George. When are you planning to leave?"

"In the next few days."

Mae said, "Jane and I believe there is a market shift in ladies' fashions. That's the reason for the diminishing demand for Jamae dresses. Modern day business women consider them old fashioned. They are not suitable for office wear. I've been working on designs for a younger consumer. You can take them with you to Hong Kong. It will attest to our recognition of the shift in ladies' fashions. That may help return us to our former status."

"What foresight Mae. I had no idea that you were working on a new innovative design series. I'll stop by this afternoon to review the designs with you before leaving for overseas."

Jane was silent throughout the discussion. Mae sensed there was something else troubling her, more than just a potential loss of business.

That afternoon George stopped at Jamae Fashions to review Mae's innovative designs of women's pantsuits, blouses, and skirts, for a new market. He liked what he saw.

George complimented Mae on her forward thinking. "These are fabulous designs, Mae. I'll present them to our Hong Kong executives. I'm sure they will like what they see. I've been in the clothing business for a long time. These are the best designs I've ever seen."

"Thanks, George."

Mae expressed to George a more urgent situation that concerned her - uncovering reasons for the false drug allegations. "No one will want to do business with us George if they believe that we are involved in illicit activities, regardless of how great our designs are. We need answers. If anyone can uncover them, you can George."

"Thanks, Mae. The Mill, Jamae Fashions, and the general economy of Lewisville are at stake. It is vital that I start soon. I'm leaving tomorrow."

"Good luck George, and bon voyage." Mae felt strange telling George what to do after all these years. She was fast becoming the driving force of Jamae Fashions and its affiliates.

A few days later, before starting work, Jane and Mae sat drinking their coffee. "Jane," Mae paused and made sure that she had Jane's attention, "You have been quiet for several days. You don't laugh and smile anymore. I'm your best friend. You have always been available for me during tough times. It is my turn to be available for you. Something is bothering you and it's not the fact that you're sixty years old, or that the business is not good. There is something personal happening in your life, and I want to help you."

Tears welled up in Jane's eyes. "Oh, Mae you're so perceptive when it comes to evaluating people. Yes, something else is going on. I'm afraid to talk about it."

"Jane, we are friends. Friends share everything. When I was going through the turmoil with Lester, you helped me to cope. Let me do the same for you. You can trust me to keep it confidential. You know that."

"Yes, I do Mae. I'll tell you. About two weeks ago, I received a phone call at home. I answered the call thinking it was you or George. You're the only two who know my private number."

Mae asked, "Who was it?"

"I did not recognize the voice. It was a man with an oriental accent." Mae kept prodding Jane for more information. Mae noticed Jane was trembling. "What did he say, Jane?"

"He demanded the shipping manifest of our last order. I asked him who he was and why did he need it. He told me it was not important. If I was not forthcoming with what he asked for, he threatened to fire-bomb Jamae Fashions. I was terrified."

"What happened next Jane?"

Amidst tears, Jane answered, "I was frightened that something bad would happen. I worried about us. You're often by yourself working in the shop Mae. If someone set off a bomb, it may have harmed you, or even killed you."

"What did you tell the caller when he asked for the manifest?"

"He told me to put it in an envelope, insert it into the middle of a newspaper, and leave it on the bench that I had erected in front of my late husband's tombstone. I did what he instructed me to do."

Mae approached Jane and embraced her. "Oh, Jane I'm so sorry that you had to go through that all by yourself. You should have told me."

"I was afraid to," Jane wept.

Jane continued to sob. She stopped trembling when Mae put her arms around her. "Regardless of what happened Jane, we are both safe," Mae assured her.

"No, we're not Mae," Jane replied emphatically. "He called back after I made the drop and demanded that I do the same thing on the next shipment."

Mae asked, "When is the next shipment?"

"Next week," Jane answered.

"Is the manifest complete yet?"

"It will be tomorrow."

"Jane, you have to trust me. I cannot say anything else right now. I'll have answers for you before this day ends." Jane looked at Mae with a questioning expression on her face. "Okay, Mae. You know I trust you implicitly."

Mae retreated down the corridor to her Design Center and closed the door. She shuffled through her Rolodex and retrieved Boris's private number, Mae gave him her identification code when he answered the phone. There was a short pause before Boris said, "Hello Mae. How can I help you?"

"My partner Jane received a phone call from somebody requesting a copy of the manifest of the next shipment of dresses from Hong Kong. The mystery caller threatened her if she did not provide it. She followed his delivery instructions and gave it to him."

"I know," Boris replied.

Shocked, Mae asked, "How do you know?"

"We monitored the line."

"You mean you had it tapped," Mae scoffed.

"You could say that," Boris replied.

"Do you have my phone tapped also?"

"We might."

"I had no idea that you went to that extent."

"We do things for the protection of innocent parties and to prevent bad guys from winning."

"Okay," Mae said. "My immediate concern is that my best friend, and business partner, is in fear for her life. I need reassurance from you she need not worry."

"It is ironic that you called me today Mae. I planned to call you later today. We have things well in hand. You can tell Jane she no longer has anything to worry about. Do not tell her what I am about to confide to you, however. You're still under oath remember."

Boris continued, "The phone call that Jane received came from a phone booth in Hong Kong. The person who called was a shipping department employee from your overseas production company in Hong Kong."

Mae asked, "How did he know to call Jane?"

"There was a mole at The Mill in Lewisville."

"Can I ask who it was?"

"It was your husband - Lester."

Mae went silent. She could not believe what Boris just told her.

Boris broke the silence and said, "I know that information comes as a shock to you. Those who seek obscurity, use those who they know are least suspecting. Often targeted are close relatives. You were a victim of Lester's evil plans Mae."

"How did he get so deeply involved?"

"He stole documents when he was working at The Mill. He passed them on to a contact at the pub near where you lived, and they ended up with Mr. Big in Montreal. When Lester went to prison he met up with Mr. Big who was serving time for trafficking. Lester put the squeeze on him for more money. That was his downfall. Mr. Big has a lot of friends inside. The fix was in to kill Lester and destroy the evidence by setting fire to the joint."

"I had no idea what was going on," Mae told Boris.

"Don't beat up on yourself Mae. Most victims don't know they are being pursued to participate in illegal activities."

"Is everything ended now? Can I tell Jane not to worry anymore?"

"The answer is yes, to both questions."

"Lester is dead. Why is somebody calling Jane for manifest details?"

"In the world of crime, there is always somebody to take up the slack. Trafficking in drugs is a lucrative business. The bad guys were looking for another way to gain access to the shipping information of Jamae dresses. Their contacts in Hong Kong dried up, and Lester was of no use to them in prison. They tried to suck Jane into unknowingly provide them with manifest information. They knew she had the information they needed, and that she regularly visited the grave of her late husband. That's why she received those phone calls."

"What is the status now?"

"The person who made that phone call to Jane has since been apprehended in Hong Kong. We are closing our files on this case."

"Thanks, Boris. It is good to know that you're watching over us."

"Thank you, Mae, for your help. If there is anything I can do for you, call me personally. Your ID code will never expire. You'll continue to be labeled, a friend of Interpol."

"Thanks, Boris. I'll remember that."

Mae hung up the phone and returned to where Jane was sitting. “Jane everything is fixed. No more harm will come to us, or to Jamae Fashions. We’ll remain safe.”

“I don’t know what you did Mae but thank you for whatever it was. I regret not confiding with you sooner.”

“That’s okay, Jane. I suggest we relax over lunch at The Club.

“Great idea Mae. Based on what you just told me lunch would be more enjoyable than what it was the last time.”

“I want to find out more about your wanting to leave Jamae Fashions,” Mae said.

“Okay, Mae. I’ll bare all my feelings to you over lunch,” Jane replied.

# 22

Mae and Jane arrived at The Club at eleven o'clock. It was too early to order lunch. Instead, they each ordered a cocktail. The extra time gave Mae and Jane time to relax and unwind a little. So much had happened, and the day was not even half over yet.

Mae started the conversation. "I sent George away with a portfolio of my new contemporary designs. I'm eager to receive their views and comments. I hope they are positive."

"I hope so too Mae. Every generation wants to create a new identity for themselves. It is difficult for the fashion industry leaders to predict trends."

"I expect George back in two days. He'll let us know what our production partners think of the contemporary designs. If they like them, chances are the rest of the world will like them also. We'll know soon if we are on the right track."

Mae took a sip of her cocktail. She continued to analyze the industry. "Unlike most businesses our product is either loved or hated. There is no halfway measure."

"How true," Jane agreed. "It is not an easy business. Sometimes I think we were better off when we were just a small dress shop. Life was simpler when we did not have to concern ourselves about worldwide fashion trends and concentrate solely on what the people in Lewisville desired."

Mae said to herself, so as not to upset Jane anymore than she already was, but The Dress Shop was going broke because ladies in Lewisville could not afford to buy your dresses, Jane.

Wanting to change the subject, Mae asked, “How are you feeling these days Jane?”

“Thanks to you Mae, I’m feeling better over what I was a couple of days ago. I’m sorry I was in such a bad mood when we met with George.”

“No need to apologize Jane. You had a lot of things on your mind. I’d have reacted the same way. That’s all behind you now. What are your plans for the future?”

“Thank you for asking Mae. I’ve been thinking a lot about the future. Up to now, I’ve not divulged my thoughts to anyone. I owe it to you, as my closest friend and partner, to tell you first.”

“That sounds troubling Jane. What is it that’s gnawing away at you?”

“I’ve been approached to run for Mayor of Lewisville. If I succeed, I’ll leave Jamae Fashions and devote all my efforts to the position of Mayor. Lewisville is a growing, dynamic city. It needs a full-time Mayor. It has only been a part-time position up to now. I feel I want to give something back to Lewisville.”

Mae commented, “What an honorable thing to do, Jane.”

“Conversely,” Jane continued, “I feel guilty leaving you alone with the trials and tribulations that a new product line brings. I’m in a quandary what to do. Part of me says, run for Mayor. Another part of me says, stay loyal to Mae and Jamae Fashions. A third tells me to, run for the hills.”

Mae smiled at Jane’s thought process. “Oh, Jane now I understand why you have been so troubled lately.”

“Do you have any advice for me, Mae?”

“The final decision is yours, Jane. I can share my feelings and give you my observations, however.”

“I would love to hear them,” Jane responded to Mae’s offer.

“First, you’re an excellent manager, Jane. You have perfected the art of multi-tasking, which few people have mastered. I cannot do that for example. As the Mayor of Lewisville that quality will bode well for you.”

Mae let Jane inwardly digest her comment before continuing.

“Second if you leave Jamae, you’re not to worry about me. I’ll find another partner or go on to other things. My life is flexible and mobile. If you leave Jamae, I’ll re-evaluate my position at that time.”

Mae resumed, "I regard Jamae Fashions to a child that needs a lot of attention when it's young. As it matures, it takes on a life of its own. Is Jamae telling us now is the time for both of us to let go? If you stay with Jamae Fashions, then I stay with you. Together we are a single, and unique entity."

"Mae, you're so astute at rationalizing situations. I always like talking with you. I've not decided yet. I'm relieved to know that whatever decision I make you'll understand, and not feel abandoned if I decide to do something else. I will tell you well in advance of leaving if I decide to run for Mayor."

"I want what is best for you Jane. If it were me having to make that decision, I know you would feel the same way."

"I would Mae. Guaranteed."

"Now that we have that settled let's have lunch."

Two days later the phone rang in the Design Center. It was George. "Hi, George. Welcome back," Mae said into the phone.

"Thanks, Mae. Are you free for lunch? I've got stuff to talk to you about."

"I'm anxious to hear what you have to say, George. I'll meet you at The Club around noon time. Okay?"

"That's fine Mae. I'll see you then."

George was already at The Club when Mae arrived. Mae was eager to hear what he had to say about the acceptance of her designs, and the drug trafficking rumors surrounding Jamae. She took no time to exchange pleasantries. As soon as she saw George, she asked, "How did things go in Hong Kong?"

"They could not have gone better Mae. They loved your contemporary designs. The overseas marketing professionals feel they will appeal to a wide market of young professional working women worldwide. They like the mixing and matching of skirts, blouses, sweaters, and pants. I left them excited about the future."

"That's good news, George. What about the illicit drug rumors connected to Jamae Fashions?"

"That became a non-issue, Mae. When I first arrived, it seemed important. Suddenly there was no more talk about it. They uncovered a problem in their organization. Everything seems okay now. Nobody wanted to talk too much about it. I got the feeling that they were embarrassed about the accusations."

Mae sensed Boris's intervention was parcel to the solution.

"When the new fashion designs go into production they anticipate that we'll be their largest client. That will eject the Jamae line into world recognition. Even the large Paris fashion houses will learn of us. It is exciting Mae. I could barely wait to get back to tell you the news."

"That's good George. Thanks for everything you did to make that happen."

Mae felt obligated to tell George about Jane. "Something happened while you were away George. I have information I want to share with you."

George had a peculiar look on his face as if to say, 'What are you about to lay on me now?'

George noticed a change in Mae over the last few months. She was no longer the meek, demure, individual she once was. Mae had become a no-nonsense business executive.

"It is nothing you have to concern yourself with right now, but Jane informed me that she might run for Mayor of Lewisville. If that happens, I must find a replacement for her. She cannot hold two positions. If she gets elected, she'll leave Jamae Fashions."

"That's unfortunate for you Mae, however, she would make a good Mayor, and give you a good contact at city hall."

George continued, "Speaking of replacements, The Mill will be appointing a replacement for me next year when I turn sixty-five years old. I'm not ready for retirement yet, but those are the rules."

"That's not good, George. I could lose both of you. I must give serious thought to my future if both of you disappear out of my life. Do you have any idea who will replace you next year George?"

"No. I'm all alone. My job is my life. I'm not ready to retire. I believe I still have a lot to offer, but the rules are the rules. I wish I had someone in my life like you Mae. I'll miss working with you. I'm not sure what I'll do with my life after retirement."

Mae commented, "It will not be easy to find someone to replace you, George. Working with somebody else will be difficult for me also. I've grown accustomed to working with you and tapping into your vast knowledge of the fashion industry."

"Thanks Mae for your kind words. They mean a lot coming from you. We know each other so well."

There was limited conversation between Mae and George as they ate lunch together, each preoccupied contemplating their respective futures. Both knew that significant changes were about to happen.

After lunch, Mae returned to Jamae, elated at the production company's acceptance of her contemporary designs.

Mae turned her thoughts to Jane and what her future might hold. Mae thought Jane had enough to think about. Knowing the size Jamae Fashions could become, Mae thought that would scare Jane even more than she already is. Mae decided not to say anything about the acceptance of Jamae's new line just yet. She would only tell her of George's pending retirement from The Mill.

Jane knew the inner workings of The Mill from when her late husband was an officer. She was not surprised that George had to retire at sixty-five. Jane, however, was concerned for Mae because of Mae's close ties to George. She wondered how she would make out working with somebody new.

Mae left Jane and walked down the corridor to her Design Center. She sat down and gazed at the innovative designs laid out on her easel.

Overshadowing the good news was that Mae would be flying solo when Jane and George moved away from Jamae Fashions. When I need them the most, they won't be here for me, she thought. Mae contemplated that acceptance of her designs meant little if she lost her two best friends in the interim. What she was hoping would be a memorable day, was turning out to be a disaster. Mae would have to find a replacement for Jane and work with a stranger at The Mill - two enormous tasks.

Mae decided not to worry until it came time to worry. She was not about to deviate from her life plans. Her priority now was to move Jamae in a new direction. If it is to be, it is up to me, she told herself.

Jamae Fashions rolled over its entire product line. It successfully moved from designing full flow dresses to a slim, closer body design of ladies' pantsuits, blouses, and skirts. A new range of matching pull-over sweaters and boleros joined the collection. Business was thriving. The Hong Kong producers could hardly contain themselves. There were barely enough hours in each day for Mae to keep up with the unrealistic demands on her time.

Jane's involvement in the daily operations of Jamae Fashions was diminishing. The business was moving too fast for her. She was more involved in campaigning for the position of Mayor. The business owners along Pitt Street supported her nomination. The out-going Mayor was popular and had a strong following. Health issues prevented him from continuing for another term on a full-time basis, however. Lewisville now needed a full-time Mayor. The out-going Mayor endorsed Jane as his successor.

Jane told Mae at their morning coffee klatch that she was leaving Jamae to campaign full time for Mayor. By agreement, Mae had the right of first refusal to buy Jane's shares of Jamae Fashions. Mae became the sole owner of Jamae Fashions.

"I'll miss you, Jane. I understand what you're doing. Serving others is an excellent bridge into retirement."

"Thanks, Mae. I appreciate your support of my decision."

With Jane no longer associated with Jamae, Mae was unsure what action to take. She was not as busy anymore. The world-wide acceptance of her designs lessened her time at the easel. The burden was on the production company to meet consumer demand.

Mae spent time with Aunt Mary rather than stay alone in the Design Center day after day. She was not happy that, due to the pressure of business, she could not spend more time with her. Mae wanted to correct that situation right away. Mae reminded herself that Mary was not getting any younger. She had outlived all her friends and Mae worried about her.

Mae drove home a little faster than usual. She wanted to see Aunt Mary. She thought she would take her out to dinner.

Mae entered the large foyer. "Hello Aunt Mary," she called out. A strange sound came from the kitchen area. Mae ran into the kitchen and found Mary laying on the floor. There was a gash over her eye, and her nose was bleeding.

"What happened Aunt Mary?"

"I made a pot of tea. I lost my balance reaching for a cup in the cupboard, I fell and ended up on the floor."

"How long have you been here?"

"Since lunch time."

Mae glanced at her watch. It was close to four o'clock. "Are you able to get up Aunt Mary?"

"If you help me I can. I can't move like I used to. I stayed on the floor until you got home. I tried to crawl to the phone, but it was too far away. I thought I might do more harm to myself."

Mae reached down to lift Mary off the floor, but it was difficult. Mary was not flexible and could not pull herself up. Mae got her seated on a kitchen chair with some difficulty and tended to her cuts and bruises.

"You're lucky you did not break any bones," she told Mary.

"I know," Mary confessed. "I must be more careful."

Mae, in a forceful tone, said, "This house is too big for you to handle, Aunt Mary."

Mary replied, "I've been feeling that for a while now. I guess it's about time I looked for some help."

Mae stated, "Getting help is not the answer. Have you ever considered moving into a senior's residence?"

"Oh, Mae. That's easier said than done. I don't know where to start. I understand there is a long waiting list."

"Leave it with me, Aunt Mary. I'll see if I can get something for you."

That night Mae slept on the couch downstairs, so she could be close to Mary if she needed help. Mae stayed home the next day to watch out for Mary.

When Mary was resting, Mae called Charlotte. "Hi, Charlotte. It's Mae speaking. Do you have a moment to talk?"

"Mae, you're the shelter's major benefactor. I always have time to talk to you. What can I do for you?"

"My Aunt Mary lives alone, and she had a fall yesterday. I found her on the floor. Her house has become too much for her to handle. She needs to find a convalescent or retirement residence. I am only here at night and Mary is alone all day. Do you have any suggestions how to get her into a nice convalescence home until she recovers from her accident, and later into a senior's residence?"

"You did the right thing Mae by calling me first. Give me a couple of days. I'll call you back."

Two days later Charlotte called back. "Hi, Mae. I found a place for your Aunt Mary. It is a convalescence home, with a residence wing. Mary can remain on the convalescence side until she is well enough to transfer to the adjoining residence. That way she can remain in the same facility, and you will not have to look for another senior's residence for her. The staff will help her move when the time comes. On the residence side, she can prepare her meals, or go to the dining room and order meals from a menu, three times per day if she wishes. Both units are fully furnished, but Mary can bring some personal furniture from home if she wishes. That will enable her to feel more at home."

"It sounds ideal Charlotte. Thank you for your help. When can she move? I know there is a long waiting list."

"Not for you Mae. The accommodation is available now."

"Thanks, Charlotte. I will wait for Ronnie to arrive on the weekend to help move Mary. Meanwhile, I'll stay home and look after her."

"That sounds like a good plan Mae. Call me if there is anything else you need. Meanwhile, I'll tell the staff that Mary will be arriving this weekend."

"You're so kind and understanding Charlotte."

When she heard what Mae had planned for her, Mary was overjoyed. She told Mae she wanted to do something like that for a long time but did not know how to go about it.

"Thank you, Mae, for tending to the details. I feel more at ease now. Is there anything more I need to do?"

Mae assured Mary there was nothing she had to do. Mae told Mary she and Ronnie would look after everything. Mary needed only to get better.

"I'll do my best Mae. Thanks for everything. I've no one else to turn to except you."

Mae felt uncomfortable staying away from work. She had not taken a vacation since joining Jane at The Dress Shop many years ago. She well remembered walking along Pitt Street with a handful of résumés. It was a long time to go without a holiday. She foolishly thought she needed to be present at Jamae every day, or the business would fail. Aunt Mary's accident proved otherwise. While she was tending to Mary's concerns, Jamae Fashions continued perking along at its own profitable pace. It confirmed to Mae it was unnecessary to spend so much time at Jamae.

Ronnie arrived on the weekend. Mae told him of Mary's accident, and the plans she arranged through Charlotte, to move her into a convalescence residence.

"You should have called me Mother. I'd have come sooner."

"You have enough on your plate, Ronnie. You have finals coming up, and you need all the time you can muster to prepare for them. Besides which, the time away from Jamae gives me time to re-evaluate things for myself."

Ronnie said, "I guess now is just as good a time as any to tell you what has transpired in my life Mother."

"What is it, Ronnie?" Mae asked in an anxious voice. Mae's mothering instinct kicked in. "I hope there is nothing wrong Ronnie."

"No," Ronnie assured her. "I just wanted to tell you that I've accepted an offer from an international group of Doctors to join their team of surgeons after graduation."

"Tell me more Ronnie, it sounds interesting."

"I'll set up my practice in a mobile field hospital in Africa."

Mae repeated in a loud, high-pitched voice, "In Africa? Where in Africa?"

"In Ranchobe."

"Where is that?"

"Ranchobe is a small landlocked country in the south of Africa. It has a population of two million souls. Problems stem from both medical and social points of view. I want to help. I think I can. The surgeon who interviewed me thought I could cope with the challenges."

Ronnie continued to recount the reasons for his decision. "The main problem in Ranchobe is starvation, which leads to other medical complications, especially amongst children. I'll be one of the pediatric team doctors. My operating room will be a tent in the jungle."

"Bless you, Ronnie. I'll miss you being so far away and working in such primitive conditions. Regardless, you make me very proud. My son the Doctor in Ranchobe. It has a nice ring to it."

Mae came over to where Ronnie was standing, she held out both arms, and said, "Let me give you a hug Ronnie." They held each other close for several seconds. Ronnie ended the embrace by kissing his mother on the cheek.

Mae asked, "What is the main social problem Ranchobe has to contend with?"

"Human trafficking," Ronnie explained. "Young boys and girls are smuggled into Europe by corrupt government officials, and sold into slavery, cheap factory labor, and prostitution."

"That's sad," Mae commented. "It is too bad something could not be done to eliminate those wrongdoings."

"Come on Mother. Now is not the time to solve all the world's problems."

"I know Ronnie. I agonize over you setting up a practice in a country with so many issues. Ultimately, conditions like those could affect your physical well-being and impact negatively on you as a Doctor."

Ronnie, wanting to change the subject said, "Perhaps, but right now we must move Aunt Mary into her new home." They both walked downstairs. Mary was waiting for them at the bottom of the stairs. Despite her cuts and bruises, she looked happy. Ronnie took a quick look at her injuries and said, "These bumps make you look like a street fighter Aunt Mary."

"Oh, go away," Mary quipped. "You have a good sense of humor, just like your mother. Thank you, for paying attention to an old lady. You'll make a good doctor because you have a sense of humor, something more doctors should have. It helps patients relax and get better faster."

Mary glanced around the big mansion for the last time before leaving with Mae and Ronnie for her new dwelling place. Upon arrival, Mae took Mary to her room. It was a spacious room, which allowed a lot of sunlight to enter. Mary recognized her furniture which Mae had moved in earlier. Mae also placed some of Mary's clothes in the bureau at the end of her bed. Mary did not know that Mae had done that. She was pleasantly surprised.

"Thank you for setting things up for me Mae. It makes me feel more at home."

"You're welcome Aunt Mary. I want to make you comfortable in your new home."

Mary had a large sitting room with a modern floor lamp shining light over a comfortable upholstered chair. Her bathroom was at the end of the sitting room. A hospital bed, strategically placed to enable nurses and doctors to gain access from either side, took up most of the room.

Mae explained to Mary, "This is the convalescence wing of the facility. There are no kitchens in this part. When you recover from your injuries, your room on the residence side will have a kitchen, where you can prepare meals, if you wish. I know how you like to cook, Aunt Mary. The residence area is larger than this section."

"That's okay with me," Mary said. "I can't believe all the trouble you went to in such a short space of time to keep me safe. I'm grateful for everything you did Mae."

Mae smiled and graciously answered, "That's okay Aunt Mary. I'm happy to do it with everything you did for me."

Mae turned to Mary and said, "When you're better Aunt Mary, we'll talk about your house and what you want to do with it."

"No need for that Mae. I've already bequeathed it to you. It is your house, Mae, to do with it as you see fit. It is the least I can do for you."

"Oh Mary, that was not necessary, but I thank you for thinking of me."

Mary answered, "No need to thank me Mae. It is I who should be thanking you."

Mae and Ronnie returned to Mary's former home. "I just acquired another problem, Ronnie. What do I do with Aunt Mary's large house? I've never owned a house before."

"Mother, you have enough to contend with now. Live in the house and concentrate on the other more pressing situations. If you sell the house now, you'll have nowhere to live. That will create another problem for you. You might have to move to Ranchobe with me and live in a tent."

Ronnie and his mother both laughed thinking about Mae taking up residence in Ranchobe.

# 23

Because he was retiring in less than a year George was busy recruiting his replacement. Mae did not think that he had selected his replacement yet.

Mae was not sure why, but suddenly, George left town without telling her. He usually kept her up-to-date on his traveling schedules. She thought he might have had to do something with the Jamae overseas production company in Hong Kong. She was unaware of any production issues, however. Sometimes the production company subcontracts Jamae products to other companies when they cannot keep up with the production demands. Could it be, George went to improve the production of Jamae designs? But, he would typically tell her if that was the case, Mae thought. Who knows, she asked herself? The business is getting too complicated for me.

Mae was happy that Jamae still has a good relationship with its Hong Kong partners and pleased that the drug issue died a natural death. Jamae Fashions day to day operations was now self-propelling. Mae had minimal input with the day to day operations. She was under no pressure to produce more designs due to the broad acceptance of Jamae's upbeat styles.

The Mill had perfected the distribution of finished products throughout North America, like the Hong Kong company's distribution throughout Europe and Asia. Jamae Fashions kept them both busy.

Mae's inactivity left working at Jamae Fashions less enjoyable than it once was. Jane was gone, and George's involvement was minuscule due to his pending retirement.

Notwithstanding the hundreds of people associated with Jamae around the world, Jamae Fashion's only representative in

Lewisville was Mae. She felt lonely – a situation she wanted to avoid as terrible things happened to her when loneliness set in. She needed to have people around her. The only person close to her was Ronnie, and after graduation, he was moving to Africa. She was happy for him on the one hand, but sad that she would be alone in Lewisville managing Jamae Fashions that no longer needed her to manage.

Mae thought about selling Jamae but then what would she do. She was too young to retire. She would have to find something else to do.

Mae was amazed at the path her life took. She never owned property, and lived only in Ontario, notwithstanding she was the owner of a giant world-wide fashion corporation. She wondered how that came about having been born on a farm and illiterate until she became an adolescent.

The name Jamae Fashions was renowned, but outside of Lewisville, nobody knew who Mae was.

My upcoming trip to Montreal, for Ronnie's graduation, will be the furthest I will have ever traveled - one hundred and twenty miles, Mae contemplated.

Jamae Fashions took up all her time and attention and left her no time for herself. Now even Jamae Fashions was pushing her away.

Mae thought she needed a change in her life, preferably something more exciting, but what? Even though she had become wealthy, she was not a business-oriented individual. She was a designer of women's fashions, working in the back room of a storefront operation, in a small city that most people would have trouble finding on a map.

Mae used to tell Lester he needed to raise his horizons. By allowing Jamae Fashions to rule her life, Mae was no better than Lester was working on the line sorting yarns. I do not want to become like Lester, with no direction in my life Mae adamantly told herself. I need to look for something else to fill my life.

A few days later, Mae got a call from a lawyer in Avonmore. "I regret to inform you, Mae, that your Aunt Wilma passed away," he said. "Wilma's primary beneficiary is your Aunt Mary. I am unable to find her. You are the second beneficiary, Mae. Thus, the reason for me calling you."

Mae paused before responding. "I'm shocked to hear about Aunt Wilma. I meant to contact her several times, but I let other things get in the way. Now she's gone."

Mae was alone in the Design Center when the lawyer called. Her eyes filled with tears upon hearing the news of Aunt Wilma's death. She asked, "How did Aunt Wilma die?"

The lawyer responded, "Nobody knows for certain. She died in her bed wrapped in a beautiful housecoat."

Mae gasped. "Wilma died wearing the housecoat I designed for her."

"Who found her?" she asked.

"Nobody found her. Your aunt was a very private person. Nobody ever got to know her well, except the bus driver who drove her twice a week into town to go shopping. A week went by without him seeing Wilma. When he drove past her house, he noticed that the mailbox was so full it could not close. The bus driver got concerned, and he went to the police and told them he suspected Wilma might need help. The police went to the house and found the door bolted from the inside. They knocked several times. The house was in darkness. They broke down the door and found Wilma dead in her bed. She had been there for several days."

"I feel terrible for not reaching out to her before this happened," Mae sobbed into the phone.

The lawyer waited for Mae to compose herself. He asked, "Do you know where I can find Mary?"

"She lives in a convalescent home in Lewisville. She's in her nineties, and unable to live on her own anymore."

The lawyer inquired, "Do you see her often?"

"Yes. I see Mary every day. Until a few weeks ago we lived together in the same house."

"Will you ask her to call me, please? She's the prime beneficiary of Wilma's estate."

"I'll have her call you tomorrow," Mae assured the lawyer.

Mae hung up the phone after getting the lawyer's name, and phone number. Tears were rolling down her cheeks.

"I was so tied up in my world that I neglected one of the principal people in my life. Wilma was the person who enabled me to achieve my goals. She took me in when nobody else wanted me.

Wilma realized that to continue living with her, in a tiny village, would impede my progress. She directed Uncle Charlie to give me a job in the bookstore. How selfish of me to abandon her. Perhaps if I had kept in touch with Aunt Wilma, she would still be alive."

That evening Mae went to see Aunt Mary to tell her the sad news about Aunt Wilma.

"I'm saddened to hear of Wilma's passing," Mary said. "I understand why you're feeling guilty for not paying as much attention to her as you thought you should have, but there is no need to feel remorse, Mae. Wilma died the way she lived her life, - alone and obscure. Over the years, I tried to reach out to her. She was Charlie's sister, you know. Whenever I tried, she rejected me. Eventually, I gave up trying."

Mary went on speaking to Mae, "You have to live your own life Mae, and let others live theirs."

"Thank you, Aunt Mary, for reminding me of that. I've been going through some turmoil lately and feeling sorry for myself. It is about time I took charge of my own life, and did things for me, instead of Jamae Fashions, which has no heart or soul."

Mary was not known to mince her words. She told Mae, "That's how you have to start thinking Mae. Otherwise Jamae Fashion will consume you, and eventually, kill you."

"You're right, Aunt Mary."

Mae explained to Aunt Mary, as the prime beneficiary of Wilma's estate, that she must speak with the lawyer in Avonmore.

"I'll do that Mae, but I'll tell him that he should be talking to you about those matters. I'm too old to be doing that stuff. You're in my will as the sole beneficiary. Anything that comes from Wilma's estate will eventually end up with you. I'll call him tomorrow, but I want you present when I phone him."

Mae told Mary, "I'll stop by tomorrow Aunt Mary, and we'll make the call together."

Mae left Mary and went back to Mary's former big, cold, and lonely house. Mae assessed that Mary's house was far too big for just one person. It needs people inside to make it come alive, she thought.

The next day Mae went to see Aunt Mary. Together they made a conference call to the lawyer in Avonmore. Mary told the lawyer that Mae had power of attorney, over her estate. Mary instructed the lawyer to direct the proceeds from Wilma's estate to Mae, instead of her.

The lawyer responded, "That's fine with me Mary. I'll draw up the documents. They will be in the mail tonight for both of you to sign. Return them after signing. It is a simple matter to disburse the assets after that."

The lawyer advised Mae, "I'll arrange for a real estate agent to list the house. Wilma had no other fixed assets, only a lot of cash. You're about to become a wealthy lady Mae."

Wilma's house sold fast. While the estate was large in total value, it was simple to settle. Mae received confirmation a week later that the payout from the proceeds of Wilma's estate, once settled, would go to her.

When George returned to Lewisville, he phoned Mae. "Hi Mae, he joyfully said to her. Are you doing anything for lunch today? I've something important to tell you."

"I've nothing planned George. What do you have in mind?"

"Let's have lunch at The Club."

"That sounds great George. I also have things to discuss with you. I'll meet you at noon."

When they met at the club, Mae asked, "What have you been up to George? I missed you. You left without telling me where you were going, not that it is any of my business."

George replied, "I was offered a job overseas, and I went to meet the people involved, and to make a decision."

Mae asked, "Did you make a decision, George?"

"I did. I'll be working in Europe."

"What will you be doing, and who will you be working for?"

"I'm not at liberty to discuss it right now, but eventually I'll be able to give you more details."

"Very mysterious George, but I respect your privacy."

Mae explained to George about Wilma's death, and how she became the recipient of Mary's house, and Wilma's estate.

"Wow, that's a lot to have happen in such a brief period. You must be happy," George assumed.

"On the contrary," Mae confessed. "I lost Jane, my long-time business partner. I'm about to lose you, my good friend, and associate. My son is moving to Africa, and I'm stuck here by myself to manage Jamae Fashions, which no longer needs me to manage."

"Why don't you sell Jamae Fashions and do something else with your life?"

"I can give you two reasons why. First, I've made no plans for the rest of my life, and secondly, I've no idea where to look for a buyer for Jamae. I don't even know what the company is worth."

"It is worth a lot Mae. Regardless of what you get for the business, it will be worth it to free yourself from its clutches and enjoy the rest of your life. You have lots of money, so use it on yourself."

George continued, "I have a similar problem. In less than a year I'll be gone from The Mill. I asked myself, what will I do with the rest of my life. The textile business is all I know. Other than you and Jane, I have nobody in my life. I fear the future all by myself. It is for that reason that I seriously looked at the overseas opportunity. It is too bad you cannot come with me, Mae. We have worked side by side for such a long time."

"I understand George. Life changes are hard to make."

George wanted to reverse the negative feelings enveloping them.

"Mae, let's talk about Jamae Fashions. I've two ideas I think could interest you. Let me work on them, and I'll get back to you."

"Thanks, George. One of the first things I want to do is get rid of Mary's big house."

"Smart move. It could take a while to sell that house. People don't want to live in big mansions like that anymore."

"I can understand why" Mae retorted. "It is a huge house and too big for just one person."

Mae was silent for a moment, and then it dawned on her that George had not told her why he wanted to meet with her.

"George, I just realized that I've been doing all the talking. You have not told me what you wanted to speak to me about."

"Well," George said in a drawn out and hesitant voice. "What I'm about to tell you is not easy, and it is not good."

"Oh dear," Mae exclaimed. "Tell me anyway George. You cannot make me feel any worse than I already am, considering all the negative things going on in my life at this time."

"That might not be true Mae, so prepare yourself."

Exasperated, Mae said, "Oh George get on with it. I'm a big girl. I can handle anything you want to tell me."

"The Mill is closing."

"Wow. You're right George, that's not good news. I did not expect you to tell me that," Mae said rolling her eyes as if to say, "What else can go wrong?"

"When will that happen?"

"When I retire next year."

"I thought The Mill was doing well."

"Only on the distribution side. As you know Mae, synthetic threads make up the bulk of most garments these days. You encompass them in your designs. The demand for natural yarns and fabrics has been dwindling over the years. While the distribution business is good, it does not warrant keeping The Mill open. The Mill used to produce large bolts of cotton for the clothing industry. There is no longer a demand for natural yarns. Asia produces most synthetic yarns and fabrics as you know. It is too expensive to produce those yarns in North America."

Mae asked, "What will happen to the distribution of Jamae Fashion garments?"

"That's what I was in Europe to try and set up. I've been talking to a large French couturier. They are interested in taking over The Mill distribution and folding it into their operations."

"Where is their distribution done now?"

"In Paris. They mass produce their garments in Hong Kong, just like Jamae does. The ironic thing is that they are looking for a new line in Canada. Hearing what you just told me, they may be interested in Jamae Fashions. I'll check it out for you if you like. It could solve your dilemma, Mae."

"I would entertain an offer from them. I can no longer run Jamae Fashions on my own, even though it does not need too much input from me anymore. I want to do something else with my life."

"I have an idea how to make that happen also, but let's solve one problem at a time. First, you must step away from Jamae. Once that's accomplished we can talk about other things."

"Do I take it from your comments George that you and I could be working together somewhere else?"

George said nothing. His reply was a smirk on his face and a twinkle in his eye.

"George, I've known you too long," Mae quipped. "You have something up your sleeve and in that bright mind of yours. I'll not pursue it until you're ready to divulge what it is. Suffice to say, that nothing would please me more than to sell Jamae and hook up with you in some other venture. It need not be in Lewisville either."

"Interesting," George remarked. "I'll get back to you soon. I'm leaving for Europe in two days. We'll talk again when I return in two weeks."

"Okay, George. Meanwhile, I'm off to Montreal to attend Ronnie's graduation."

"That's nice Mae. You must be proud."

"I am," Mae answered. "Unfortunately, after graduation, Ronnie's leaving for Ranchobe. I wish he would start a practice in Canada - even in Lewisville. Ranchobe is so far away."

"Things have a way of working themselves out Mae. Who knows what the future will bring?"

"You're right George. Look at today for example. I did not understand things would transpire as they did."

George and Mae left The Club together. Outside Mae said, "Can I give you a hug, George? You have been my close friend for many years. I'm afraid I might lose you like I did Jane, Wilma, and Ronnie. That's a scary thought."

George reached out and embraced Mae. "Don't worry Mae. I think we'll be friends for a long time. I'll do everything I can to make that happen. I don't want you to walk out of my life either."

"I hope not George. Have a safe trip. I'll look forward to your return."

"Thanks, Mae. Enjoy Montreal and Ronnie's graduation exercises."

Mae returned to her Design Center. "This has been an eventful and revealing day. I wish I knew what the future has in store for me."

Looking around the Design Center, she told herself, I am lonesome here by myself, and if this keeps up, I'm going to become depressed again. I hope George can find a solution for me. Whatever happens, I need to dispose of Mary's big house. I'll ask her tonight when I visit her. She might have an idea what she wants me to do with it.

# 24

Mary recovered from her injuries and was living in the residential area of the retirement home. Mae knew her meal schedules. Mae looked at the clock in the Design Center workshop and figured out Aunt Mary was having dinner now. She concluded, there is no point to visit with her until she finished eating.

Mae had personal matters to discuss with Mary which she would feel more comfortable talking about in the privacy of Mary's room, and not in the dining room where other people could hear their conversation.

Instead of visiting Aunt Mary, Mae called Jane and asked her to have dinner with her. They had not seen each other for a long time – better than eating alone Mae resolved.

"Hi, Jane. Are you available for dinner tonight? I was thinking of Chinese food. Can you join me?"

"What a wonderful idea Mae. I was sitting in my office wondering about dinner. Your call is well-timed."

Mae and Jane agreed to meet at a new local Chinese restaurant. Mae arrived first. The restaurant was full of diners, as most restaurants were on Pitt Street at dinner time. Lewisville had gained a reputation for excellent restaurants, and delicious cuisine, in the last few years. The hostess directed Mae to a table at the rear of the restaurant. She ordered a glass of wine and waited for Jane to arrive. Jane arrived five minutes later. They fell into each other's arms like they had not seen one another for an eternity.

Jane ordered a glass of wine, and the two long-time friends talked. Although the restaurant was full of people, Mae and Jane were oblivious to them. They had so much catching-up to do.

"My life has moved in a different direction since leaving Jamae Fashions," Jane said.

"Are you happy?" Mae inquired.

"Somewhat. I wake up every morning hoping my decisions will help the citizens of Lewisville. It is a satisfying feeling to have. At Jamae, I never experienced the satisfaction clients derived from wearing Jamae creations. With growth comes challenges, however. I work long hours, attend meetings, and meet lots of people. I'm still trying to get used to that aspect of the job."

"I'm somewhat jealous of you Jane," Mae said.

"How so?" Jane questioned. "George told me that business has never been better."

"That's true. Business is great. It is me that's not so great."

"Are you not well Mae?"

"I'm lonely Jane. I miss working beside you at Jamae. I miss our morning coffee klatches. I miss sharing things with you. When I go to work each morning, I'm all alone, and remain alone in the back room looking at my easel. I do little design work any more because the production company cannot keep up with the demand for my present designs. They get back-ordered, and George gets mad at them for not keeping up production schedules."

Jane asked, "What is George doing these days? Can he not find another production company where you can submit new fashion designs and start a new line?"

"George is away a lot. I have little contact with him any more. He'll retire and disappear in a few months. Someone new will take his place. I will surely miss working with him."

Jane suggested, "What about looking for a new production company Mae?"

"Therein lies one of my problems Jane. I'm still just a simple farm girl who learned how to design dresses. I've limited business experience. What I know, I taught myself, or you taught me. I'm not business minded Jane. I always relied on you and George to look after the business end of things."

"Mae stop beating up on yourself," Jane demanded. "You lived on the farm when you were a little girl. Granted you had humble beginnings but look at all you have achieved since then. "I remember when you left Lester. You wanted to change your life around — and you did. You promised Ronnie a better life than what he was born into – and you did. In a few weeks, people will be addressing him as 'Doctor Ronnie.'

"While you may not regard yourself as an astute business person you need only to ask the citizens of Lewisville what they think of you, especially the small business owners along Pitt Street. Mae, you're admired as the one person who turned this town around with your avant-garde designs. You got The Mill up and running in new directions, to where today, it is one of the finest distribution centers in the country."

"Oh Jane, I know why I call you my best friend, it's because you are so upbeat. You always make sense when you talk. That's what makes you a good Mayor. I wonder if the fine folks of Lewisville know how lucky they are to have you running this city. You have given me a lot to consider. Your words of wisdom have rejuvenated my thought process. George told me that The Mill will be closing and that he's negotiating with another company to take over the North American distribution."

Jane commented, "Yes, I know about the up-coming Mill closure. I've been trying to negotiate tax relief to encourage them to stay, but to no avail. When it closes, I hope the impact won't be too devastating on Lewisville. I don't think it will. There is a diversified business base in Lewisville now. Unlike it was when you and I first met Mae. You had an indirect impact on the Lewisville business community Mae. I've another thought for you to process."

"What is it, Jane?"

"If Jamae Fashions is causing you a lot of grief then just walk away from it. That's what I did. I regretted having to leave you and George and the business behind, but it was the right time for me to go."

"It is funny that you should say that Jane. George told me the same thing. The company he's negotiating with to take over the distribution is interested in securing a client base in North America. George said he would speak to them about Jamae and let me know if they are interested in purchasing Jamae's North American book of clients and designs."

"There's your answer Mae. Once away from Jamae, and all its problems, you'll be amazed at what opportunities are laying out there for you."

"Thank you, Jane. The food was delicious, and your pleasant company even better."

"Thanks, Mae, we'll do it another time soon I hope."

"For sure we will Jane. I'll call you next week."

Mae drove over to the retirement home to visit with Aunt Mary before she went to bed.

Mary was sitting up in her upholstered chair watching TV when Mae arrived.

When Mae entered Mary's room, Mary greeted her, "Hi, Mae. I'm glad to see you."

"It is nice to see you too Aunt Mary. Have you been keeping well?"

"As well as can be," Mary replied. "I have a cold which is holding me back a little, but aside from that I'm well."

"Make sure you stay warm Aunt Mary. I don't want you to get sick."

"Thanks, Mae. I'll look after myself. You're always so concerned for me."

"I have another concern I need to talk to you about."

"What's that Mae?"

"It is about your house. You asked me to look after it for you. I'm very grateful for your generosity but, it is too much house for me. I was thinking of selling it, but I don't want to do anything before checking with you. Do you have anything in mind, Aunt Mary?"

Mary thought for a minute and said, "Well Mae if you don't want the house - sell it. You can do what you want with the money you get for it. It's your house to decide what to do with it."

"I don't need the money, Aunt Mary. It is your house, and therefore the money belongs to you."

"Then give it to charity. I'm an old lady, and I don't need the money. I'll leave it to you to decide."

"Okay, Aunt Mary. I'll try to sell it, and when it sells, we can discuss what to do with the money."

"That's fine, Mae. Thank you for looking after that for me."

"You're welcome Aunt Mary. You're looking tired. I'll leave you now, so you can go to bed and get to sleep. I'll visit you tomorrow night. I hope you'll feel better by then."

Mae leaned over and kissed Mary on the cheek. Mary returned a kiss to Mae.

"Good night Aunt Mary."

"Good night Mae."

The next day, Mae contacted a real estate agent and listed Mary's house. The agent warned Mae, "There is not much demand for houses of this size and vintage."

"List the house for three months only. If it does not sell by that time, I'll rethink my options," Mae instructed the agent.

"Very well," the agent replied. "I'll do my best to get it sold in the next three months. It may not be easy to find a buyer willing to spend that much money on a big old house like that."

That evening, Mae returned to Mary's residence. Mary was in bed when she arrived.

"Hi, Aunt Mary. You're in bed. Are you still not feeling well?"

"I've not been too well today. I was tired. I got undressed and went to bed."

"Have you told anybody on the staff that you're not feeling well?"

"No. I did not want to bother them with something so trivial as a cold."

"That's their job Aunt Mary. I'll tell them you're not well. They will come and check on you."

Mae left in search of someone to look at Mary and discover why she was still sick. A few minutes later, she returned with one of the resident nurses.

The nurse examined Mary and said, "You have a lot of fluid on your chest. That's why you're tired and having trouble breathing. I'll give you something to relieve it. You'll feel better in the morning."

"Okay," Mary replied.

A few minutes later the nurse returned and gave Mary a penicillin injection.

"I'll make a note on your chart Mary to have someone check on you tomorrow morning. If you need help in the night, push this red emergency button. I'll pin it to your bed for easy access."

"Thank you," Mary said in a soft, weak voice.

After the nurse left, Mae sat beside Mary's bed.

"I'll not stay long Aunt Mary. I want you to rest. Before I go, I just wanted to tell you that I listed the house. It could take time before it sells. When it does, we'll talk further."

"Okay, Mae. Thanks for everything you're doing for me."

"No need to thank me, Aunt Mary. I'm happy to help."

"I'm leaving now. I'll be away for a few days. I'm going to Montreal for Ronnie's graduation."

"Oh, how nice Mae. Please extend my congratulations to him. He'll make a fine Doctor."

"I'll be happy to pass on your best wishes, Aunt Mary."

Mary and Mae embraced each other and wished each other a good night, as usual.

When Mae got home, she packed a small suitcase for her trip. She was excited about going to Montreal to see Ronnie graduate. Ronnie reserved a room at the Ritz Carleton Hotel for his mother. She would arrive a day early. It was Ronnie's idea to spend time with Mae exploring Montreal. Mae had never been to Montreal before.

# 25

The next morning Mae boarded the train destined for Montreal. It was a three-hour journey.

The train pulled into Montreal's historic Windsor Station. Ronnie was waiting on the concourse.

"Welcome to Montreal Mother," he gleefully shouted to Mae when she walked through the gate from the platform.

"Hi, Ronnie. I'm glad to be here with you. Do you realize this is the first time we have spent time away from home together?"

"Yes, I know. I'm looking forward to spending the next couple of days together."

Ronnie took his mother's suitcase and ushered her out of the North end of the station to a line of waiting taxicabs.

"My goodness, Ronnie. I've never seen that many taxis cabs in one place before. Lewisville has only two taxicabs, and they must be reserved a day in advance."

Ronnie smiled. He went to the first taxi in the line. He reached around Mae and opened the rear door and motioned his mother to enter. Ronnie followed her into the back seat. The driver placed Mae's suitcase on the front seat.

They drove North on Peel Street through Dominion Square. Mae was awestruck with the hustle and bustle of the large city. She marveled at the size, and height, of the buildings. She was awestruck with the, 'Mary Queen of the World Cathedral,' and the twelve apostles carved in stone across the top.

"This is different than the buildings on Pitt Street Ronnie. Do you like living here? It is so noisy and busy."

Ronnie looked at her and said, "I've been too busy studying, and getting ready for Ranchobe. I spend no time in the city. That's why I'm happy to have you here Mother. We'll both see the city for the first time together. My friends tell me that you only need to be in Montreal for a day and you will fall in love with the city and want to return."

The cab pulled up to the front door of The Ritz Carleton Hotel. The doorman snapped to attention as he opened the rear door of the cab. Mae paid the cab driver. She knew that Ronnie had no money.

The entrance to the Ritz was spectacular. Gorgeous furniture and chandeliers adorned the lobby. After checking in at the ornate registration desk, a bellboy took Mae's suitcase and led her and Ronnie to Mae's room. It overlooked Sherbrooke Street.

"I've never stayed in such a beautiful room, Ronnie. Thank you for reserving it."

"No problem Mother. I'll leave you now and return to the University. It is just up the street. I can walk back to the campus. After you get some rest, I'll meet you in the lobby at six o'clock. I thought we would go downtown for dinner. I know a good steakhouse which I think you'll enjoy."

"That sounds great Ronnie. You have taken care of every detail. Just like a good doctor."

Ronnie blushed and said, "Thank you, Mother. You're biased, however."

"Oh, go away with you Ronnie. I'll see you at six tonight."

Mae wept when Ronnie left. I've never been away with my son, and it may be the last time, she sobbed out loud. Ranchobe is so far away. In a few days, he will disappear out of my life, Mae sadly thought.

Determined not to let Ronnie see how sad she was about his moving to Ranchobe, Mae took a hot bath in the luxurious big tub, dressed for dinner, and went down to the lobby to meet Ronnie.

Mae waited for Ronnie in the luxurious lobby adorned with tapestries and museum quality furniture. She sat in a high-backed, upholstered green chair.

Ronnie arrived right on time. "Hi, Mother. Are you ready to party?"

"The party began when I met you at the station this afternoon Ronnie."

Ronnie laughed. "Well let's keep the party going then," he said.

Ronnie and Mae exited the hotel through the revolving doors, onto Sherbrooke Street.

The doorman asked Ronnie, "Taxi Sir?"

"No thank you, we'll walk."

"Excellent, Sir."

Ronnie and Mae walked along Sherbrooke Street and turned onto Stanley Street. "I hope you like steak Mother?"

"I love steak Ronnie, although I don't have it too often. There are no steak restaurants in Lewisville."

"I think you'll like this restaurant."

"What is the name of it Ronnie?"

"Joe's Steak House."

"That's a simple name for a restaurant," Mae commented.

"Only simple in name," Ronnie answered. "The steaks are far from simple. That's all they serve."

Joe's Steak House was everything that Ronnie said it was.

"This is a great meal, Ronnie. It is so nice to share times like this with you. I'm sorry that it will be short-lived. You'll be moving halfway around the world in a few days. I'll miss you."

"You can come and visit me in Ranchobe Mother. It will allow you to view first-hand the work I do."

"I'd like to do that Ronnie, but I think it might pose a problem for you to have your mother present."

Ronnie replied, "Doctors who work in remote places are encouraged to invite family members to observe what is taking place. It is a form of fundraising for the organization."

"How does the visitation by family members encourage funding?"

"Family members observe the work that's going on and return home and tell their friends. The more news that gets broadcast about the work at the Ranchobe Center, the more financial support it receives. In my interviews with the founder of the clinic, Dr. Taylor, he suggested that I invite you to visit The Center in Ranchobe. That's why I'm discussing it with you now." Ronnie giggled, "He's probably looking for a little financial encouragement from you also."

"How interesting," Mae commented. "It sounds like a different world. A world I might find interesting. I'm excited at the prospect of seeing you performing miracles in the jungle. You can tell Dr. Taylor he can expect to receive a donation to help finance the work the clinic is doing in Ranchobe."

"When you decide Mother, you only need to give me a week's notice. It is not like there is a long waiting line."

Mae and Ronnie walked casually back to the Ritz in the warm Montreal summer air. At the hotel, Ronnie asked, "Can we do breakfast tomorrow morning, Mother?"

"That would be nice Ronnie."

"Good. Meet me in the lobby at nine o'clock. We'll eat in the Garden Restaurant. I understand it is the most prestigious restaurant in Montreal. I'll make reservations for us."

"Thanks, Ronnie, but only if you let me pick up the tab."

Ronnie laughed, "I was assuming you would do that Mother. I'm a struggling medical student who eats pork and beans out of a can."

Mother and Son laughed for several minutes at Ronnie's remarks.

"Oh, you're so much fun to be with, Ronnie. I'll miss our times together. When I come to visit you in Ranchobe, I may not want to leave."

"That won't be a problem, Mother. There is always work you can do."

The next morning Ronnie and Mae met in the lobby. The Garden Restaurant was one floor below the lobby level. The head waiter, dressed in a grey cut-away, greeted them at the door. He led them to a table and professionally removed the reserved sign off the table before seating Mae and Ronnie.

Live swans swam gracefully by in a narrow stream beside them. Mae and Ronnie dined on crepe suzettes. After breakfast, they walked through Old Montreal, and Place Jacques Cartier.

Back at the hotel, Mae commented, "Ronnie a few problems with Jamae Fashions have emerged recently. Spending time with you, away from Lewisville, has allowed me time to put aside my concerns relating to Jamae Fashions. It has been wonderful. Thank you for making it all possible Ronnie."

"It is not over yet Mother. Tomorrow is convocation night. I'm looking forward to it, and happy that you'll be there to see me. Without your dedication to ensure I acquired a good education, tomorrow night would never have happened."

"I'd not miss it for the world, Ronnie."

Ronnie told Mae he had a few last-minute things to do before the ceremonies began. He also had a meeting with Dr. Taylor. He asked Mae to go directly to the University. It was just a short walk down Sherbrooke Street. He would catch up with her at the ceremonies.

"That's fine Ronnie. I'll just stroll down the street and enjoy the sights."

"Okay, Mother. I'll see you tomorrow evening. Don't forget to bring your invitation."

Mae reached into her purse and said, "Here it is Ronnie. I will not let it out of my sight." They both laughed and went their separate ways.

The next morning Mae went for a walk. The hotel was in the Fashion District of Montreal.

Montreal women prided themselves on being well-dressed. Mae noted that many were wearing her designs. She walked past several small boutiques who carried the Jamae line. Montreal women loved Jamae clothes.

Mae returned to the hotel at three o'clock. She ordered room service of selected cheeses, and bread, at four o'clock. After her snack, she got ready for the biggest night of her life. The graduation of her son Ronnie, from McGill University receiving his Doctorate Degree in Medicine.

Mae designed a dress for the evening. She wanted Ronnie to view her as somebody unique. There would be nobody else wearing a dress like Mae's. She made sure of that.

Mae strolled along Sherbrooke Street toward the University. She went through the Redpath Roddick Gates, the main entrance to the McGill campus, off Sherbrooke Street. Mae had lots of time to take in the sights, sounds, and smells of the world-famous University. She stopped and read every memorial plaque. One achievement plaque caught Mae's eye. It listed famous graduate Doctors who contributed to help make the world a better place to live. Mae contemplated

Ronnie someday having a plaque honoring him for his work in Ranchobe.

Mae sauntered into Convocation Hall and looked for her reserved seat. The ceremonies were very formal. There were lots of speeches and individual introductions. None of that mattered to Mae. She did not know who all those people were anyway. She only had eyes for Ronnie – her son the Doctor.

She sat ten rows away from the dais and admired Ronnie in his cap and gown, snapping pictures of him and his graduating class throughout the ceremonies. When the exercises ended, Ronnie joined his mother in the audience. They embraced each other for several minutes. Both were in tears.

Ronnie spoke first and said, "Thank you, Mother, for everything you have done for me. You gave me everything you promised - a better life than what I was born into."

Mae, tears still flowing from her eyes, said, "I was determined to accomplish what I promised, Ronnie, even though at times there were doubts I could pull it off."

"I never doubted you, Mother. You're the best. I'm so grateful to you for believing in me. I'm also very proud of you."

A smile came across Mae's face, and she told Ronnie, "Just think Ronnie, you could have ended up sorting yarns at The Mill like your father." They both laughed at the thought.

Ronnie remarked, "I remember Lester telling me that I'd never amount to anything. If he could see me now, I wonder what he would think? His negative attitude drove me to work hard to excel. Contrary to Lester, you were always there for me Mother."

"Thank heavens you did not let Lester influence you to stop learning Ronnie."

At that moment, a tall, distinguished gentleman wearing a graduate gown, approached Ronnie and Mae.

"Good evening Doctor Taylor," Ronnie said. "I want you to meet my mother."

Ronnie turned to Mae and said, "Dr. Taylor is the Chief Medical Officer of the Ranchobe project. He and his wife Carol founded the project. He'll be my boss."

Dr. Taylor shook hands with Mae. "Congratulations Mae. You must be proud of what Ronnie has achieved so far in his young life."

"Indeed, I am," Mae answered with eyes gleaming and looking at Ronnie all the while.

Dr. Taylor said. "Ronnie has told me a lot about you Mae. You have quite a story yourself to tell. My daughter wears your fashions and loves them."

"Thank you for telling me, Dr. Taylor."

"Are you wearing one of your designs now, Mae?"

"I am and thank you for noticing, Dr. Taylor."

"Ronnie told me this afternoon that you might visit the Ranchobe Project, is that correct Mae?"

"Well I've not made any definite plans, but yes, I'd like to visit Ronnie and see firsthand the work that you and he are doing over there."

"That would be great if you could arrange it, Mae. You can expect a warm welcome. Thank you also for your generous contribution to the Center and congratulations on raising such a brilliant and dedicated son Mae. I have plans to propose to him for the future."

The following morning Mae and Ronnie had breakfast together. Afterward, Mae checked out of the hotel and took a taxi to Windsor Station for the train trip back to Lewisville. Ronnie was leaving the next day on his long journey to Ranchobe. They shed many tears between them.

The return trip to Lewisville was not as pleasant for Mae as the trip in the opposite direction a few days earlier.

After spending three days in Montreal, Mae noticed how slow the pace of life was in Lewisville, compared to Montreal. She never realized that before. Mae felt that Lewisville was a little backward. Nothing new ever happens in Lewisville, she thought. It is the same old thing from one day to the next.

The hustle and bustle of Montreal appealed to Mae. Ronnie was right. It only took a day to fall in love with Montreal. I could come to like living in a cosmopolitan city like Montreal. The French-Canadian culture adds excitement and flair to everyday living. People in Montreal are so fashion conscious. Mae brought away fond memories of Montreal and Ronnie's graduation exercises.

********************

Mae was dabbling with some design ideas when the real estate lady called.

"I just want to keep you up-to-date," the agent told Mae. "There is a potential buyer interested in Mary's house. They just need to get their financing in place, and then they will make an offer. Will you be remaining in Lewisville for the next few days?"

"I will," Mae replied. "It will be a relief to get the house sold. I have a lot of things on my mind these days. If the house sells, it will be one less thing to deal with."

"I'll do my best to speed things along," the agent reassured her.

Mae remained at Jamae for the rest of the day. Nothing happened. It reminded her of the last days she spent with Aunt Wilma. She had out-grown the small village atmosphere of Avonmore, and now she has outgrown the small city of Lewisville.

"I hope George brings good news about a prospective buyer for Jamae Fashions. After spending the weekend with Ronnie and reveling in the excitement of Montreal, it was a let down when Mae returned to Lewisville. I want to visit Ronnie in Ranchobe, she told herself. That will be exciting. I miss him already.

Before that can happen, Mae told herself, there is a lot of work to clean up here first.

# 26

The phone rang at Jamae Fashions. Mae answered it.

"Hello, Mae, I am the head nurse at your Aunt Mary's residence."

"Hello," Mae responded. "Is there something wrong?"

"Your aunt has contracted pneumonia. She's not feeling well. I thought you should know. Perhaps you may want to see her."

"Thank you for calling me. I'm leaving now."

Within minutes Mae was at Mary's bedside. A nurse was checking her vital signs. The nurse came over to Mae and whispered, "She's drifting in and out of consciousness. It started last night."

Mae sat down beside Mary's bed. Mary opened her eyes a few times, but Mae was unsure if Mary knew that she was there beside her. It did not matter. It was plain to see that Mary's life was ending. Mae decided to stay with her until the end came.

Mary was having difficulty breathing. There was a rumbling sound coming from deep within her body. It got louder as the night grew longer. It was painful for Mae to sit and watch her slowly drift away. Her skin color was turning a strange reddish color. Nurses came in and out of her room all night. After sitting with Mary all night, the head nurse entered Mary's room and whispered to Mae, "Prepare yourself, my dear."

Less than an hour later Mary passed away. Mae was in tears. Other than Ronnie, she just lost her last family member. A feeling of sadness and loneliness enveloped her, and she began crying profusely.

Mae spent the next three days making funeral arrangements. She had no idea what was happening at Jamae and furthermore did not care. Her priority was to tend to Mary's final arrangements.

The funeral took place three days later. The church was full. Lewisville had lost one of its long-time citizens.

The next day was quiet for Mae. She felt she should be doing something, but she didn't know what. She went from being overly busy, to now suddenly, having nothing to do. She went into Jamae Fashions, not because she had to, but because she needed something to keep her mind occupied.

Mae sat and stared at her easel. She could not believe what was happening in her life. She felt like a cork on the ocean, bobbing around with no direction, and no idea what would happen next.

Mae was unsure how long she had been daydreaming before she realized that the phone was ringing. "Jamae Fashions, Mae speaking," she said into the phone.

"Hello, Mae. It's George. I just got into town. I heard about your Aunt Mary's death. My sincerest condolences Mae."

"Thanks, George. It is so nice to hear your voice. I need a friend to talk to right now. Is there any chance we could have lunch together?"

"There is every chance," George said. "I'll drive over right away and pick you up. You're a dear friend, and I want to do whatever I can to help get you through these tough times. I also have some news which you might be interested to hear. We can talk about it now, or we can wait until you're feeling more receptive to talking business."

"Is it good news George?"

"I think so, but I'll let you be the judge of that."

"Come over right away George. I want to hear good news. In the last few days, my life has been full of sad news. I need that to change."

"I'm on my way, Mae."

George arrived fifteen minutes later. He walked through the Jamae showroom and found Mae where she usually sat, all alone, in front of her easel. George noted that her eyes were red from crying. He put his arms around her and held her tight for several minutes.

"Mae, rather than go to The Club for lunch like we always do, let's break with tradition and go somewhere different. You need a change of scenery."

"What a wonderful idea George. Let's get out of here."

George drove Mae in his car to the other end of town. He talked little. He wanted to give Mae some personal space for her thoughts.

George wheeled the big black Cadillac up to a mobile chip wagon. "Can I buy you a hot dog and fries?" he asked Mae.

"I'd love it. I can't remember the last time I ate a hot dog and fries."

"After you finish this one I'll be able to answer you." George quipped.

"Oh George, thank you for trying to humor me. You have always been good at that. You are a good friend."

"I'll always be your friend Mae. You have inspired me over the years to remain positive. It is my turn to do it for you. Let me go and order some food for us. It will be fun to have lunch together in the fresh air. Something I have not done for a long time. There is a picnic table over there where we can share our lunch with the ants and spiders." Mae laughed at George's remark.

George brought two hot dogs and two orders of fries to the picnic table. He made a second trip back to the wagon to pick up two paper cups of soda. They ate their lunch at the table, in glorious sunshine, and gentle breezes, amongst songbirds and pigeons looking to share food with Mae and George.

"This is delicious," Mae exclaimed. "The fries taste great. They are nice and greasy. They taste wonderful."

George quipped, "That's because they have lots of heart-stopping ingredients." Mae and George laughed heartily together, which is what George wanted, to lift Mae's spirits.

"The fries sure beat that limp green salad that The Club serves up," Mae said.

"Yes, and at only a fraction of the price, and no tip."

George soon got Mae relaxed with his light-hearted conversation.

"You're so kind George to help me overcome my grief. What a wonderful idea you had to do something different. I must relax like this more often. I don't know what will happen next. I'm out of control, and I don't like it."

George replied, "You don't like it because you have never been there before. You're always in control Mae. Ever since I first met you. You always have a plan and know exactly how to implement it. Suddenly you have no plan, and you're having difficulty dealing with it."

"You're so right George."

"I can help you make some plans if you like Mae."

"Please do George. I need all the help I can get."

"Have you ever heard of, Couturier La Monde?"

"Of course. La Monde is the renowned fashion house in Paris."

"That's right. When I retire from The Mill, I will become La Monde's new Chairman. I'll live in Lyon, France."

"Why Lyon? I thought La Monde was in Paris."

"That's where the runways are. Headquarters is in Lyon."

"Congratulations George that's a prestigious step up for you. La Monde made a wise choice to put you at the helm."

"Thanks, Mae."

"I've also been talking to them about you. Your designs are famous around the world. The European shops cannot keep them on the racks. They watch for the courier truck to arrive so that they can get your fashion pantsuits, and accessories, on their racks quickly. They know that your designs will attract clients to their shops. European women especially love your designs. When I mentioned your name, they recognized it at once and associated it with Jamae, of Lewisville, Canada. There is not another Canadian designer who has amassed such a wide following around the world. You have put the small town of Lewisville on the world map, Mae."

Mae smiled and took another bite of her hot dog. George noticed Mae had relaxed from when they first arrived at the chip wagon. He continued talking to her.

"La Monde are interested in establishing a new product line. They admire your designs, Mae. They noted that Jamae has a strong and loyal North American clientele."

George watched Mae's reaction as he spoke. He noted she had become more upbeat at his news.

"La Monde wants to expand their facilities throughout the world, including into Africa. One of my duties, as Chairman of La Monde, is to seek out new markets. They prefer to buy existing, successful, businesses, and they will pay top dollar for profitable companies with a preferred market share, and clientele."

George could see he had Mae's undivided attention now. He explained La Monde's market plan and his new role as Chairman.

"I recommended you, and Jamae Fashions, Mae. They liked that you and I know each other so well, and we have worked together for many years. They would like us to continue to work together under the La Monde banner, if possible. Does that appeal to you Mae?"

"Oh, George what a wonderful thought. The timing could not be better for me. What must I do to make it happen?"

"Well, Mae there are some strings attached. You must sell your interest in Jamae Fashions to La Monde. You would have to give up your clients. The valuable name, Jamae Fashions, would not change, however. In return, they are prepared to appoint you as a Director of La Monde. You will have a seat on their board, and you and I will continue to work together, doing the same as we are doing together now. The deal is contingent upon you staying associated with the Jamae line and creating your fabulous designs. The only difference is that you'll be creating them for La Monde instead of Jamae Fashions."

"I've not heard anything yet George that could be a deal breaker. I keep waiting for the other shoe to drop."

Mae listened to George intently. Her sadness turned to optimism, and then to exhilaration. George saw Mae move from grief to excitement before his eyes. The creative designer of contemporary fashions had returned. George was pleased to see Mae's positive reaction.

"There is something else Mae that I hope won't be a deal breaker," George said.

"What is it, George."

"As a Director, you must reside in France. It is company policy. You'll have to move from Lewisville and take up residence in France."

"Where in France would I live?"

"In Lyon. It is about two hundred and fifty miles from Paris. La Monde's world headquarters are in Lyon."

"Is Lyon where you'll be living and working George?"

"Yes. I already have a company apartment there. If you agree to sell Jamae and become a Director of La Monde, you'll have a staff of designers reporting to you, creating your beautiful fashions. You and I will continue working together just like we always have. The nice part is only you, and I will do the negotiating. You'll not have to deal with strangers, thousands of miles away, in France."

"What a delightful thought," Mae commented. "When can we start negotiating George?"

George answered, "We already have."

"That's terrific," Mae told George. "La Monde is one of the largest designers of women's fashions in the world. I'm flattered that they want to buy Jamae Fashions and fold it into their organization. The fact that their offer is contingent on including me as part of the deal pleases me. I've only got one concern, George. I have no place to live in Lyon. I would have to look for a place to stay. That may be difficult because I know nothing about Lyon or where to look for a place to live."

"You can stay with me," George said. "As Chairman, I am entitled to a company apartment. It is far too big for me. If you wish, you can move into my place until you find a place of your own. Since I can read and speak French, I can help you integrate into the French culture. If you enjoyed Montreal, you would enjoy Lyon as well. They are like twin cities."

"That sounds like a good plan George. I'm okay with that."

"That's great Mae. We know each other so well. It'll be good to continue working together. I like the idea of moving in together also. I admire and respect you so much Mae, not just in business, but personally as well."

"I feel the same way, George. What else must we do to make this happen?"

"The deal is all but done Mae. All that's left is for the lawyers to dot the I's and cross the T's."

Mae leaned over and wiped a speck of mustard from the side of George's lip. She kissed him on the cheek.

"You're the most important man in my life George. Thank you for your understanding. I liked you from the first time we met. My admiration for you has grown even deeper since then. Regardless of where our paths lead, I believe we'll always be a part of each other's life."

"I believe that also Mae. Let's drive back into town. It was a great lunch, but we each have work to do, and plans to make."

"You're right, George."

Mae was a different person when they left the picnic table. They had a stimulating conversation on the drive back to Jamae, unlike their trip in the opposite direction about three hours earlier.

When Mae got out of the car, George said, "I'll give you a couple of days to get your thoughts in order Mae, then we can sit down with the lawyers and complete the deal. Call me if you need me for anything."

"Thank you, George, for the wonderful lunch and conversation. You have no idea how good you made me feel."

"I think I do," George said smiling. "I feel the same way after having had a unique lunch and a dynamic conversation with you today."

Mae waved to George as he drove away. She opened the door, and danced between the rows of fashion garments, to her familiar spot in front of her easel.

Mae sat alone thinking about what had transpired over lunch with George. Finally, she thought, there is a light at the end of my tunnel. Moving from Lewisville will be good for me. There are too many unhappy memories here now. I'll miss my friend Jane, but she's content to remain in Lewisville. She was born here and has no desire to move. I must tell her soon of my intentions to give up Jamae Fashions and move to Lyon, however. It will come as a surprise to her, but I know she'll be happy for me.

# 27

About fifteen minutes after Mae returned from her thought-provoking lunch at the picnic table with George, the phone rang in the Jamae Design Center. It was the real estate lady calling.

"Hi, Mae. I've got terrific news for you. We have an offer on Mary's house."

"That's good news," Mae answered joyfully.

"It is a young couple who owned a house in Toronto, which they sold for a small fortune. They have lots of money to buy Mary's old house, and they are prepared to pay your asking price."

"Is that the only offer received?"

"Yes."

"Why are they moving to Lewisville from a big city like Toronto?"

"He's the new Vice-President of Marketing at The Mill, replacing George Smith, who will be retiring soon. Some changes are about to occur at The Mill, and this young executive will be implementing them."

Mae said nothing about knowing George and his retirement plans. She asked the real estate lady, "Why do two young people need such a big house? Are they planning on having a large family?"

"I don't know about that, the real estate lady said. I only know that they intend to bulldoze the house down and build a new modern home for themselves. They are buying it for the property. They are not interested in the house."

Mae said nothing. She silently asked herself, what Mary would think if she knew her house was about to be torn down?

The long pause prompted the real estate lady to ask, "Are you still there Mae?"

"Yes. I'm still here," Mae replied. "I'm trying to get over the shock of what you just told me."

"What did I say to upset you, Mae?"

"I cannot allow Mary's house to be bulldozed down. It is a Lewisville landmark. It belonged to one of its early citizens, and business owners of this town. Demolition is out of the question. What would Mary think?"

Frustrated, the real estate lady said, "Mae, it is only a house. When you sell it, the buyers can do whatever they want with it. It becomes their house."

In a firm voice, Mae said, "Tell the prospective buyer that the house is no longer for sale."

The real estate lady was shocked. "Do you mean that Mae?"

"I certainly do. Remove the house from the market at once," Mae ordered.

"Okay. I will remove it right away. I think you are making a big mistake not to take this offer. Mary's house is not the easiest piece of property to sell. People do not want to own houses like that anymore."

Mae answered emphatically, "I do not want Mary's house destroyed. I'll find something else to do with it."

Angrily, Mae said goodbye and hung up the phone.

Now, what have I done to complicate my life, Mae asked herself? She decided to call Jane for advice on Mary's house. She wanted to tell Jane anyway about her intention to sell Jamae Fashions to La Monde. Mae didn't want Jane to hear about the sale of Jamae from somebody else first. It won't take long for word to get around Lewisville about the deal for Couturier La Monde to take-over Jamae. It's a small town, Mae reminded herself.

Mae remembered the last time she and Jane met for dinner, and how enjoyable it was. They ate Chinese food at a new Lewisville Chinese restaurant.

Mae heard the click on the phone and Jane's familiar voice. "Hi, Jane. Do you feel like Chinese again tonight?"

"I sure do. Is six o'clock okay?"

"Sounds great. I'll see you there. I've got a lot to tell you."

Mae arrived at the restaurant early, like she did the last time. She relaxed with a glass of wine while she waited for Jane, who arrived a few minutes later.

"Hi, Jane. Glad, you could make it on such short notice."

"Thank you, Mae. I've been thinking about you. How are you holding up after Mary's funeral?"

"Up until noon today, I was in bad shape. Then George called and invited me out to lunch. We had hot dogs and fries."

"Hot dogs and fries," Jane exclaimed. "Did he blow last month's budget?"

Mae chuckled at Jane's sense of humor. "No," Mae said. "He thought that going somewhere different would help pick me up."

"Did it work?"

"Yes. It relaxed me. George is such a sincere and convincing talker, as you know."

"Yes, I know. What did you talk about?"

"Most of the conversation was taken up talking business, although there was some personal stuff discussed also. I'll tell you all about it over our egg rolls."

Mae and Jane went together to the buffet and picked out their egg rolls. Back at the table, Jane said, "Okay Mae, out with it. You are bursting to tell me things, let's hear them."

Mae smiled and excitedly told Jane of the new events about to unfold in her life. "As you know George is retiring. He has a new job. He asked me to join him."

"Who will you and George be working for?"

"Couturier La Monde," Mae answered. "In Lyon, France."

"Wow," Jane exclaimed. "Will you live in Lyon also?"

"I'll be living in George's large, company-owned apartment until I can find a place of my own."

With a smirk on her face, Jane asked, "Is there something going on between you and George?"

"No, not exactly," Mae answered.

Jane pursued the subject, "Would you like there to be something between you, Mae?"

Mae told Jane, "We've come to know each other well. I don't know how George feels about having a closer relationship."

Jane continued prodding Mae to encourage her to look for a more permanent arrangement between her and George when they move together in Lyon. "If you gave him a positive sign, I think he would react positively. You would make an ideal couple."

"Enough of that Jane. Let's talk about my new career path."

"As you wish Mae, but don't forget about working with George under a better personal arrangement. It would be good for both of you. Now tell me about your agreement with La Monde."

Mae outlined to Jane the La Monde offer.

"Mae, I'm delighted at the news. I'll be sorry to see you leave Lewisville, but I understand. I know you have not been happy with everything that's going on in your life.

"On a brighter note," Jane said, "I'll have a reason to travel to France and visit my two best friends in Lyon."

Jane leaned across the table and embraced Mae. She was happy for her friend's success. Mae thought she detected a sign of regret coming from Jane, wishing she could still be a part of Mae's life. Her best friend was about to exit from her life.

"As my best friend, and Mayor of Lewisville, I need to tap into some of your wisdom," Mae said.

"How can I help," Jane offered.

"As you know, I put Mary's big old house up for sale. I received a call from the real estate lady to say she had an interested buyer."

"That sounds good," Jane commented.

"Well, it sounds good Jane. The only thing is the new owners want to demolish the house."

"Oh dear," Jane exclaimed.

Mae continued, "That house is full of history, and a landmark of Lewisville. I did not feel comfortable letting it be torn down. It has historical value."

"What did you decide to do Mae?"

"I told the agent to take the house off the market. I'm back to square one. I own this big old house that nobody wants. As Mayor of Lewisville, do you think the city would like to take it over for its historical value?"

"That would be hard to get approved, Mae. The council will say we have more urgent matters to spend money on. I have an idea for you though."

"What is it, Jane?"

"Why don't you give Charlotte a call? I'm sure she could make use of the house and property. She's always looking for more low-cost housing. Housing costs have doubled in Lewisville over the last five years. Many of Charlotte's clients are having a tough time making ends meet. The cost of housing in Lewisville is expensive now. You could ease the housing shortage, Mae, by offering Mary's house to Charlotte."

"What a brilliant idea Jane. I knew if I asked, you would come up with a solution. I'll call Charlotte first thing tomorrow."

Mae and Jane finished their meal, wished each other a good night, embraced, and left the restaurant. The next morning Mae called Charlotte.

"Hi, Charlotte. It's Mae speaking."

Charlotte answered, "Hi Mae, how can I help you?"

"I've got a big old house on York Street that I inherited from my Aunt Mary. I want to give it away. I don't want it torn down. Can you use it for your clients, Charlotte?"

There was silence at the other end of the line. Mae heard Charlotte sobbing through the phone.

"Charlotte, are you okay?"

"Yes, thanks, Mae. You overwhelm me with your generosity, Mae. You're so kind and thoughtful. Some women and children need accommodation as we speak. We cannot help them due to lack of space. You're the answer to our prayers, Mae. The growth of Lewisville is good on the one hand, but not so good for those needing help to get away from abusive husbands and boyfriends. You know how it is Mae."

"I know very well Charlotte. I was there once myself. I'm indebted to you, and the shelter, for turning my life around."

"Mae the answer is, 'Yes.' We will modify the interior to accommodate multiple families of mothers and children. I promise you Mae, Mary's house will always remain standing on my watch."

"That's all I need to hear Charlotte. I'll instruct my lawyers, to contact your lawyers, and make this happen quickly."

"Bless you, Mae," Charlotte blubbered into the phone.

Charlotte asked, "Where will you live after you donate the house to The Women's Shelter?"

"I'm hoping to take a position with Couturier La Monde. If that takes place, I'll be leaving Lewisville."

"Where are you going?"

"Lyon, France."

"That's far away."

"I'll be working with George Smith who is retiring from The Mill in a few months. He also is taking up a new position with La Monde."

"I'm shocked Mae, but happy for you. You have outgrown Lewisville. I always knew that someday you would. You're far too ambitious to stay stagnant in a small city like Lewisville. Nevertheless, Lewisville will miss you."

"I'll miss Lewisville as well. I want to remind you, however, Charlotte, that although I'm moving away, my charity will remain to service your needs. In that regard, I'll still be here for you. Don't forget to contact them if you need anything. I will hire an administrator before I leave, but I'll be returning to Lewisville regularly. You and I will keep in touch."

"Mae, I want to propose to The Shelter's Executive Board that we name Mary's residence, 'Mae's Place.' Would you be agreeable to that?"

"I'm flattered Charlotte. If your board agrees, I'd love to have my name associated with The Woman's Shelter.

"As you know Charlotte, the Women's Shelter means a lot to me. It taught me I was more than just a punching bag for Lester. I hope it can inspire others as it did me."

"Consider it done Mae. Henceforth, Mary's residence will become, Mae's Place."

Both women were crying on the phones. "Oh, Charlotte, how I wish that Mary was still with us to witness the transition of her home from an out-dated monster home into a haven for Mothers and children."

Charlotte remarked, "Perhaps she knows already Mae."

"Perhaps," Mae consented.

Both ladies said good-bye. As Mae hung-up the phone from Charlotte she thought, if only she could conclude the sale of Jamae as fast as she did Mary's house, then she would be free to travel to Ranchobe and visit with her son – the Doctor.

Mae wondered how Ronnie was doing in his first days as a new Doctor, far off in Ranchobe. Mae longed to visit him. She missed him.

# *DIRECTIONS*

*If you have nowhere to go*
*- any road will get you there.*

# 28

The next day George stopped at Jamae Fashions to speak with Mae. "Hello, Mae. La Monde agrees, in principal, to the terms of sale."

"Fabulous," Mae shouted with joy. "When can we complete the deal?"

"Not so fast," George warned. "La Monde must do their due diligence on all aspects of the agreement. There is paperwork to complete, and there is one last hurdle."

Mae asked, "What now?"

"Do you remember the time when there was a drug problem with our Hong Kong production company?"

Mae did not mention the meeting she had with Boris in Ottawa. If she did, she thought she might violate the confidentiality agreement. Mae was unsure if that agreement was still valid. Rather than take a chance, she said nothing to George.

George said, "La Monde wants to make sure there are no outstanding issues. They don't want to buy into any existing problems. It is part of their due diligence."

Mae asked, "How do we do that?"

George replied, "You'll have to go to Ottawa and meet with a government official. His name is Boris. He's the head of the Canadian Espionage and Sabotage division of CSIS. He's also connected with Interpol."

Mae found it ironic that Boris was heading up the investigation on the sale of Jamae to La Monde. After the Hong Kong incident, she thought she would never see, or hear, from Boris again. Pretending she knew nothing about the inner workings of international policing, Mae asked George, "Who is CSIS?"

George replied, "The letters C. S. I. S stand for, The Canadian Security and Intelligence Service. Boris heads up the Canadian division. CSIS works with Interpol, the international police organization. Ironically, their headquarters are in Lyon. The two entities work hand in hand to combat international crime."

George continued explaining CSIS's role to make sure Mae understood. "Jamae and La Monde are registered as International Companies. All take-overs are scrutinized by Interpol, before implementation to avoid money laundering activities."

Mae did her best to act surprised at George's explanation, even though she knew all along what CSIS stood for, and who Boris was.

"When do I meet with this Mr. Boris, and what kind of information is he looking for George?"

"The La Monde executives made arrangements for Boris to contact you. He'll call you in the next couple of days."

"Okay. I'll wait for Boris to call. Is that the only thing holding up the sale of Jamae to La Monde?"

"Yep. That's it, Mae. After approval from Boris, Jamae Fashions will be no more. You'll join me as a Board Member with La Monde and move to Lyon with me. I don't foresee any problem with Boris," George reassured Mae. "It is a mere formality to ensure no illegal activities are going on. That often happens in international corporate deals like this. La Monde is extra cautious because of the former drug activity in Hong Kong."

"I hope you're right George. I don't want this deal to fall through. Jamae Fashions had nothing to do with the illegal activity. It started in Hong Kong and ended in Montreal."

"I'm sure Boris knows that Mae. Boris will ask you a few questions. Just answer his questions and go from there. There is nothing to worry about."

"Very well George. I'll wait for Boris to call me."

As George said he would, Boris called Mae the next day.

"Hello, Mae. It's Boris from CSIS. How are you? I understand you are going through some rough times. I was sorry to hear of the death of your Aunt Mary. My condolences."

"How do you know about my Aunt Mary's death?"

"I know a lot of things Mae. I want to share some with you before the sale of Jamae to La Monde is concluded."

"I don't understand," Mae confessed to Boris.

"You'll know soon after we talk," Boris replied. "Are you able to come to Ottawa tomorrow morning?"

"I guess so."

"Good. We will make the same arrangements as the last time. The officer will call you from his car parked across the street. Simply drive in your car to the Lewisville Airport as you did before. The officer will follow you."

Questions kept Mae from having a sound sleep that night. Why am I summoned to Ottawa again? How does Boris know about Aunt Mary's death? What else does he know about me?

The next day, Mae sat in the display area of Jamae Fashions watching for the agent to arrive. She saw the black Ford Victoria turn the corner and drive down Pitt Street. It stopped directly across the street from Jamae Fashions. Just as Boris said it would. Within a few minutes, the phone rang. Mae answered, "Jamae Fashions, Mae speaking, how I can help you?"

The voice on the phone, without emotion or fanfare, said, "I'm across the street. I'll follow when you leave for the airport."

Taking no chances, Mae said, "I want to make sure I know who I'm talking to, please wave to me."

The officer raised his left-hand part way and made a waving gesture. He kept looking straight ahead so as not to show who he was waving at.

"I'm leaving now," she replied and hung up the phone. Very intriguing, Mae thought.

Mae locked the door and walked to her car parked in front of Jamae Fashions and drove to the Airport. The black Ford Victoria followed a short distance behind. At the airport, she parked the car and boarded the government plane for Ottawa.

At the Rockland Ottawa Airport, a limo whisked her to CSIS headquarters. A young, unsmiling, and insincere looking civil servant ushered her into a small interview room. Mae thought she might be Boris's secretary.

A square table and two sets of chairs were the only pieces of furniture in the room. A closed door and a large mirror filled the opposite wall. Mae presumed it was a one-way mirror, which someone was using to watch her. She wondered what was going on.

A few seconds later, Boris bounced through the door into the small room, his arm outstretched, and in a jolly tone said, "Hi Mae. How nice to see you again," while firmly shaking her hand.

"Hello Boris," Mae said. "I was not expecting to see you again."

Boris sat down across from Mae. He grinned and continued talking. "I understand that you're moving to Lyon, France."

"Where do you get your information?" Mae inquired.

Boris ignored Mae's question and carried on. "We at CSIS and Interpol are grateful for your help last year on the illegal drug activity between Hong Kong and Canada. With your help, we shut down that criminal operation."

Mae told Boris, "I had a personal stake because the illegal activity was impacting negatively on my business. Our dress orders got delayed, and customers were complaining."

"Your business grew at a fast rate after that issue got resolved did it not, Mae?"

"Yes. Our overseas business increased to the point that we could not keep up with the orders. It has maintained that high volume ever since I'm pleased to say."

"That did not happen by accident," Boris said.

"What do you mean?" Mae asked.

"We are not as callous as you might think. We reward those who work with us as intermediaries. After you agreed to help us, word spread around the world that Interpol approved Jamae Fashions. We publish a confidential, honorable mention list to large corporations like Couturier La Monde. They love to receive that annual list. It saves them having to perform excessive due diligence. They know that the officers of the companies listed have been pre-screened."

Mae was astonished. "I had no idea you went to that extreme."

"Why do you think that your negotiations with La Monde went so smooth? They knew that you were trustworthy, and therefore let George, their new Chairman, do the deal directly with you."

"Wow. You know about George also." Mae sat in bewilderment. "If I'm such a suitable candidate why are you holding up approval of the sale of Jamae to La Monde?"

"Oh, we are not holding it up, Mae. We have approved the transaction." Boris explained, "I never know who is listening or watching. I purposely created a false setting so as not to arouse suspicion. I wanted to speak to you. It was my way of getting you to Ottawa discreetly so that we could talk. I wanted to talk with you before you left for Lyon."

"I'm confused," Mae told Boris. "Why do you need to talk with me so urgently? Could we not have spoken on the phone? I'm not comfortable with this cloak and dagger stuff."

"I called you in because I need your help once more."

"What is it this time?" Mae asked impishly.

"You're moving to Lyon, France. Lyon is Interpol's World Headquarters."

"I know that," Mae responded. "How do you want me involved?"

"Your son, Ronnie, is starting up a practice in Ranchobe. Some things are going on with some Ranchobe Government Officials which is all I can tell you now. When you get to the Ranchobe Medial Center, I would appreciate a call from you, and I will provide you with more details at that time. It is close to your heart Mae. I believe that when you hear what the project is you will not object. Suffice it to say that you're an ideal candidate to help Interpol in another international crime investigation."

"How did you know Boris that I was going to Ranchobe before moving to Lyon? I would like to know where you get your information from," Mae inquired.

"All in good time," Boris answered. "You are an ideal CSIS contact person Mae."

Mae asked, "How do you figure that Boris?"

"You're a well-known designer who keeps a low profile. We regard you as a CSIS and Interpol safe contact. Even when George baited you yesterday, you did not let on that you knew who I was. You even pretended that you knew nothing about CSIS or Interpol. Through George, we were testing you. George is also a CSIS reliable contact person. You passed with excellence. Commendable.

"Other than your son Ronnie, you have no other relatives that will attempt to pry information from you. It is a lot easier to withhold information from strangers than it is from family. You're as free as a bird Mae. We need someone like you in Lyon as a messenger to receive confidential information and pass it on to us. We like that you and George will be living together in the same apartment."

"How will I receive information and how will I get it to you?"

"We'll let you know when we get all the dots connected. It is a worthy task, however. We understand how charitable you are through your foundation in Lewisville. We noted your recent generous donation to The Women's Shelter. The shelter can use Mary's old house.

"You're under no obligation to accept the assignment, Mae. Before making a final decision, however, please wait for all the pieces to come together."

"Alright, Boris count me in even though I've no idea what you have planned for me. I'm proceeding on blind faith."

"I'm pleased that you consented Mae.

"Congratulations on your new position with La Monde. They are good people."

"You're welcome, Boris. Am I going to see you again?"

"Maybe. You can always contact me if you need help with anything you know."

"Thanks, Boris."

Mae flew on the government jet back to Lewisville. She was tired. Mae decided not to return to the Design Center. Instead, she went home to Mary's big house, poured a glass of wine, kicked off her shoes, put her feet up on an ottoman, and wondered what next would happen in her life. My life has been a whirlwind of events, she said to herself.

Mae was eager to visit Ronnie before moving to Lyon. Poor Ronnie, she thought. He knows nothing about what has happened since he left. He is so far away. I miss picking him up at the train station and spending weekends with him. I will make plans tomorrow to visit him in Ranchobe.

Mae decided to write a brief note to Ronnie to tell him she was coming to The Ranchobe Medical Center to see him perform miracles in the jungle.

Mae reached over to the end table and removed a flowered piece of stationery from the drawer. She picked out a matching envelope. The envelope and paper reminded her of Aunt Mary. It was her writing paper. Poor Aunt Mary. I miss her as much as I do Ronnie. I need to get away from here

# 29

The next morning Mae left for Jamae Fashions. On her way, she mailed her letter to Ronnie. Mae wondered how long it would take before Ronnie received it. She had never sent a message to such a distant location before.

Upon arrival at Jamae, Mae unlocked the door and turned on the lights. Present designs were sleek and simple. They looked nothing like they used to when Mae and Jane established Jamae Fashions. Clients are more demanding and fickle now. Life seemed so simple, Mae recalled, when her only duties were designing dresses. She lost track of the number of designs she created. The Producers stopped her from developing anything new until consumers decided that they no longer liked Mae's current fashions. Mae's business designer clothes are mass produced somewhere in Hong Kong, and other localities in Asia.

Mae felt she lost control of her own business. What a strange world I've created for myself, she often thought. Only people with an appointment came into the Lewisville shop these days. Most designs sold in places around the world with names Mae could not pronounce or spell. She guessed that was good in some ways. Because of Jamae's international exposure, it induced La Monde to make an offer to buy Jamae.

Mae told herself that she should never fear for the lack of money. It was only after she and Ronnie took control of their lives that money was no longer a concern.

She remembered the time when married to Lester that the lack of money was the cause of all their woes. She thought, if Lester was more ambitious, and made more money, she and Lester would still be married – then again maybe not. Lester had other problems also.

Reminiscing back to when she was married to Lester, she recalled how adamant Lester was that she not return to work after Ronnie was born. How foolish he was to let his pride stand in the way of making a better life for everybody, she thought, including himself. Poor Lester.

Mae had a good life, good friends, and a smart and caring son. What more do I need, she asked, doubtless not more money. I want my money used to help make this world a better place, she told herself.

Mae remembered the abuse she received at the hands of Isabel and Lester. Her present problems were minuscule compared to those days as a teenager living on the farm with Father and Isabel. She felt she had no right to complain, but still, she felt there was always something missing in her life. Why am I so lonely, she asked herself? I've got everything I could ever want, but again, I'm alone. Except for Ronnie, who is living somewhere in the wilderness of Africa, I have no other family members.

She hoped Ronnie got her letter and that he replies right away. She wanted so much to see him. It takes a lot of planning to travel from Lewisville to Ranchobe. I hope nothing happens to prevent me from visiting him, she told herself.

Mae turned her thoughts to her lack of involvement at Jamae Fashions compared to several years ago when she was so busy designing new markets for changing demographics. She thought, when I take up my new position with La Monde, I will return to being active again. Someone else will look after the business stuff, and I can go back to just designing women's clothes.

Three weeks elapsed. Mae still had not heard from Ronnie. She was getting anxious, wondering if he ever received her letter. She had no other means to contact him.

She could not make plans until she heard from him. She was getting desperate and inquired at the Lewisville Post Office, how long it usually took for a letter to get to Ranchobe.

The postmaster told Mae, "It takes a long time to get anything into Africa, especially a remote country like Ranchobe. There are no roads beyond a ten-mile radius of each village, then they abruptly end.

A letter could take up to four weeks before it reaches its destination. Passageways flood in the rainy season and sometimes mail is stolen by marauding gangs looking for money and drugs."

Mae was not happy with the information she received. Conditions were worse than she thought. She wondered what prompted Ronnie to start his practice in such an isolated location. I must find another way to communicate with him, she told herself.

Two days later George and Mae were sitting at The Club concluding the sale of Jamae. After the meeting, Mae asked, "George, I want to get in touch with Ronnie. I was hoping to visit him before moving to Lyon. I wrote him a letter, but I've not received a reply. I'm beginning to worry. Do you have any suggestion how I can reach him, other than by mail?"

George replied, "I think I do but leave it with me for a couple of days. I have some diplomatic contacts I can call on."

"Thanks, George. You have so many contacts around the world that you can call on for help. You never cease to amaze me."

Two days later George called Mae and said, "There is a modest number of landlines that Ronnie's group of doctors can access. Close to Ronnie is a radio-telephone communications tower. All the doctors in the camp have emergency call access through the tower's communication system. I'll get Ronnie's call number and give it to you tomorrow." A broad smile crept across Mae's lips at George's news.

The next day George and Mae met at The Club. "Hi, George. We'll have to find a place in Lyon like this to meet."

"I already have a place in mind Mae."

"You're unbelievable George at the attention you pay to details. That's how you got to become so successful."

"It is my training Mae."

In a timid voice, Mae asked, "Did you get a chance to obtain Ronnie's number in Ranchobe?"

"I told you I would, and I have," George said in a voice indicative of, 'Did you doubt me?'

George reached into his vest pocket and pulled out a folded piece of paper. "Here is Ronnie's calling code Mae. Remember that Ranchobe time is six hours ahead of Canadian time. I'd suggest that you call between five and six o'clock tomorrow morning."

"Oh, George you have no idea how happy, and relieved, you made me feel."

Mae stood up and hugged George and kissed him on the cheek. "I still don't know how you managed to get this information. I'm grateful regardless of how you got it. It will be so good to talk to Ronnie tomorrow morning. I can hardly wait."

Mae did not sleep well that night. Early the next morning, sitting on the side of her bed, she called the number that George gave her. It seemed to take forever for the call to connect. There was a lot of static on the line. Then she heard Ronnie's familiar voice say, "Hello, this is Doctor Ron speaking."

"Ronnie. It is me, your mother in Lewisville."

"Hi, Mother. How are you?"

"I'm well Ronnie. Are you okay?"

"It is stifling hot and steamy here. The weather is not pleasant. We are at the end of the rainy season."

"Are you busy Ronnie?"

"We treat about a hundred patients a day. The work is hard, but the results are rewarding. I'm happy to be here. Most of my patients are children who need a lot of medical attention. Their ailments stem mostly from malnutrition." Mae gasped into the phone.

"Ronnie, I want to visit with you in Ranchobe. When can I come?"

Humorously, Ronnie answered, "Tomorrow would be fine Mother."

"Oh Ronnie, you know that's not possible, even though I wish it were."

"Get here as soon as you can Mother. I miss you and will welcome you whenever you can get here. Give me the details when you know them, and I'll meet you at the airport in Bokang. That is the only international airport in Ranchobe. We will drive from Bokang in the Medical Center's jeep. It will be a bumpy ride, but there is no other way to get to here. Do not wear any of your designer clothes. The road is muddy, and the voyage long. There are no windows, or doors, on the jeep. Everything is open. When you get here, you can stay in a guest cottage for as long as you like. Instead of rent for the cottage, guests can volunteer time helping at The Center, if they are able. Be prepared to work Mother."

"Nothing would make me happier than to work beside my son, the Doctor. It will enable me to see firsthand the wonderful work that you're doing."

In a motherly tone, Mae asked, "Where do you live and sleep at The Center Ronnie? Are you getting enough rest?"

"The Doctors stay in the bunkhouse, and yes Mother, I rest enough."

"Okay, Ronnie. I expect to be there in three weeks. Will that be okay?"

"That will be fine Mother."

Before hanging up the phone, Mae wanted to know about the letter. "Ronnie, I sent you a letter. Did you ever receive it?"

"No. Not yet. It takes a long time for mail to get here, sometimes never. Gangs of road thieves intercept the mail looking for money, jewelry, and passports. When you come, do not let your passport leave your sight once you arrive in Africa. Be prepared for a culture shock Mother."

"Okay, Ronnie. Thanks for the warning. I'll be in touch soon to give you my itinerary."

"Goodbye for now Mother. It was great talking to you."

"For me too Ronnie. We will talk soon. Goodbye for now Ronnie. I love you."

"I love you too Mother. Stay safe."

Mae hung up the phone. She fell back across her big bed looking up at the ceiling thinking how happy she was that Ronnie was safe and well. He had taken on a mammoth task for someone so young. She was very proud of him.

She had to make plans to fly to Bokang. There was a travel agency on Pitt Street. I'll go there when they open this morning, she thought. The sooner, the better.

# 30

The young lady at the travel agency smiled when Mae entered. "Oh, Good morning Madam," she said recognizing Mae.

"Have we met before?" Mae inquired.

"Not officially, but everybody in town knows you. It is nice to have someone of your stature walk into the agency."

"Well thank you Miss, and what is your name?"

"My name is Helen."

Mae took a seat in front of Helen's desk. The two ladies shook hands.

"How can I help you, Mae?"

"I want a one-way ticket to Bokang in Ranchobe, and an open ticket from Bokang to Lyon, France."

Helen told Mae there was little accommodation in Ranchobe. Mae proudly explained that her son was a Doctor in Ranchobe and that she would travel with him inland from Bokang by jeep.

"That's quite a voyage. I've never arranged such an itinerary. People in Lewisville do not travel far from home. When do you want to return to Lewisville Mae?"

"I'm not returning to Lewisville. I'm moving to Lyon, France."

Helen was surprised that Mae was leaving Lewisville. "When do you want to leave on your trip, Mae?"

"In three weeks. I'll pack only one suitcase."

"Okay," Helen said. "I'll get working on this right away and phone you when it is ready."

Mae left the travel agency and returned home. She thought it strange not going to Jamae Fashions, but it did not belong to her anymore. As of yesterday, Couturier La Monde was the owner. They would be staffing it with new people. Mae felt no remorse, however. Her focus now was to reunite with Ronnie, in Ranchobe.

She would call George and buy him lunch for enabling me to speak with Ronnie. She was indebted to him for his help.

When Mae called George, they both agreed that it would be fun to return to the chip wagon for hot dogs and fries.

"I spoke with Ronnie this morning George. I was happy to hear his voice. It sounded like he was in another world over the radio-telephone system."

"He's far away Mae. I am glad you connected with him. I know you were worried after not hearing from him for such a long time."

"I met with the travel agent this morning to make plans to travel to Ranchobe, and then to Lyon. I want to provide Ronnie with my itinerary."

George suggested, "When you get back to Lyon Mae, the first thing we have to do is find a little bistro to replace this chip wagon. Maybe we can find a place with a picnic table like the one we are sitting at now."

They both laughed at George's suggestion. Both of their lives were on the verge of transformation. A change was imminent.

Two days later, Helen called. Mae's tickets and itinerary were ready for her. "You'll depart from Toronto in eighteen days Mae. Come in anytime to go over your itinerary."

"I'll come in right away Helen. I must give my son the details, so he can make his plans to meet me. He has a three-hour journey over bumpy roads to the airport in Bokang."

Early the next morning, Mae tried to call Ronnie to provide him with her travel plans. The line was dead. Mae did not know what was happening. Yesterday there was no problem, she recalled. She kept trying to reach Ronnie all morning but to no avail.

I'll call George, she said to herself. He can give me an explanation why I cannot connect to the tower.

"Hello, George. I need your help once more. I cannot connect with Ronnie through the tower. Am I doing something wrong? Do you have any suggestions on what else I can try?"

"I'll investigate and call you back."

Twenty minutes later George called back. "Mae, there is a civil war going on in Ranchobe. There has been turmoil between the tribes for a long time. Occasionally, it flares up into combat. Tensions have escalated in the last few days. The rebels have taken over the government communications in Ranchobe. There is no communication until the restoration of the system. I would suggest you not travel to Ranchobe until hostilities cease. It is not safe to travel there now."

George shocked Mae with the news about the downed communications in Ranchobe.

Mae's first concerns were for Ronnie. She asked George, how she could discover if Ronnie's safe?

"I'll make some diplomatic phone calls. That is the best way to get answers under the circumstances like this. I will call you the minute I hear anything. Stay near the phone, Mae."

"Thanks, George. I hope you call back soon."

"Leave it with me, Mae. I will work on it right away. I know you're eager to speak with Ronnie."

Later that day George called back. "Hello Mae, I have more news. There are some local uprisings confined to a small area. That often happens. Law and order in Ranchobe are almost non-existent at the best of times. By cutting communications, it allows the rebels to gain control. Ronnie and his colleagues do not seem to be in harm's way. The only problem is a lack of communication. I have left word for Ronnie, through embassy backlines, to call you as soon as he is able. Crews are restoring contacts for The Medical Center.

"Thanks, George. It will be good to hear from Ronnie. I hope he's safe and well."

"I'll keep on top of things for you Mae."

"I don't know what I'd do without you George. I'm out of my realm with things like this."

"Keep calm Mae. I'll call you back."

Mae went downstairs to the kitchen and made a cup of tea to relax. She asked herself, why did Ronnie have to move so far away? He could have started his practice in Lewisville on Pitt Street rather than a tent in the depths of Africa. Ranchobe seems such a dangerous place to live and work.

Sitting alone in Mary's big house Mae questioned her motives for leaving Lewisville. Why do I want to move to Lyon, away from Lewisville, where I must speak French all the time? Ronnie will still not be in my life. I fear loneliness may raise its' ugly head again.

The pleasant part, however, Mae thought, is that I'll be close to George. George and Ronnie are the only two men in my life. I wonder what George would think about us having a permanent living arrangement, as Jane suggested.

Mae's thoughts returned to the present situation. I am so confused and upset, she thought, I wish I could speak to Ronnie. I have everything ready to go. I even have my suitcase packed.

The phone rang. Mae jumped up from the table in the kitchen and ran into the living room expecting to hear Ronnie's voice on the phone.

She lifted the receiver to her ear. "Hello," she said into the mouthpiece. "Hi, Mae. It is Jane speaking. I thought I'd call you to learn how you're doing with your plans."

"My packing is all done, but I can't leave yet."

Mae's response surprised Jane. "Why Mae?"

"There is an uprising taking place in Ranchobe. Communications are down. I cannot reach Ronnie. I am waiting for a call from him. I am a nervous wreck. I hope he's okay."

"It sounds like you could use a friend. Would you like a visit from me sometime Mae?"

"I could use a visit from you right now Jane. This house is so big and cold. I don't enjoy living here alone."

"I'll be there in a few minutes," Jane said.

As promised, Jane arrived at Aunt Mary's old homestead a few minutes later. She had baked cookies and buns earlier that morning and brought them to share with her good friend.

"As usual Jane. You think of everything. I'll miss these spontaneous meetings when I move."

"I'll miss them too Mae."

"I'm beginning to question myself, Jane."

"What about?"

"Am I making the right decision to leave Lewisville and live in Lyon? Other than living in this huge house, I am comfortable living in Lewisville. Why do I want to leave? I wonder if I could convince Ronnie to return to Canada where it is safe. If he did that, I would not move away. Everything would remain the same."

"I'd not advise deciding on that yet, Mae," Jane suggested. "Your emotions are running high. Let your feelings settle down a little. Wait until you speak with Ronnie. Discover how he feels about giving up his activities in Ranchobe. Do not forget Mae it is his choice to work in Ranchobe. You cannot expect him to make a choice that will make you happy and leave him sad. He has his own life to live."

"Jane, you have always been straightforward with me with your wise suggestions, and I appreciate it. You are right of course. My emotions are in the stratosphere. Now is not the time to think about other options. Oh, I wish so much Ronnie would call me. I need to hear his voice. I hope that no harm has come to him. You never know in situations like this."

"Calm yourself, Mae. Think positive thoughts."

Jane reached for the plate of cookies on the coffee table. "When troubled I eat cookies. Here, have another one Mae."

Just as Mae was reaching for a cookie, the phone rang. The sound made both ladies jump.

"Hello Mother," Ronnie's voice sounded through the phone.

"Ronnie," Mae exclaimed. "I'm so happy to speak with you. Are you safe?"

"Yes Mother, I'm fine. There was a coup overnight, and the military is now running the country."

"Is there any fighting where you are Ronnie?"

"Not now Mother. We are a medical facility and assured protection. Dr. Taylor has been through this before. He thinks the military will restore order to the country. There are still a few pockets of conflict. The shooting has subsided where we are. I treated about twenty individuals this morning for gunshot and shrapnel wounds. No more cases have arrived in the last two hours. That's a good sign."

"Ronnie, you're so blasé about the situation. Is it safe for you to remain there amidst all that fighting?"

"Of course, Mother. I have dedicated my life to saving lives. I want to try to make this world a better place to live. There is no better place on earth than here to carry out my goals and fulfill my ideals. I hope this little skirmish does not deter you from coming to visit me, Mother."

"People have been advising me not to go, but I refuse to listen. I want to see you, Ronnie. It does not matter where I travel. I am all packed and ready to go. I leave Toronto in three days. Are you able to meet me at the Bokang airport?"

"I'll meet you outside the customs building. Bring nothing of value like jewelry, cameras, or expensive cosmetics. There is a huge black market for those things here."

"I will leave all that stuff in Lewisville, Ronnie. I do not want anything to slow me down from seeing you." Mae outlined her itinerary over the phone to Ronnie.

"I'm anxious to show you the work that we are doing here Mother. It will enable you to understand better why I want to remain here."

"I can hardly wait to see you Ronnie and see for myself the work that you're doing. I know that you cannot stay on the phone too long. I will be there soon Ronnie. Goodbye for now and be careful."

"I will Mother. We will talk soon. Goodbye for now."

When Mae finished talking with Ronnie, Jane asked, "Do you feel better now that you have spoken with Ronnie?"

"I do. I am excited all over again about traveling to the far reaches of the earth to be with my son, the doctor, in Ranchobe. I had never heard of Ranchobe until Ronnie told me about it. It is an eerie feeling. Had I not needed to speak with Ronnie I would not have known about the problems that lurk in Ranchobe. I should see and hear more when I get there. The sad part is that when I leave from Lewisville, I will not return. I'm leaving you behind Jane, my long-time friend."

"I'll not allow you to forget me, Mae. I am planning to visit you when you get to Lyon. Lewisville will always welcome you back Mae. You are leaving Lewisville better than you found it. As the Mayor and your best friend, we are grateful for everything you have done to help this city prosper."

Mae inquired, "When your term is over are you planning to run for a second term?"

"I don't think so, Mae. The job entails more than I realized. I find it difficult attending meetings and dealing with people with hidden agendas. I am not as political as I thought I was. I have set up a good base for a younger person to take over from me. I'm not sure what I'll do when my term is up."

"I have a suggestion," Mae offered.

"What would that be Mae?"

"I need somebody to run my foundation. I can think of no better person than you Jane."

"Oh, Mae. I would love to do that job. It will also enable us to remain in contact."

"I have a few days before I depart. I will set up the paperwork to have you take over as my representative. It is not a difficult job. I have an administrator to look after the day to day activities. You need only to act as my advocate and ensure the proper allocation of charitable funds."

"Thank you, Mae, for the confidence you have bestowed in me. It is an ideal job for me at this point in my life."

"You're the best person for the job Jane. You have your fingers on the pulse of the city. I feel very comfortable putting you in charge."

"Things always have a way of working themselves out Mae. Neither of us knows what the future will hold. It looks like we will see more of each other than we thought. That makes me happy."

Jane remained with Mae for another three hours. They went over the plans to transition Mae's charity to Jane.

"I've got to leave now Mae. I have a meeting to attend."

As she was leaving Jane said, "Instead of running off to a boring council meeting, I'll be happy when I can devote my attention exclusively to your charitable foundation Mae."

"Me too," Mae answered.

Jane and Mae embraced in the hallway. They waved to each other as Jane pulled out of the driveway.

Alone once more in the big house Mae thought to herself, Change has been a decisive factor in my life. It goes back to those early days on the farm. Since then my life has been in continuous change. It is about to occur again. I never know when a change will happen. I've not regretted any changes, and I don't expect this one will be any different. I am happy the way things are developing in my life. What makes me most comfortable is that I will be with Ronnie. He too is experiencing significant life changes. He seems happy doing what he has chosen, however.

# 31

Mae spent the next day arranging the transfer of power in her charitable foundation to Jane. After that, she devoted her time getting prepared for her long voyage to Ranchobe. She was not only traveling to another country but another way of life, a life she knew nothing about. The highlight of my trip will be when I meet Ronnie in Bokang, Mae told herself. She was eager to know how he was coping with his new position. Mae hoped his enthusiasm would continue considering he was living and working in an unaccustomed environment, frocked with complications.

The following morning Mae took a taxi to the train station. From Lewisville, it was a two-hour journey by train to Toronto's Union Station and another half-hour to Pearson Airport, Toronto's international airport.

Helen had arranged for Mae to fly from Toronto by BOAC to London's, Heathrow Airport.

At Pearson Airport Mae looked for the BOAC counter. It was at the far end of the terminal. She picked up her suitcase and headed towards the sign.

There was a long line-up at the BOAC counter. She stood in line for twenty minutes before reaching the counter and speaking with the agent. Mae admired how smartly dressed he was in his BOAC uniform. "Good day Madam," he greeted her. "Where are you traveling to today?"

Mae handed her documents to the agent and answered, "To Bokang, then on to Lyon two weeks later."

"Not many passengers fly to Bokang. What is your reason for going to such a remote location?"

"My son is a doctor in Ranchobe. I'm on my way to visit with him at the Ranchobe Medical Center."

The agent asked, "Are you traveling alone, Madam?"

"My son is meeting me at the airport in Bokang."

The agent lifted his head from the paperwork in front of him, and said, "There are severe problems in Bokang now. The authorities shut down the airport yesterday. Be careful Madam. It is not safe for a lady to travel alone in that part of the world."

"I'll be careful. It's important I see my son."

Mae felt that everybody was trying to keep her from visiting Ronnie. She refused to listen and kept going.

The agent stamped her documents in several places, handed them back to Mae, and directed her to the departure gate.

"Good luck to you Madam and be careful."

"Thank you, sir."

Mae unzipped her jacket pocket and carefully stashed her documents inside and refastened the pocket for safe-keeping. She remembered Ronnie warning her to protect her documents, especially her passport.

Mae proceeded to the departure gate as instructed. I'm on my way to Ranchobe, Mae said to herself. Here I come Ronnie, she whispered under her breath.

After an hour into the flight Mae relaxed. The flight attendant asked if she would like a glass of wine. "Yes please," Mae answered. The wine, followed by a nice meal relaxed her more. The drone of the big Rolls-Royce engines, the effects of the wine, and a full stomach of food, made her feel drowsy. She had been awake since early morning.

She remembered Helen telling her to get sleep on the plane. When I get to London I will be ahead of Lewisville time by six hours, Mae reminded herself. Helen told her that jetlag could be hard to overcome on a long voyage.

Mae put her head back and fell asleep. She was awakened by a public-address announcement.

"Good Morning Ladies and Gentlemen. This is your captain speaking. We are expecting to arrive at London Heathrow Airport in one hour and twenty-seven minutes. We are right on schedule. The weather in London is cool and rainy. We will touch down at nine a.m. local time. I suggest that you set your watches to London time now."

Mae rubbed her eyes to wake herself up. She lifted the blind on the window and stared at the puffy white clouds far below.

The big plane landed at Heathrow Airport on schedule. The airport was a lot bigger than the Toronto Airport. The plane taxied to the terminal. Mae joined two hundred other passengers in the baggage area to retrieve her luggage. After several minutes, her suitcase popped from under the floor, and rode the noisy conveyor belt, with what seemed to be, a thousand other pieces of luggage. With her bag in tow and the first part of the journey over, she contemplated her next step. I must find the South Africa Airlines counter on the departure level, she said to herself.

With her suitcase in tow, Mae rode the escalator to the second-floor departure level. There was no lineup at the South Africa counter. The agent was standing behind the counter with nothing to do. He looks to be about Ronnie's age, Mae thought.

"Hi," she said. "I'm traveling to Bokang. Here are all my documents."

The agent looked strangely at Mae.

"Are you traveling alone?"

"Yes."

"There is a problem Madam. There are no flights, in or out, of Bokang Airport except for emergency planes carrying medical personnel and supplies."

"Oh dear," Mae exclaimed.

"I notice from your papers that you're related to a doctor practicing in Ranchobe. Will he be meeting you at the airport?"

"Yes, Sir. My son is a doctor at the Ranchobe Medical Center. I'm on my way to visit him and do some volunteer work while I'm there."

"I think I can help you, Madam. I will classify you as a medical passenger. When the airport reopens, you will have priority passage. The bad news is that nobody knows when the airport will open. Do you have a place to stay in London?"

Mae quietly answered, "No."

"It could be a while before things return to normal in Bokang. I will let you know the minute I hear anything," the agent said. "Can I try to contact your son to let him know you're here?"

"Yes, please," Mae graciously replied. "My son is at a field hospital in the interior of Ranchobe. Here is his tower code for easier access."

Mae wrote down Ronnie's contact number on a piece of paper and gave it to the agent.

"Let's see if we can make contact," the agent said.

"Oh, I hope so. My son will be so worried if he does not hear from me. I do not want him to worry. He has enough on his mind."

The agent tried several times to reach Ronnie. "I'm not having any luck. I will keep trying, however. Meanwhile, I suggest you get something to eat and some rest. You must be tired and hungry."

"I'm more tired than hungry, but I'll take your advice."

"Listen to the announcements. I'll call you when I contact your son."

"Many thanks. You're very kind and considerate."

Mae picked up her suitcase and left the counter to get something to eat. She was glad Ronnie told her only to pack one bag. She did not know what she would have done if she had another case to look after. Mae was having enough trouble lugging around only one. Heathrow is such a large airport, she said to herself.

Mae decided on a ham sandwich at one of the airport cafeterias. It tasted good. She did not realize how hungry she was. After she finished eating, she returned to the bench near the South Africa Airline counter. She hoped the agent would make contact soon with Ronnie.

When Mae checked with the agent, he told her that communications were still down in Ranchobe because there was still a lot of shooting going on at the Bokang Airport. "As long as there is gunfire present, flights will not land," he told Mae. "It is not safe to do so."

"Not even medical flights?" Mae asked.

"Not even medical flights," the agent repeated.

The agent went on to say, "I'll be closing at midnight, Madam, which is in ten minutes. I will try one more time, but that will be the last time I can do so tonight. This desk will reopen tomorrow morning at six a.m. Since you do not know anybody in London, I suggest that you go to a hotel. You can come back tomorrow. Things in Bokang may be better by then. If you leave the airport, remember that you must go through security again tomorrow morning."

"I don't want to leave in case there is a chance of getting out during the night," Mae told him.

"Suit yourself," the agent said. "You will have to sleep on a bench if you elect to stay here. I suggest you claim one now before they are all taken. They go fast. Lots of people are forced to spend nights sleeping at the airport."

"Okay," Mae said. "Thanks for your help."

"I wish I could have helped you more Madam. Good luck."

Mae found a bench near the counter. She laid her suitcase at one end, took off her shoes, and put them under her case. Mae was thankful she was wearing travel slacks. Mae was not counting on having to sleep on an airport bench.

Mae's suitcase served as a pillow. She tried unsuccessfully to go to sleep. Even though there were few travelers at the airport during the night, an army of maintenance people milled about all night. Their activities kept Mae from going to sleep for a long time. After what seemed an eternity, Mae dozed off to sleep. She woke up when she heard her name called over the public-address system. It was directing her to go to the South Africa Airline counter.

"Something is happening," she told herself. "I hope it's good news."

Mae ran to the counter and identified herself. The daytime South Africa Airline attendant told Mae, "I have an emergency call for you from the airport at Bokang," the agent told Mae. "The reception is bad. You have to pay close attention to the person talking," the agent instructed Mae.

Mae took the hand-held receiver from the agent. "Hello," she said into the receiver.

"Hi Mother, this is Ronnie. I cannot talk long. I am on a battery-operated phone. There is somebody with a hand-held sign with your name on it. He'll meet you at the South Africa Airlines counter."

Mae looked around. She saw a man carrying a homemade sign with her name scribbled on it.

"I see him, Ronnie."

"Good," Ronnie said. "Identify yourself to him Mother, and he will fly you to an airport near Bokang. I'll be there to meet you."

"Are you okay and safe Ronnie?" Mae inquired in a concerned voice.

"Yes, Mother. I am fine. I have been busy treating casualties from the recent uprising. There is a change of flight plans. It is uncertain when the Bokang Airport will reopen. The Center is using a smaller airport to receive supplies. I made plans for you to travel on our medical supply plane into the smaller airport. I'll be at the airport with a jeep to meet you."

"Thanks, Ronnie. I can hardly wait to see you. Be safe my darling."

Mae just finished speaking her last words, and the phone went dead.

Peering across the concourse, Mae waved at the tall, thin man holding a sign with her name on it.

"Hello, Miss Mae. I am your pilot. I will fly you to Ranchobe in the medical airplane. My name is Lea. I work at The Center in Ranchobe. I fly the airplane which carries supplies for the Medical Center."

"Pleased to meet you Lea and thank you for looking for me in this big airport."

Lea picked up Mae's suitcase and walked to an exit door. Mae followed him.

"We must hurry Miss Mae. There is not much time left in our take-off window. If we miss it, we must wait until tomorrow. Lea emphasized that the supplies need to get to The Center urgently. Dr. Ron and Dr. Taylor are waiting for them.

Mae said, "I'm going as fast as I can Lea," as she tried to keep up with him running through Heathrow Airport.

Lea led Mae through back passageways between terminals at the large Airport complex.

When they arrived at terminal three Lea opened a door marked, emergency exit only. He guided her to a plane with its engines rumbling, and a narrow staircase leading down from the plane onto the tarmac.

Mae climbed the stairs behind Lea. It led to a cramped flight deck. Once onboard, Lea pulled the rope that caused the stairway to fold up into the plane. He grabbed the long red handle on the door and swung it from 'open' to 'locked.' He folded down the jump seat and over the noise of the engines, shouted for Mae to sit down and fasten her seat belt. No sooner had Lea jumped into the pilot's seat when she heard the tower usher clearance over the radio for the emergency medical flight to take-off.

There were no further words spoken. The roar of the engines as the plane taxied into the darkness, made it impossible to talk.

Lea sat in the pilot's seat in front of Mae. A co-pilot sat beside him. Mae looked around. They were the only people on the plane.

Mae did not understand what was happening. All Ronnie told her to do was to follow the man carrying a sign with her name on it. She did not know who he was, or where he was flying her. It was dark outside and no lights below. Her safety rested in the hands of the two unknown pilots flying her through the darkness to an unknown destination. Mae hoped they knew where they were going, because she didn't.

After being airborne for twenty minutes, Lea said something to his co-pilot in Afrikaans dialect. He loosened his seat belt and turned to Mae. "Welcome aboard miss Mae. My co-pilot's name is Okafor. We call him Oka for short."

Oka looked over his shoulder and smiled at Mae. Mae smiled back.

"Is Dr. Ron safe and okay?" Mae asked Lea.

"Yes, he's okay, but he is very rushed. There is a war in my country and many people hurt. Dr. Ron makes them better. The government closed the Bokang Airport, because of the shooting. We will land at another smaller airport near Bokang. Dr. Ron will be there to meet us. The small airport only accepts medical supply planes like this one. That is why we can fly, and others can't. The only airplanes in the sky destined for Ranchobe are military, and medical supply planes."

Mae looked behind and peered into the dark fuselage. Behind her was a stringed bulkhead securing crates with Red Cross decals on each.

"What is in those crates," Mae inquired.

"Medical supplies donated by the British Government for Dr. Taylor, and Dr. Ron, to save lives. We must get there fast."

Mae noted that the airplane was only a fraction the size of the plane she flew on from Toronto to London. The medical plane had two noisy sounding engines, one under each wing. The airplane rolled and bumped its way through the night sky to some obscure airport in Ranchobe. It was unlike the smooth and well catered BOAC flight.

Mae asked Lea, “Does Ronnie know that I’m on this airplane?”

Lea answered, “Yes. Dr. Ron asked us on the radio to pick you up at Heathrow. We are not supposed to, but nobody in the government will know.”

“Thank you, Lea and Oka, for letting me ride with you,” Mae said.

“We’ll be landing in three hours. You must be tired, Miss Mae.” Lea suggested that Mae try to go to sleep.

Mae laughed to herself. What a joke, she thought. Lea was asking her to dream an impossible dream.

Lea told Mae, “It is a long trip by jeep to the Medical Center. You will ride in the jeep with Dr. Ron. Oka and I will stay to unload the supplies and follow you in two trucks. Two other pilots will take the plane back to Heathrow.”

After winging her way for three hours closer to Ronnie, Lea said, “We are going to land soon, Miss Mae. Tighten your seatbelt and be prepared for a hard landing.”

The ground was rising closer. Mae could not understand why she didn’t see signs of an airport or a runway. With no warning, Mae felt the wheels touch the ground with a heavy thump. She looked out of the small cockpit window. Oh, my God, she said to herself. We have landed in a grass field. Is it any wonder I could not see a runway.

When the plane came to a stop, Lea released the rope that let down the stairs. Mae clutched her suitcase and descended. She saw a small hut at the end of the airport fence. In front, she saw Ronnie waving frantically to get her attention. They both ran towards each other and fell into one another’s arms. “It is wonderful to see you, Ronnie.”

“Likewise, Mother.”

“It was a long and difficult journey to get here, but seeing you makes it all worthwhile. I have not been this happy for months, Ronnie.”

"It is too late to travel to The Center, Mother. We cannot complete the journey before nightfall. It is not safe to travel at night."

Ronnie reached down and picked up Mae's suitcase saying, "You must be tired after your long journey, Mother."

"A little," Mae confessed.

"I've reserved two rooms for us at a lodge about two miles away. The medical personnel stay there when traveling in and out of this airport. Be forewarned, however, Mother, it is not the Ritz in Montreal."

Mae laughed. "It does not matter Ronnie. I am happy to see you. I'd sleep on a bed of rocks if I had to."

"When you get up in the morning you might think that was what you slept on," Ronnie joked.

Mae laughed.

Before leaving the tiny airport, Mae had to go through customs. The agent did not speak to her. He opened the first page of her passport, closed it, and handed it back to her. With a wave of his hand, she exited customs and onto Ranchobe soil.

On the way to the lodge, Ronnie remarked, "I appreciate your traveling so far to visit me, Mother. I am eager to have you see what I do in this remote part of the world. Be prepared for a shock. It is a different world here."

The jeep was right-hand driven. It desperately needed a wash. Mae guessed Ronnie had more important things to do than wash the Center's dirty jeep.

Mae and Ronnie checked into the lodge. There was no lobby, only a small entranceway with a sleepy desk clerk sitting at a small round table. Behind his desk was an old vending machine housing a few chocolate bars and cookies. Ronnie threw a few coins into the machine and told Mae to choose something. Two chocolate bars and some cookies made up Mae's supper. It was the only food she had to eat all day. She did not tell Ronnie she had not eaten before now, or that she spent the night sleeping on an airport bench. Ronnie ate the same food as Mae.

Ronnie arranged for two rooms next to each other. "I hope you sleep well tonight Mother. We have a long journey over dirty, barren, and bumpy roads tomorrow. We'll leave right after breakfast."

"What time are you planning to have breakfast in the morning, Ronnie?"

"Five o'clock," Ronnie answered without hesitation.

"Okay," Mae answered, surprised at the early hour.

Ronnie told her, to go to bed early and he hoped she could sleep. "My room is right next door if you need me for anything," Ronnie said to keep Mae at ease in desolate surroundings.

# 32

The next morning Mae and Ronnie had bangers and mash for breakfast. They ate in the small dining area of the lodge. When they left, the sun was just rising.

Mae had a better look at the jeep about to transport her and Ronnie to the Medical Center. There were no doors on either side. Roll-over bars with a tarpaulin strapped to them served as the roof.

Mae thought it strange that the windshield laid flat on the hood of the jeep. Comically Mae imagined, that was to ensure that the inside of the jeep remained as dusty and dirty as the outside.

A spare wheel sat on the hood in front of the folded windshield.

The jeep sat high off the ground. Mae stepped onto the rung where a running board is on a regular vehicle. She fell into the bucket passenger seat. She looked for a seat belt. There was none.

Ronnie fired up the engine. Black smoke spewed from the rear of the jeep. It backfired twice, lurched forward, and took off like a gazelle throwing Mae's head back against the headrest.

"We're off," Ronnie exclaimed excitedly.

Mae and Ronnie zigged and zagged over roads that rarely saw motorized vehicles. They passed mule trains carrying fruit and produce destined for village marketplaces. "You did not exaggerate when you said the road was bumpy, Ronnie."

Ronnie just answered, "It will get worse."

The road consisted of two ruts with grass and weeds down the middle. Water filled the holes making it impossible to tell how deep they were. The jeep bounced and rolled along the road dodging rocks and ruts on its way to the Medical Center. Generating any speed was impossible.

Occasionally Ronnie and Mae met other vehicles traveling in the opposite direction. When that happened, someone had to back up, or move into a clearing at the side of the road and let the other one pass. There were few places on the way where two vehicles could pass side by side.

Limited communication took place between Ronnie and his mother. It was too noisy to talk. The jeep sounded like a truck ten times its size. Ronnie was too busy maneuvering around obstacles on the road to engage in conversation.

They passed soldiers, dressed in green battle fatigues, carrying machine guns and riding in broken down military vehicles. Others marched along the sides of the road. Mae thought they looked tired and tattered. Most were very young – some only teenagers. They paid no attention to Mae and Ronnie. Mae was thankful the soldiers did not stop them. She expected that the faded Red Cross on the side of the jeep showed they were harmless. Ronnie seemed undeterred.

The deeper into the jungle they traveled, the worse the road became. About three hours into their journey, Ronnie pointed and shouted, "Look Mother. You can see the Medical Center ahead."

Mae saw buildings in the distance. It was the first sign of civilization seen since boarding the jeep at the lodge.

Ronnie pulled into the entranceway and stopped in front of a long white building and shut off the motor. It backfired a few times before it realized its' services were no longer needed.

"Welcome Mother to the Ranchobe Medical Center," Ronnie said hugging his mother.

Mae responded, "Thank you, Ronnie. It was a long journey but worth it to be here with you. I'm looking forward to spending time with you and observing what you do in this desolate part of the planet."

"Thanks, Mother. Let me show you where you will be staying then we can talk all we want. I have no patients today. I reserved the day for you and me."

"Ronnie, you're so considerate of me."

"No Mother. My patients are the ones who are considerate. When they heard that my mother was coming to visit today, they agreed to postpone their treatments and inoculations so that we could spend time together. Family means so much to these people. You'll see what I mean tomorrow."

"How kind of them to do that, Ronnie. Your patients must hold you in high regard, Ronnie."

"They are part of my extended family, Mother. Even though I've only been practicing here for a short while, I've gotten to know most children and mothers by name."

"What about the fathers?" Mae inquired.

"It's a different culture here, Mother. Most children and mothers do not know who their fathers or husbands are. The women and girls who live in the villages are not held in high esteem by the men in the villages."

As Ronnie and his mother were talking, Ronnie was leading his mother toward a row of cottages behind the facilities. They stopped at the first one. "This is your place, Mother. You should find everything you need inside."

"This is nice Ronnie. Where do you stay?"

"There are four doctors in total. We are all single except for Carol and Dr. Taylor." Ronnie pointed to a larger building behind the cottages. "The single guys stay in that bunkhouse over there."

Pointing to another building, Ronnie said, "That's where Carol and Dr. Taylor live. Their unit has a stove, washroom, and eating area. There is a private meeting area in there also. When Dr. Taylor wants to discuss private matters with his assistants, that's where he does it. His home is the headquarters building for the Ranchobe Medical Center. Dr. Taylor is not home right now. He is attending government meetings in Bokang, trying to get extra funding for The Center.

"Carol is probably sleeping now. Her last four nights were spent tending to patients."

Mae had a confused look on her face. "Why were there patients to look after during night time?"

"There is a civil war going on. We are the only medical facility for hundreds of miles around. We were treating soldiers with gunshot wounds."

"Where are those soldiers now?"

"If they were able, some went back to fight. We passed a few on the road who I recognized. Others got air-lifted by helicopter to a hospital in Bokang. Some of those were so badly injured I doubt they survived the journey. Some were beyond help and died."

Ronnie pointed to a hill in the distance. "We have a graveyard on the other side of that hill. We bury the deceased patients quickly to prevent the spread of disease.

"Carol works as the triage nurse among her other duties. She keeps busy. She is the only full-time Medical Assistant at The Center. Dr. Taylor is trying to get her more help. Carol never complains though."

Mae told Ronnie, "She's a special lady. I could not do what she does."

"Yes, you could Mother. I've seen you work under many adverse conditions. You and Carol are two strong-willed ladies. The world needs more women like the both of you."

"More than half of my patients are children. I'm the pediatric surgeon."

Ronnie opened the door of the cottage with a key and handed it to Mae, saying, "Even though The Center appears secure, keep your door locked at all times, Mother. People do desperate things when they are starving."

"Okay, Ronnie. I'll be careful."

"Take time Mother to get some rest. I will stop by in two hours. We'll have a bite to eat and talk."

"Thanks, Ronnie. I am tired. The last few days have been a little frenzied. Also, I got up earlier this morning than I usually do."

Ronnie placed Mae's well-traveled suitcase in the corner of the room. "You'll find the conditions rather spartan Mother. There is a toilet behind the screen over there." Ronnie pointed to the far corner of the room. "Showers are only allowed three times a week to conserve water and electricity. They are in the white building you saw when you arrived. There are only two showers. One is for doctors and medical staff. Only use the one marked public. Be aware Mother, the showers are gender neutral, on a first-come, first serve basis. Make sure you have a towel nearby before you enter, or you may have to shower longer than you expected, waiting for the guy next to you to finish."

Mae laughed and giggled, "I never imagined my son having to talk to me like that. I will heed your warning Ronnie."

"I'll give you a tour of the facilities later," Ronnie told his mother.

Mae noticed Ronnie's stethoscope draped around his neck. "Before you leave Ronnie I want to tell you something. Before now, I was unable to visualize you as a Doctor. You were always Ronnie, my son. Now you are Ronnie - my son the Doctor. You make me proud, Ronnie."

"Mother, I'm glad you're here. I am going to leave you for a brief time. Don't forget to lock the door behind me."

"Okay, Ronnie. I'll look forward to having supper with you later, and you can tell me all about your life as a Doctor in Ranchobe."

Mae locked the door when Ronnie left. She glanced around the single room cottage. Behind a flimsy faded curtain Mae found the toilet and a bucket of water for flushing. On a hook beside the bathroom hung two clean washcloths. Mae presumed that they were to replace the conspicuously absent toilet paper. A faded red linoleum covered the floor. The walls were unpainted. A few plates constructed from hammered tin and some homemade tin pots and pans sat in a wooden closet with no doors. A table big enough for two people sat on one side of the room. Close by was a double hot plate to heat food. Two hooks fastened to the back of the door served as a clothes closet.

Mae noticed the cottage held only the barest of essentials. She told herself, Ronnie was not kidding when he said the conditions were crude, Mae thought. Conditions on the farm were better than this, she said to herself. We in North America do not understand life in this part of the world. Even the poorest people in Lewisville have more than the people of Ranchobe. I've no right to complain about my problems, she assured herself.

Mae kicked off her shoes and laid down on the hard cot. There was no pillow, but she was so tired it did not matter. She fell asleep right away.

# 33

As the sun was setting, there was a knock at the door. Mae peeked through the window. It was Ronnie. She smiled and unbolted the door. "Are you hungry?" Ronnie asked coming through the door.

"A little," Mae replied.

"We don't have a menu to choose from," Ronnie said laughing. "We have a dining room, however. Supper will be whatever our cook Sarahani decides."

"Where is the dining room, Ronnie?"

"Follow me."

Ronnie took his mother to the long white building near the entrance to The Center. He led her to a door on the back side of the building. Ronnie inserted the key into the lock and opened the door. They entered a small dining room. The room was set up in cafeteria style. It had a refrigerator and an electric stove. Two long wooden tables and six chairs on each side were set up in the middle. There were no windows in the room. The kitchen was at the far end of the room from the entrance. A long counter separated it from the eating area.

"This is a secret room Mother. It is only accessible to doctors and assistants. We eat in this room behind locked doors. Food is not eaten or taken beyond these walls."

"Why?" Mae asked.

"We have hundreds of patients who walk for miles from surrounding villages. They may not have eaten for two or three days. It is unfair to allow them to see us eat.

"There is another factor also. When people have no food in their bellies, they will resort to violence, to get something to eat. It could incite rioting. To avoid both scenarios, we eat secretly."

"How do you keep the food cold in the fridge, and where does the power come from for the stove?"

"The fridge is operated by propane gas. There is a generator outside that gives power to The Center. The generator is a vital piece of equipment for The Center. Without it, we could not support our facilities or do any surgeries. Several times we have caught locals trying to steal it. If you listen closely, you'll hear it humming."

Ronnie and Mae stood silent listening for the generator. Mae said, "Oh yes. I hear it now."

Mae opened the fridge door to look inside. It was full of food. Mae saw chicken, beef, lamb, fresh fruits, and vegetables. It even held North American fast food items like hot dogs, and hamburgers. A dairy section included milk, yogurt, and butter.

"I'm startled at all the food you have to eat Ronnie. How do you keep the fridge so full of food?"

"We work through, 'Doctors Without Borders' who supply us with everything. The food is good and nutritious. We must keep up our strength and stamina for the job at hand. If we get sick, The Center closes, and hundreds of people will die."

"How do you transport food and supplies into the middle of Ranchobe?"

Ronnie smiled at Mae's question. "They fly it into the small airport near Bokang, the airport that you arrived at this morning. Dry ice keeps the food frozen in insulated containers, the same goes for drugs and vaccines that need to be frozen.

"Much of the food you're looking at in the fridge traveled with you on the airplane this morning. For the same reasons that we do not eat in front of the native population, we hide the food and hard drugs amongst the medical supplies and equipment. A few trusted souls bring the food and supplies in from the airport by trucks. Deliveries arrive every ten days from Geneva."

Ronnie continued introducing Mae to the Medical Center's various functions. "Sarahani is our cook when he's not driving the jeep or one of the trucks. He will be here shortly to prepare our supper. Sarahani feeds his own family first.

"When Sarahani arrives, I'll ask him to get dinner going right away. You must be hungry."

Mae and Ronnie sat at the end of one of the long tables waiting for Sarahani to arrive. They were the only ones in the room.

When he arrived, Ronnie introduced Sarahani to Mae. He was a small man and spoke with a thick dialect. Mae found him hard to understand. Ronnie had no trouble conversing with him.

Mae and Ronnie feasted on fried chicken, mashed potatoes, peas, and carrots. They had sweet buns for dessert. Ronnie had a glass of milk with his meal. Mae drank tea.

Mae complimented Sarahani on his culinary skills. He was overjoyed that she liked his cooking. "Madam, you come back tomorrow, and I make you another nice dinner," he cheerfully invited Mae.

"Thank you Sarahani. I'll be back tomorrow to taste your fine cooking."

Mae was curious how Ronnie ended up at The Medical Center in Ranchobe. "What drove you to take this job, Ronnie? I'm sure it is not for the big money they pay you to practice here."

Ronnie laughed. "No, you're right Mother. I'm not the highest paid Doctor in the world." Ronnie explained, "Dr. Taylor was a guest lecturer at McGill last year. I listened intently to him at a conference talking about his work in Ranchobe. I was intrigued. I spoke with him afterward and told him that I was interested in learning more about his work at The Center. We had breakfast the next morning. Dr. Taylor is a legend in Africa, and I marveled at the work he was doing. I asked him for permission to work beside him at The Center. He agreed to my request to work in Ranchobe with him. That is how I ended up at the Ranchobe Medical Center.

"It is the best decision I ever made Mother. I feel called to do this work. Dr. Taylor spoke to me about taking over from him in two years. I am giving it serious consideration. I want to try and make a difference in the lives of people who were born into a life of poverty, with little opportunity to escape. I can start by keeping them well."

With tears in her eyes, Mae said. "I did not realize that you were so committed, Ronnie. I am amazed at your deep dedication, and passion, to improve the lives of others. It is reminiscent of your own life as a child growing up in poverty, Ronnie."

"The poverty that I encountered growing up pales to that which these people have to endure. I wish I could do more, but resources are scarce. I am happy Mother that you can see firsthand the work that I do. I wish I could do more. We can talk more in the next few days. Meanwhile, we should get rest. We have a busy day tomorrow."

Ronnie walked his mother back to the cottage. It was dark outside. Ronnie carried a long flashlight to light the way.

Mae sat on the side of the cot and thought about her first day at The Center with Ronnie. She shuddered at the desperate conditions Ronnie told her that people must live under to sustain life. Ronnie and Dr. Taylor can only do so much, she pondered. There is much left undone. Ronnie can keep his patients well, but there is little he can do to improve their economic life. The rest of the world has abandoned Ranchobe, she said to herself.

The next morning Mae woke up to the sound of a rooster crowing. I have not heard roosters crowing since I was a young girl on the farm, she thought. The people in Lewisville won't be awakened by a crowing rooster this morning. It is fun to hear him crow. It brings back memories.

Mae let her mind ramble over the events of the last few days. I have lived a very sheltered life, she concluded. I thought my life was hard living on the farm. I knew nothing of how people in other parts of the world lived. Had I known what others had to contend with, I would never have complained as I did. There must be a way to help turn things around in this part of the world.

Mae and Ronnie had an early breakfast of mango juice, cereal, and tea. They finished eating at five thirty. Ronnie had been up since four. The rooster woke Mae up at four thirty.

On the way to the dining area, Mae noticed people were lining up outside the hospital building. After their breakfast, the line had grown by at least a hundred and stretched outside The Center's border.

"Who are all these people?" Mae asked Ronnie.

"They are Medical Center patients served by the four doctors at The Center. Many are my patients. Would you like to work with me today Mother? You'll learn what a typical day is like for me."

"I'd love to Ronnie. Just tell me what to do."

"You can register the patients when they arrive. Most cannot read or write. You must record all the information for them and fill it onto this form. I usually fill out the form myself as each patient comes to me. I can see more patients if you pre-screen them for me."

Ronnie placed a handful of forms on the table. "Don't worry about the correct spelling of names. Use your spelling. Note if they are male, female, adult, or child and record their ailments. When the form is complete, send the patient in when the previous one leaves. One thing more. The patients will call me Dr. Ron. Do the same Mother, even though it may seem awkward. They will not know who you are referring to otherwise. Malnutrition affects their memory."

"When do I start sending them in?"

"Right now. We have a lot to see."

"Okay, Dr. Ron. I will follow your directives. I hope I can live up to your high expectations."

Ronnie smiled and entered the examination area pulling the curtain behind him. The number of mothers and babies needing medical attention astounded Mae. The line was never-ending. Most could speak English, but they were far from fluent. At first, Mae had difficulty understanding what they were telling her. After a brief time, she got the jest of what they were saying.

Mae wondered why there are no fathers in line. The only men seeking medical help are old men, she noted. I must ask Ronnie tonight, she said to herself.

Most children suffered from malnutrition. They had swollen bellies, and their heads were abnormally large. They had multiple medical problems. Inoculations, broken bones, and eye problems took up most of Ronnie's time. Some needed cataract surgery. Ronnie set aside Thursdays for eye surgeries.

Mae marveled at how Ronnie coped with all the medical complexities. He knew most of his patients by name, and he was friendly to them. In return, mothers and children adored him. Mae noted that his patients exited the medical tent happier than when they entered.

Mae thought Ronnie is far busier than most doctors in North America who work in limited disciplines and consider a couple of dozen patients a busy day. Mae noted Ronnie was more dedicated to his calling than many of his North American counterparts.

Mae and Ronnie worked until sundown. When Ronnie quit for the day there was still a long line-up of patients waiting to see him. Neither Mae nor Ronnie stopped for lunch.

"What will the patients do that you were unable to see today Ronnie?"

"They will go home and come back tomorrow."

"How far away do they have to travel?"

"Some walk as much as five miles to get here. They live in unbelievable conditions. This place is safe and clean. Unlike the filthy villages, with open sewage, and disease runs rampant."

Mae asked Ronnie, "Why are there so few men seeking medical attention Ronnie? There were a few old men, but not many."

"Men consider themselves superior to women and girls."

For a fleeting moment, Mae recalled, that's how Father and Daniel regarded Mother and her when she was a little girl on the farm.

Ronnie continued, "They believe that their role in life is to produce babies. They brag about how many babies they fathered. Women are subservient to them and are on this earth only to serve men, both sexually, and economically. Most of the men, especially the younger ones, refuse medical advice because, in their minds, it makes them less than a man. They fear rejection by the other men in the tribe. It's a culture thing. Because of not seeking medical attention most men die at an earlier age than the women in the tribe.

"Most mothers have experienced the death of at least one child. They will do anything to avoid losing another. They know that the Medical Center will keep them, and their children alive. Unlike their male partners, they are not shy to seek medical help and advice. The Center makes birth control information available. It is not strongly adhered to, unfortunately. I can tell you more over supper tonight Mother.

"We will eat in the doctor's dining room in an hour. Dr. Taylor is home now. He wants to meet with all The Center's Doctors and bring us up-to-date on his trip to Bokang. I hope it's good news."

"That's fine Ronnie. I want to hear more about your life and work here in Ranchobe. It is a different world here. I'll meet you in the dining room after I rest a little from a busy day."

Mae and Ronnie ate supper together. Sarahani prepared a lamb stew with a beet salad side dish. Mae had an opportunity to meet some of the other doctors and assistants who, like Ronnie, had dedicated their lives to helping others. After dinner, Ronnie said, "Come, Mother, I'll walk you to the cottage. We will be more private there."

Mae wondered what Ronnie wanted to talk about in private. She noted that he was more subdued than the night before. Something is troubling him, she deducted.

At the cottage, Ronnie and Mae sat at the small table. "Something is bothering you, Ronnie. What happened when you went to speak with Dr. Taylor?" Mae noted there were tears in Ronnie's eyes.

"Dr. Taylor told us he has been trying to get government funding to enable us to expand our facilities and improve the lives of the people of Ranchobe. Corrupt politicians denied all of his requests for funding."

Mae asked, "Other than medical help Ronnie, what other type of help is needed?"

"These people have no future Mother. I can mend their broken bones, and restore them to good health, but The Center cannot give them jobs, schools, and fresh water to drink. The lack of those items are the causes why they are sick. They have no chance of living a long, and healthy life under present conditions. That is why you see no old people. The age expectancy is forty-three. Low compared to the standards of the rest of the world. They die young, but they don't have to if only their living conditions could be improved."

"I can see Ronnie that the lack of care and help touches you deeply," Mae said.

"Dr. Taylor feels like I do also, Mother. He was certain that he could ignite passion in the minds of the officials whom he was meeting. They claimed there was no money available."

Ronnie added, "They have lots of money to buy guns and fund a civil war amongst the population, however. They all drive expensive cars even though there are no suitable roads to drive them on. They just park them in front of their homes and offices. They brag and show-off to the people they are supposed to serve."

"What about foreign aid?" Mae asked.

"The officials claim that money goes to pay expenses. The expenses they refer to allow corrupt politicians to live in lavish living conditions. The people living in the villages, never see a cent of any foreign aid money. The whole country is corrupt. It has been going on for generations."

"I'm sorry for you and Dr. Taylor, Ronnie. You are both so dedicated to the needs of others. It is unfortunate that the government is so corrupt."

"Mother, I'm happy that you're here with me during these troublesome times. There is no one else that I can confide in. If you were not here now, I would have to go through this alone. You have always been close when I needed you."

"And I always will be Ronnie. I promised you the day you were born I would make life better for you. I'll continue to do that Ronnie."

"I know Mother. Just by being by my side now makes my life better. I'm grateful for all you have done for me."

"I want to do more Ronnie."

Ronnie sighed, "There is nothing more to do at this point, Mother. It is the Ranchobe culture that must change. That could take generations to change. Meanwhile, I'll keep doing what I was trained to do and hope for the best."

Mae noted that Ronnie was becoming withdrawn like the time Lester beat her up in front of him. I want to raise his spirits now as I did then. I must give it some thought. This situation is complicated. Is there anything I can do, she wondered?

"It is getting late Mother. You should get some rest. You worked hard today. Are you able to help me again tomorrow?"

"Of course, Ronnie. I enjoyed every minute I worked with you today. I observed first hand, a smart, and gifted doctor at work."

"Thanks, Mother. It was just like old times. You and I against the world."

"Before you go, Ronnie, I've some business to look after. I would like to make a call to Lyon, and to Lewisville, before going to bed. Can I use your tower code to call?"

"You'll have to return to the dining room and use the call-box from there. Just dial in my code."

Ronnie took a card from his pocket and gave it to Mae. He also gave her the long flashlight. Ronnie and Mae left the guest cottage together. Mae went to make her calls, and Ronnie went in the opposite direction to his bunkhouse quarters.

"Good night Mother. I'll see you early tomorrow morning."

"Good night Ronnie. I will see you tomorrow. Remember things can only get better. Stay strong my darling."

# 34

The next morning the rooster woke Mae up again. Still half asleep she thought, that the rooster was fun to hear yesterday, but the novelty has worn off now. It was early, and Mae went to bed late the night before. She could have used another hour of sleep.

She hoped that Ronnie was feeling better this morning. She remembered how troubled he was last night. He wants to do more, she told herself, but the resources are not available to enable him to do so, and corrupt politicians are hampering the Foreign Aid funding.

The rooster continued taunting Mae to rise from her bed and get ready for a new day. Mae wondered if Ronnie wanted her to register patients again like she did yesterday. Mae was still in awe of the primitive conditions that the villagers undergo, and the distances they travel to receive medical attention, especially the women and children.

Later Ronnie knocked on Mae's door. "Good morning Mother. Are you ready for breakfast?"

"I'm ready Ronnie. I have been ready for two hours. The rooster made sure of that. How did you sleep after our discussion last night?"

"I did not sleep well, Mother. I tossed and turned most of the night thinking about our conversation. The problem is the lack of resources and commitment from the Ranchobe government. The people of Ranchobe have tons of obstacles to overcome. It is impossible to know how they will ever get out from under their burdens."

Mae said, "You'll recall Ronnie when you were growing up we too faced problems. Albeit not of the magnitude faced by the people of Ranchobe, but obstacles requiring attention nevertheless. Do you remember how we addressed those problems?"

Mae did not wait for Ronnie to respond. "They were conquered by seeking help and advice from others, building self-confidence, and exercising a strong work ethic. We set goals for ourselves and made plans how to achieve them – education plans for you and design plans for me."

Ronnie commented on Mae's remarks, "I remember how determined and diligent you were Mother to make a better life for us."

"Not just me," Mae answered. "But you too, Ronnie. You worked and played hard to excel, and you succeeded."

Mae challenged Ronnie. "Is the plight of the people of Ranchobe any different than the confrontations we faced Ronnie?"

Again, Mae answered her question. "No. They are the same, only on a larger scale. The people living in Ranchobe must overcome their limitations, just like you and I did. They must address their shortcomings. If not, their life path will not improve."

Ronnie replied, "Therein lies the problem Mother. The ways to amend the situation, require resources far beyond what the Medical Center can provide."

Mae told Ronnie he and Dr. Taylor need more resources to effect change.

"We are entering a phase of deep discussion, Ronnie. Too deep to indulge on an empty stomach. I want to share with you some of my thoughts. We can do it over breakfast."

Ronnie could tell his Mother was serious about something. He had seen that look in her eyes and heard the tone of her voice often enough to know that something was brewing in her mind.

"I'd be interested to hear your views and comments Mother. I remember how strong-willed you were when I was a young boy. You had a clear vision of what to do to achieve your goals and aspirations. I believe you have grown even stronger over the years."

"That's true Ronnie. Throughout my life, I was goal-oriented. I made sure that you escaped from a life of poverty. The people of Ranchobe need a similar escape mechanism."

"You guided me well Mother."

"Did I succeed Ronnie?"

"In spades."

"It would have been easy to do nothing and live day to day having no plans for the future like Lester lived his life. Had I followed Lester's example, what would I have achieved? You would have grown up in poverty, Ronnie, and lived a life as Lester did."

Mae continued, "That's what has happened to the people of Ranchobe. They have given up. They see no way out. They have nobody to show them a better way. Dr. Taylor's Medical Center has laid a strong foundation. I have some further thoughts and ideas to share."

Ronnie turned and faced Mae saying, "You're incredible Mother. I saw no light at the end of the tunnel when I came in, and now, after only ten minutes in your presence, I am higher than a kite hanging on to your every word. I know your views and comments will be insightful. They always are, Mother."

Ronnie and Mae walked to the dining room. Sarahani was cooking breakfast. The aroma of bacon cooking filled the air. They filled their plates with food and sat at the end of one of the long tables. Other medical personnel sat at another table. Mae selected a spot where she and Ronnie could talk privately.

"Ronnie, I want to support you in all your endeavors as I've always done. It upset me last night when I saw how devastated you were for your patients and the people of Ranchobe. You see first-hand the other side of humanity. Being sad is natural. I too became sad when you told me about the hardships your patients had to endure. I did not believe that conditions like this existed in the world. I understand what caused you to break down last night, Ronnie. You want people to live decent, and healthy lives. There are countless numbers of factors hindering you from completing your mission. You do not know when, where, or how, to start. Am I right so far, Ronnie?"

"As usual Mother, you're right. In contrast, I am only one person. I can mend their bodies, but I cannot educate them, teach them skills, or provide them with better housing."

"You're right Ronnie. You cannot be all things to all people. If you try, you will fail. You are in the healing business. Stick to what you do well."

"What's your point Mother?"

"Tools are needed to help the community to better their lives. They lack self-esteem."

"You need to explain in more detail, Mother. What tools are you referring to?"

"More help is needed. You cannot change a person's mind by just telling him to change. He must know that it is beneficial for him to change, even if it is difficult and uncomfortable to do so."

"Mother these people have lived like this for generations. What magic formula do you propose that will entice them to change?"

"They need money, experts, and a whole lot of inspiration."

"There is not a lot of that around here," Ronnie sarcastically commented.

"You sound cynical Ronnie, but your assessment is correct. Money, experts, and inspiration are required by Ranchobe to turn things around."

Ronnie answered in a skeptical tone, "I think you are dreaming an impossible dream, Mother."

"I used to have impossible dreams, Ronnie. Then Charlotte, at the women's shelter, entered my life. She told me that if I do nothing to change my life, that is what I will end up with - nothing. I engaged Charlotte's help to compose a résumé, and I went up and down Pitt Street dropping off my résumés to prospective employers. I eventually landed a job at, The Dress Shop. Our lives changed for the better after that, Ronnie."

"I remember those days at the shelter Mother. You were determined to succeed and make a better life for me."

"Exactly, and now you can do the same for your patients, Ronnie. You can help others make a better life for themselves over what they were born into. Like I did for you, Ronnie.

"You have been exposed to both sides of life, Ronnie. The bad, and the good. Not everyone has had that opportunity to observe life from both sides."

Ronnie gave his mother a strange look and said, "But Mother where do I start? You had Charlotte and Jane as resource people to guide you. Who do I have? Only Dr. Taylor, who is running out of resources."

"You have Dr. Taylor who holds you in high regard. He has dedicated his life to bettering the lives of people by keeping them healthy."

"That's right Mother. Dr. Taylor and I can keep them healthy but who will keep them safe and secure?"

"You have forgotten one of your main resources Ronnie."

"What's that?"

"Me," Mae answered emphatically.

"Thanks for your encouragement, and enthusiasm, Mother. The fact remains that more, on hands, involvement is required than what even you can provide."

Mae peered into Ronnie's eyes and said, "You underestimate me, Ronnie."

"You need to explain Mother."

Mae reached into her pocket and pulled out a crumpled piece of paper, with some writing on it.

"I made a list," she told Ronnie. "The people of Ranchobe remind me of Lester, living day to day with no plans. They need to take ownership of their lives and not rely on corrupt politicians to rule their lives. They need jobs and money, and a strong desire to mold their destinies."

Mae paused and then continued, "I spoke to George, in Lyon, after you left me last night, Ronnie. I convinced him to have Couturier La Monde build a new production facility in Ranchobe, and train and employ locals to work in it. The facilities will instill pride, confidence, and loyalty, into the hearts and minds of the employees."

"We could then increase our capacity to serve," Ronnie commented.

"It will also enable the employees to buy food for their families with the money they earn from the La Monde Production facility, and acquire, or build, better accommodations to live in."

Ronnie added, "That would reduce the threat of malnutrition and disease which runs rampant in the rainy season."

"George guaranteed that the employees wouldn't be taken advantage of like they are at present by corrupt politicians. They will receive a fair wage and have a health care package. As a Director of the company, I will oversee the Ranchobe project.

Ronnie interjected, "Does that mean The Center would get paid for its services?"

"You're beginning to get the picture, Ronnie. The Center could eventually become self-sustaining." Mae explained further, "I told George that La Monde would have to train the employees on how to sort yarns and operate the looms. George assured me that would happen.

"Africa is a largely untapped market where La Monde is anxious to gain a foothold. La Monde is a benevolent company and would be pleased to participate in the development of Ranchobe."

Ronnie was awestruck at what Mae was telling him. "Mother I cannot thank you enough for your help. Wait until Dr. Taylor hears about this."

"I made three phone calls last night, Ronnie," Mae said.

Inquisitively, Ronnie asked, "To whom, Mother?"

"I made the second call to Jane in Lewisville."

"What for?" Ronnie wanted to know.

"I instructed her to set up a new foundation and to name it, The Ranchobe Project. Its' purpose will be to fundraise for the mothers and children of Ranchobe, with emphasis on schools, daycare, and nutritious eating habits. The Ranchobe Medical Center will receive a portion for future expansion into other parts of Ranchobe. Jane is putting that into place as we speak."

"Mother, you are wonderful. I cannot believe how you put all this stuff together in such short order. You never cease to amaze me.

"You said there was a third call. Who else did you talk to last night Mother?"

"I have a good contact at Interpol. His name is Boris.

"Boris left a message for me through George. Without going into too much detail, Ronnie, suffice it to say that Interpol is aware of the corruption in Ranchobe government circles, and the misuse of aid money. I can guarantee you Ronnie, Dr. Taylor's dealings with Government Bureaucrats in the future will go much better. Interpol is determined to eliminate Government corruption in Ranchobe."

Overwhelmed and sobbing profusely from listening to Mae outline her plans, Ronnie asked, "How can I ever thank you, Mother?"

"There is a way you can thank me, Ronnie."

"Name it Mother. Whatever it is, I'm certain I can accommodate you."

"You can give me away at my wedding."

Ronnie stared at his mother in disbelief. "What are you talking about Mother?"

"Before leaving for Ranchobe, George and I agreed to move in together. I did not want another relationship like the one I had with Lester. I love George, and before leaving Lewisville, I told him so."

"On my journey, I had lots of time to think. When I spoke to George last night, I told him I was ready to start a new life with him in Lyon. He was overjoyed at my decision, as I am also. I have been secretly in love with George ever since I met him, many years ago. I got very involved with Jamae Fashions and pushed aside the feelings I had for George. They resurfaced at a picnic table, near a mobile chip wagon, when he told me he too was secretly in love with me. I gave him my answer last night. George was happy with my decision. I am also glad Ronnie.

"If you agree to it, Ronnie, I'll stay another month to coordinate the plans we talked about for the new facility. George will join me to help pull everything together.

"When I return to Lyon, George and I will make our wedding plans together. It will not be an elaborate affair. I want a church wedding, however. Something I never had with Lester.

"I'd love to have my son, the Doctor, give me away."

Ronnie stood up and threw his arms around his mother. They embraced and cried together.

"I'm so happy for you Mother. George will make a wonderful partner. You and he belong together. There is nothing I'd like better than to walk you down the aisle Mother."

"Thank you, Ronnie. It is comforting to know that you approve."

"That will be fine Mother. I'm ecstatic with all the good news you have announced, and it is still early in the morning."

"Speaking of which Ronnie, I must leave you and get things prepared for today."

"Like you have not done enough already, what must you do that's so urgent Mother?"

"I have work to do before you start seeing patients."

"Again, I ask. What do you have to do?"

"I have bedpans to wash."

Ronnie laughed and said, "I wonder what the officers and executives of the world's largest fashion house think about one of their Directors, and renowned Fashion Designer, washing bedpans in the wilds of Africa.

Mae paused contemplating what Ronnie said. They both burst out laughing together.

* 1 3 1 9 1 9 4 1 1 *A